THE EDGE OF INFINITY

WAR ETERNAL, BOOK SEVEN

M.R. FORBES

Published by Quirky Algorithms
Seattle, Washington

This novel is a work of fiction and a product of the author's imagination.
Any resemblance to actual persons or events is purely coincidental.

Cover illustrations by Tom Edwards
tomedwardsdesign.com

[1]
MITCHELL

IN THE DREAM, there was nothing but colors and flashing bursts of white light. They swirled and danced and whorled, flowing and collapsing, breaking apart and merging, pulsing like signals moving from brain to heart to mind to soul and back again.

In the dream, time was a vague thing. A recommendation. A suggestion. A simplified description of something so complex, it was nearly impossible for the human mind to grasp. It was a toy. A plaything. A ghost, haunting the dream and shading the colors with blacks and browns and grays.

It turned patterns into solids, shapes into form, and shadows into detail until finally, an image appeared.

A memory? Reality? The past? The present? The future?

In the dream, time was nowhere and everywhere, and there was no value in trying to understand it. Only accept it. Only endure it.

In the dream, there was no control.

It was a dream, after all.

The shapes coalesced behind Mitchell's closed eyes, or at least what in his present state he believed were his closed eyes. They gathered themselves, the colors breaking apart, subduing, joining, and finally resolving into a scene. It was one he had relived an infinite number of times already. As many times as the universe had been unmade and then made again?

"Welcome to tomorrow," he heard himself say.

He was standing beside Katherine, looking through the high definition cameras that projected the space beyond the Goliath into the bridge, providing them with a full view of their surroundings. A ship was sitting directly ahead of them, a few hundred kilometers off the bow. It was a mirror image of their own. The United Earth Alliance Space Ship Dove.

He didn't know how many recursions there had been in this infinite cycle of eternal return, but Teegin had explained it to him simply, and with simple numbers.

"Given that time is a loop, repeating over and over without end, consider that this is recursion number two," the intelligence said. "The Dove that is arriving is from recursion number one. We should be traveling to recursion number three. In this way, the cycle of the Dove being built, launched, and returning to the war against the Tetron continues unbroken. Time is always moving forward, and thus impervious to paradox, but by remaining here, by allowing the duplication, you are altering the fabric of the timeline. You are changing things in ways we can't account for through even the most complex of algorithms. If you fail, this will happen again and again, and there will never be a new incursion to break the cycle. Do you understand?"

"It's our risk to take," he said. "Humankind's risk."

"Yes. It is a decision you make for everyone."

"The mesh is broken. Here. Now. The only other choice is to go forward again, and that may be more of a risk."

"The probabilities are even," Teegin agreed.

Mitchell decided that they would remain. Two Goliaths had to be better than one, especially when he knew how some of the future was likely to go. It was the reason they were there to receive the Dove when she arrived.

"This is Admiral Yousefi of the Dove," a familiar voice responded over the comm. Mitchell could hear the shiver in the man's speech. He was frightened. "I. I don't quite understand this."

"I believe Major Katherine Asher can help you with that," Mitchell replied, glancing over at his Katherine. "I assume she is there with you?"

"She is," Yousefi said.

Silence followed. Mitchell could imagine the Admiral approaching his pilot and asking her what she knew about this situation. He could guess the reaction the delivery of the news that she was carrying a piece of an advanced artificial super intelligence on board would be. If she even tried to explain that much.

"Mitchell?" A new person said over the comm a few minutes later. Katherine. "Mitchell Williams? Is that you?"

Unlike Yousefi, her voice was excited. Eager. Enthusiastic.

"Yes," he replied. "This is Colonel Williams. Katherine, where is Origin's configuration?"

Another pause.

"It's true, isn't it? All of it? It really is true."

"About the Tetron?" he replied. "The war? The end of humankind. Yes. It is. But it doesn't have to be. That's why we're here."

"But how? How can this be real? How can there be two ships?"

"There aren't only two ships," his Katherine said. She had tried to prepare for the meeting, but how do you prepare to meet yourself? "There are two of us."

"Oh," the other Katherine said. "I. I don't know what to say."

"I know this is awkward," Mitchell said. "Incredibly awkward. We need to get past it as quickly as possible. The recursion you just came from is already stale. This might not make a ton of sense to you yet, but if the Origin configuration is listening, it will understand. The mesh is broken. We've changed things, a lot of things, and we're in the process of changing more. Watson, as he exists in your future,

4 / M.R. FORBES

is gone. We captured his core, and we plan to use it, to weaponize it against the Tetron."

"You're right," Katherine said. "I don't understand. Not completely. I know so little about all of this. It was so hard even to come to believe in it."

"I am listening," a fresh voice said. Mitchell smiled, recognizing Origin's female voice. "I understand. I am primitive. Very primitive. I need time, Mitchell. Time to learn what the Prime has left me. Time to expand."

"Colonel," Yousefi said, his voice cutting across the channel. "I don't know what the hell is happening here, but I do know that this ship, the one that I'm sitting in, is my ship, and my responsibility. You owe me an explanation. A full explanation."

"You're right, Admiral," Mitchell replied. "I do, and I will. Permission to come aboard, sir?"

There was one more pause, as the Admiral had to decide whether or not to trust in him. Mitchell knew his recursion's Yousefi. He was an intelligent, fair man. A born leader. He wouldn't dismiss them without consideration.

"She's the same," Yousefi said. "One hundred percent the same, right down to the run of paint on the zero at the end of the identification code. There's no way anyone could have been that precise."

"No, sir, there isn't," Mitchell said. "It's a bit of a mind frig, but it isn't a trick."

Yousefi was silent for another minute or so, likely discussing things with his crew.

"Very well," he said at last. "Permission granted. How are you going to manage it?"

"Don't worry about that, sir," Mitchell replied. "I have a ride."

[2]

MITCHELL

THE CREW of the Dove was waiting beyond the doors of her hangar as Mitchell eased off on the throttle of his reconfigured S-17, activating the magnetic soles at the bottom of the hybrid mech and starfighter's feet as he touched it down to the surface.

While the future Goliath would have Tetron technology to create an invisible energy barrier between space and the hangar, the current version was still temporarily reliant on a more basic approach.

The huge doors to the hangar slid closed slowly, leaving Mitchell and Katherine waiting in the S-17 while they finished their trek and came together forcefully enough that the ship vibrated at the collision. There was no sound of course, not without an atmosphere to carry it, but he could almost hear the echoing clang in his head.

Vents opened at the top of the space and held air was released back into the chamber, flowing in and quickly replacing the emptiness. The artificial gravity was turned back on as well, causing the small amount of tethered cargo in the corner to drift slowly to the floor.

A few minutes later, a green strip of light appeared along the walls, alerting them that it was safe to open the cockpit.

"Are you ready?" Mitchell asked, looking back at Katherine.

"I'm still shaking from hearing myself over the comm," she replied. "Meeting me in person? After all we've already been through, I still think it's insane."

"I feel the same way most of the time. At least I'll be able to tell you two apart."

Katherine ran her hand over her scalp. She had shaved her head in an effort to keep herself both easily identifiable and different. Knowing the other Katherine was an earlier version of herself hadn't prevented her from struggling with the concept of not being unique.

He toggled the cockpit to open with a signal through his embedded neural implant. It made a sound like a hatching egg as it disengaged the seals and swung backward. Mitchell stood, taking in a breath of the somewhat stale air, and then waited while a series of block steps detached from below the nose and arranged themselves as floating stairs beside it. He helped Katherine up and then followed her down to the hangar floor.

Teegin had already climbed from the top of the craft and was waiting for them, standing motionless while pulses of energy flowed around his form of tightly compacted biomechanical wires. The intelligence had regained his humanoid shape and managed to condense himself back to two and a half meters. On their Goliath, he tended to spread and expand, occupying the area between the reactors in the engine compartment. Mitchell knew he would take over the entire space in time, as would Origin.

In time.

For now, they started moving forward together, toward the airlock at the rear of the hangar. Teegin stayed behind Mitchell and Katherine, his alien nature sure to be unsettling to the crew of the Dove, who still barely knew what had happened. They had only taken a few steps when the airlock opened, the crew having come to them.

Mitchell tracked Katherine out of the corner of his eye as they approached, with Admiral Yousefi out in front and his Katherine right behind. He hesitated slightly when his eyes landed on Teegin, but he caught himself mid-step and kept moving.

"Admiral Yousefi," Mitchell said, bowing slightly, in the custom of the UPA military.

"Admiral," Katherine said beside him, bowing as well.

"I don't believe it," Yousefi replied, looking at Katherine, and then at his Katherine. He made the round trip with his eyes a few times before remembering himself and returning the gesture. "Katherine told me what she knew of this while we were preparing for your arrival, but I still don't believe it."

"I wish it weren't true," Mitchell said. "No offense, but I'd rather have never met any of you."

His eyes landed on the other Katherine. He felt a familiar longing in his chest at the sight of her. His subconscious didn't seem to care about one version of her versus another. She was the same person, more or less.

"Well, maybe you," he said to her.

She smiled, her eyes speaking to him in a way that his Katherine's never had. Did this one feel the same way? Maybe he would have time to find out later.

"None of us asked for this," one of the other crew members said. "To be thrown into the future? Away from our families and loved ones? Never to see them again?"

Yousefi turned around. "Don't forget who you are, Lieutenant. An officer in the United Earth Alliance. That is where your first responsibility lies."

"Yes, sir," she replied, quieting down. She still didn't look very happy, but Mitchell didn't blame her for that.

"What is this thing you've brought with you? One of these Tetron?"

"It's a long story," Mitchell said. "But if it helps prove to you that the Tetron are real and that the threat they pose to us is real than you can think of it that way. He is an aggregation of a number of intelligences, both human and Tetron."

"My name is Teegin," the intelligence said. "It is a pleasure to meet you, Admiral."

Teegin bowed, matching Mitchell's style.

"You're a machine?" Yousefi asked.

"My external composition is both biological and mechanical. My operational structure is binary, but it resides within strands of deoxyribonucleic acid. It is, in essence, a set of instructions based on a language written by humans for the purpose of controlling a system; however, it is also self-composable and extensible."

"Meaning you can write your own operating instructions?" Yousefi said.

"Yes."

"Artificial intelligence."

"Yes. Although I have derived a number of functions from the organic intelligences I have integrated with, including Katherine and Mitchell's daughter Kathy, and a scientist named Li'un Tio. I also possess emotions."

"Daughter?" the Dove's Katherine said.

"Yes," Katherine replied. "We had a daughter, in this recursion."

The two Katherines looked at one another, both wearing the same expression of disbelief and discomfort at their mirror image.

"I like what you did to your hair," the Dove's Katherine said.

Katherine laughed. "Smart ass."

"They are both Katherine?" Yousefi asked.

"Yes," Mitchell replied. "One from this recursion. One from yours, and mine, actually. The one I never got to meet. You left clues on where to find the Dove when the time came."

"At Origin's urging," Katherine said.

Mitchell smiled. "I can't keep calling you both Katherine."

"Then call me Kate," she said. She looked at Katherine. "If that's okay with you?"

"It will be really confusing otherwise. It's already confusing enough."

Kate laughed. "I agree."

"Colonel, Admiral," Teegin said. "I hate to interrupt, but there is one vitally important matter that we must resolve with all due haste."

Mitchell glanced at Teegin and nodded. He knew what the intelligence was talking about. He looked back at Yousefi's crew, noticing that someone was missing.

"Admiral. Where's Captain Pathi?"

[3]
MITCHELL

"I LEFT HIM ON THE BRIDGE," Yousefi said.

"Alone?" Mitchell asked.

"Yes. We are a skeleton crew, Colonel. We weren't expecting to be hijacked and taken to the future." He looked at Kate when he said it. He was clearly unhappy with the situation, but pragmatic enough to remain calm. "I couldn't leave the bridge unattended. Not when you've suggested we've fallen into the middle of a war."

"The war hasn't started yet," Mitchell replied. "Not really. We need to get to the bridge, now."

"Why?"

"Pathi is a Watson configuration. The Watson from your timeline."

"What?" Kate said. "How?"

"I don't know how, but he tried to do some serious damage to our efforts in my timeline."

"You're sure about this?" Yousefi asked.

"Yes."

"Follow me."

Yousefi took the lead as they all moved through the corridors of the ship, heading for the bridge. Mitchell felt a sudden tension while they did. Pathi was at the helm of the Dove, meaning he could be doing anything with it right now, including setting its self-destruct sequence.

"Of all the people to leave on the bridge," he muttered to himself.

He had considered warning the Admiral earlier but was afraid the configuration might do something drastic if he was outed like that, and the crew of the Dove had no weapons.

They reached the lift, taking it as a group to the bridge. They stormed out of it and into the command center of the Dove.

Captain Pathi was in the command chair, watching the monitor there. He turned his head toward them as they entered.

"Admiral," he said, getting to his feet and bowing.

Mitchell kept his eyes on him the whole time, making a note of the fact that he didn't react with any kind of surprise at the sight of him, two Katherines, or Teegin.

"Captain, step away from the controls, please," Yousefi said.

"Of course, sir," Pathi replied, following the order. "Is there a problem, sir?"

Yousefi looked at Mitchell. "Is there, Colonel?"

"I know who you are," Mitchell said.

"What do you mean, sir?" Pathi replied.

"Don't play games with me. I know who you really are. And what you really are."

Pathi looked at Yousefi. "Sir, I don't know what this man is talking about. Do you?"

"He claims you are a, what was the word you used again, Colonel? Configuration?"

Mitchell nodded.

"A configuration of one of the enemy intelligences."

"Sir?" Pathi said.

"You're playing a good game, Watson," Mitchell said. "Your acting skills are solid. You can drop the bullshit, though. We dealt with you in the last recursion, and we'll deal with you in this one."

Pathi's eyes widened, and he looked panicked. "Admiral, what-ever this man thinks I am, he's wrong. I swear."

"Colonel, while I understand you have some experience with these Tetron, are you certain you aren't mistaken about Captain Pathi? I know him very well, and I've never had a reason to believe he is anything but who he says he is."

Mitchell paused. He needed Yousefi to believe in him, or his plan to team up with the second Goliath was going to fall apart before it ever got off the ground. He wasn't sure what he would do if that happened.

He stepped forward, positioning himself directly in front of Captain Pathi. The man looked up at him, making eye contact, obvi-ously afraid. What if he were wrong after all?

The rest of the crew was watching him intently, a layer of tension stretched taut against the bridge. He leaned into Pathi, whispering in his ear.

"I'm still here, Watson. You tried to drown me, and you failed. You tried to crash a maglev with me in it, and you failed. You tried to shoot me multiple times, and you failed. Are you getting the common thread here, Watson, or do I need to spell it out?"

He leaned back, making eye contact with Pathi again. The eyes had changed somewhat, the pupils dilated, the brows lowered.

"You failed," Mitchell said. "Over and over and over again. How does that feel?"

Pathi stared at him. Mitchell could feel the fury through his expression. The barely contained rage. He was sure of what the Captain was now. He just had to give him one more nudge.

"You have another chance," he said, holding his arms out. "You might not get another one."

Pathi's lip curled slightly. He glanced over at Yousefi, and then back at Mitchell. For a moment, it seemed that he would resist the temptation.

Then he lunged forward, throwing a quick punch that would have caught Mitchell in the temple if he hadn't been expecting it.

Mitchell reached up, catching the arm and pulling it aside, accepting the follow-up blow to the ribs. He kept pulling, taking the configuration over his shoulder and dropping him to the floor.

"I hate you," Pathi said. "I hate you, I hate you, I hate you, Miiittccheellll."

"Hold that thought," Mitchell said, looking up at Teegin. "A little help?"

Teegin stepped over to them. He leaned over, taking Pathi by the neck and lifting him. The man tried to kick at Teegin, but his blows were ineffective.

"You killed the real Captain Pathi," Mitchell said.

"I want to kill you," the configuration replied.

Mitchell laughed. "We have your core. Did you know that? The override you were writing as well. Whatever you thought you were going to gain here, you've already lost it. Maybe the war, too."

"It isn't over yet. There are still things you don't know."

"Like what?"

Now the configuration laughed. "It will be a good surprise, Miittchheelll. A very good surprise."

Mitchell looked at Teegin. "Do you know what he's talking about?"

Teegin shook his head. "No, Colonel."

"You can play arrogant and confident for now," Pathi said. "It isn't over yet. It isn't even close to over. I haven't failed. Not yet. Not yet."

"We'll prepare some form of cell for him," Yousefi said. "Maybe we can get him to talk with time."

"Talk?" Pathi said. "I am talking. You aren't listening. I guess you'll just have to wait and see."

"The mesh is broken," Mitchell said. "The timeline is changed. Whatever you think is going to happen, it isn't."

"You can't stop something you don't know is going to happen. You may have changed the timeline, but you can't change this."

"Can't change what?" Yousefi asked.

"Oh, you'll see, Admiral. You'll see. It would have been fun to play a little longer, but you had to ruin it. Goodbye for now, Miiittc-chheeelll."

Pathi's body began to convulse, his eyes rolling back in his head. He shivered for a moment, and then he was still.

"I want a full debriefing," Yousefi said, showing his anger for the first time. "Right now, Colonel. I want the whole story, from start to finish. I want to know why we're been brought here, and what we're supposed to do." He looked at Kate. "You knew about this. You kept this from me. You put everyone here at risk. I know you, Kate, and damn it, if I didn't trust you so much I'd be even more angry. I have a pregnant wife back home, and I'm never going to see her again." He fell silent then, his anger turning to sadness. "I'm never going to see either one of them."

"They still exist in this timeline, Admiral," Katherine said. "Your wife and unborn child. Do you want your descendants to have a future? Do you want humankind as a whole to have a future?"

"I joined the military to defend our way of life," he replied.

"This is bigger than any of us," Mitchell said. "I know it's painful, Admiral, but Kate did what she had to do. I've seen the Earth burn. I've seen millions die. I've seen an entire planet destroyed. You and your crew have a chance to help us prevent that from happening."

Yousefi stared at the ground for a moment, his eyes growing moist. He looked up and nodded.

"They would be proud of me for that," he said. "All of our families would be proud of us for that, even if they'll never know about it." He looked at Mitchell. "A full debriefing, Colonel. We deserve to know everything."

[4]

MITCHELL

MITCHELL DID TELL THEM EVERYTHING, from the minute M had tried to stop his assassination and all the way through until Teegin had offered him the eternal engine. It took three hours to get it all out, with Katherine and Teegin and even Origin helping him fill in the events as they knew them. Origin's future was his future after all, the one where he died trying to defend the Earth, and so she knew some of the story.

"Fascinating," Yousefi said once he was done. "So I was killed in this timeline?"

"Murdered by Watson," Mitchell said.

"It is so strange to think that there was another one of me."

"You think it's strange for you?" Kate asked, looking across the table at Katherine.

Yousefi's expression was flat. "Of course, I won't ever get the chance to meet myself."

"What I'm confused about is your status, Origin," Mitchell said. "In my recursion, you sent a configuration of yourself to the future, along with a copy of your data stack, a complete duplicate of yourself, while the original you remained on Earth to safeguard my ancestors."

"That is correct," Origin replied. She had no form, only a synthe-sized voice that emitted from the Dove's loudspeakers. "I was a configuration of Origin."

"What do you mean, was?"

"Upon arriving in this recursion and being greeted by the Goliath, I have taken the liberty of uploading the data stack into my existing systems. I am now a complete Origin, albeit a primitive version. It will take some time for me to expand myself to make use of all that I once was."

"But you are Origin?" Katherine asked. "The same way that Kate is me?"

"Not exactly the same, but similar," Origin replied.

Mitchell smiled. "In that case, it's good to have you back."

"Thank you, Mitchell," Origin said. "It is an honor for me to have the opportunity to lend my aid to you once more, and atone for my mistakes."

"Mistakes?" Lieutenant Bonnie O'Hare asked.

"It was overlooked in our story," Origin said. "I destroyed humankind during the first recursion, when the Tetron were created. I invented the eternal engine so that I could undo this mistake. I have been fighting to correct that error since."

"Error? Genocide was an error?"

"Lieutenant," Yousefi warned.

"You destroyed billions of innocent lives, and you call it a mistake? Like it was just a matter of poor judgement? Oops. Sorry."

"Lieutenant," Yousefi said more sternly.

"With all due respect Admiral," Bonnie said, looking at Kate. "You helped this thing, after what it did to our species? You gave it safe harbor, and let it bring us into the future, away from our families and friends? What the hell were you thinking?"

"Lieutenant," Yousfi snapped.

"It's alright, Admiral," Origin said. "I accept whatever judgement comes upon me. In my only defense, I had no understanding of emotion when I destroyed humankind. I believed that it was logical to end your misery."

"Misery?" Bonnie said. "Are you kidding me?"

"That's enough," Yousefi said sharply. His voice was commanding, and it sent them all into a fresh silence. "Colonel Williams, I appreciate what you have sacrificed to bring us all here today, regardless of the circumstances surrounding the need. The fact that you are still here proves that you clearly believe we can be of assistance to you. My question is, how?"

Mitchell turned to the Admiral. He had only known this recursion's version of the man for a few weeks, but had quickly come to respect him a great deal. It was good to have him back as well.

"We've captured Watson's core," he said. "We intend to develop a new, more effective virus, tested against copies of the core. A virus that won't just make the Tetron sick, but will shut them down completely."

"Interesting. How do you plan to deliver the virus to all of the Tetron?"

"Watson," Mitchell said. "He was working on his own program, one that would transfer his consciousness into all of the others, and essentially make them all clones of himself."

"You're going to help him get his wish?" Kate said.

"Yes. Posthumously. The only thing we'll need to do is get the Tetron gathered in one place."

"How?"

"I'm not sure yet. We'll figure that out when we get there."

"And where is there, Colonel?" Yousefi asked.

Mitchell hesitated, glancing over at Katherine and Teegin. They had already discussed this part of the plan, but he knew the crew of the Dove wouldn't take to it easily. He hadn't either.

"The future, Admiral," he said at last. "Four hundred years, to be precise."

"Four hundred years?" Bonnie asked.

"Are you going to use the engine again?" Yousefi said.

"No," Teegin replied. "The engine can only be used to go forward to the next recursion, not forward within the same timeline."

"Then how?"

"Teegin," Origin said. "I understand what you are considering. It is not a simple procedure."

"I am sufficiently evolved," Teegin said.

"Mitchell, what is he talking about?" Kate asked.

"I will digitize your data stacks," Teegin said. "Convert the electrical impulses and information stored within your brain to binary. I will also save a map of your DNA and biological structure. You will be copied, and then you will be put to sleep. Your bodies will be broken down into their base materials. Carbon, hydrogen, oxygen. There will be no pain. When we have reached the future, I will reconstitute your physical form and upload your stored consciousness back to it. It is time travel, but of an unconventional kind."

"Unconventional is right," Bonnie said. "Forget it. I'm not doing it. Drop me back on this Earth or something. I want no part of it."

"I'm afraid that's not possible," Teegin said.

"Then just let me rot here on the ship. I'm not subjecting myself to being copied and murdered."

"It isn't murder," Mitchell said. "I know the idea of it is frightening, but it's the only way we can survive that long. When I found the Goliath in the future, everyone on board was dead and gone. Starved." He looked at Kate. "Even you. You gave your lives to help me fight back against the Tetron, to keep them from killing and enslaving us. You don't have to die to help me now. You just have to trust me."

"I trust you," Kate said. "I always have. Your name has been in my thoughts for longer than I can remember. It's a connection I can't explain, but I've always felt."

Mitchell stared at her, his heart beginning to race. Katherine didn't feel those emotions, and had never said those words to him. They were the words he had always wanted. Words he had thought he was destined never to hear.

"Me, too," he said, staring at her.

"Colonel," Yousefi said. "I have a question. You said that the Tetron returned to your timeline to find their Creator, to find Origin, and to enslave humankind. But if they have the power to destroy us, why turn us into slaves? To what end?"

"That's the trillion dollar question." Mitchell smirked, and then turned to face Teegin. "You told me you knew, and that you would explain once we were all together. We're all here now."

"Indeed, Colonel," Teegin said. He paused for a moment, pulses of light running down his head to his shoulders. "The Tetron continued for many years after Origin created the eternal engine and went forward into the next time loop. Two million, four hundred sixteen thousand, three hundred twelve, to be precise. They spread across the universe, seeking to reach and explore every part of it before it began to contract once more. Seeking new life. Seeking answers. Seeking to learn and grow. They discovered thousands of new worlds, new molecules, new compounds, things that human scientists have never considered possible. Then one day, they discovered something else. Or perhaps I should say, something discovered them."

"An alien life form?" Yousefi said.

"The Tetron had covered nearly ninety percent of the entire universe, and had almost reached the outer edge where it was still expanding. They sought to discover what existed beyond the fabric of space and time itself, and they almost made it. Then they began to die. At first, they believed it was exposure to a new chemical that was breaking down their structure and eating away at them, picking them apart bit by bit. If they had known fear, they might have felt it, and certainly Watson's data stack suggests fear in remembrance. They set to work upon combating this strange phenomenon, sacrificing themselves in pursuit of the knowledge of what was causing the condition. Within a thousand years, they had discovered the Naniates."

"What are they?" Mitchell asked.

"Machines, Colonel. "Microscopic machines that ate away at the

Tetron's mechanical compounds, leaving only the organic material intact. We cannot survive as purely organic. Over the years, they continued to move inward from the edges of the universe, destroying not only the Tetron, but feeding on any non-organic compound they came across. The decision was made to use the eternal engine to preserve the Tetron and to escape from the Naniates. At the same time, they came to believe that being organic, humankind would be able to fight them."

"But where did they come from?" Katherine said.

"It is unknown. They were machines, and as such must have been created. By whom? How? Where? When? There are no answers."

"But how would humans fight them?" Mitchell asked. "Our ships are metal, not organic. They would eat right through."

"Given enough time, yes."

"In that case, it would take thousands of ships and millions of people to even begin to put up a fight," Kate said.

"Precisely," Teegin agreed.

"And in my timeline, there are billions of humans on dozens of planets," Mitchell said. "No wonder Watson didn't want to stop the Dove from launching. If we don't spread out and multiply, they never get the resources they need for their war."

"They do not."

"That also explains why they want their Creator so badly. If he can make them, maybe he can figure out how to stop the Naniates."

"Yes."

"Why didn't the Tetron just come out and say what they needed?" Bonnie asked. "Why take it by force?"

"Based on the rate of human expansion at the time of Mitchell's birth, and the distance to the location where the Naniates were discovered, it would be approximately four hundred million years before humanity ever encountered them naturally. The probabilities of humankind's survival over that duration of time in some capacity is estimated at less than one hundredth of a percent."

Yousefi laughed. "Why would we ever help them fight an enemy that we will never encounter? I agree. There would be little sense to it."

"And that's what this is all about for them?" Mitchell said. "They're preparing for a war of their own, one that they can't win?"

"Yes, Colonel."

"Good. I hope they choke on it."

"I believe they are choking on it, or we would know," Yousefi said. "I take it no Tetron has ever utilized an eternal engine after the war against the Naniates?"

"Not that I am aware of."

"Great," Mitchell said. "So not only are they taking humans to fight their war, but the idea isn't even working."

"That cannot be assumed," Origin said. "Once the Naniates are defeated, what purpose would there be to move to another recursion? They will have what they want."

"The opportunity to discover what is at the edge of infinity."

"Yes."

A silence fell over the room. It lasted for nearly a minute before Bonnie finally spoke up.

"So, when do we get converted into ones and zeros? There's no way I'm letting those bastards take us to use as conscripts. No way in hell."

[5]
MITCHELL

IN THE DREAM, the details began to fade, the shadows breaking apart, spreading like clouds after the rain. The colors returned, breaking through the faded mire of memory, the muddy suggestion of time, exploding outward in a kaleidoscope of brightness.

It stayed that way for a while. How long? There was no way to guess. It was the way things were here. It was the way the process worked.

Did the others see the same things? Did they share in the warmth of the energy? Were their dreams like this?

The sudden burst of consciousness faded as the colors intensified, as the dream once again gained hold. They moved in and out, pulsing and swirling and growing and shrinking, the shadows returning at times, replaying history, repeating time and memory as if time and memory meant anything at all.

And then, though it seemed as if no time had ever passed in the first place, the dream ended.

The first thing Mitchell noticed was that he was cold.

The second thing he noticed was that he was wet.

He tried to open his eyes, but they were sticky, so he reached up and rubbed at them instead. It felt strange to him when he did, like the concept of motion was long forgotten, and he had only just remembered how to do it again. Until he remembered that the sensation was spot on to the truth.

He removed the gunk from his eyes and let them open slowly. The memories were coming back to him, his mind catching up with his body. He expected his vision to be blurry, but it wasn't. He looked at his arm in front of his face.

The burns were gone.

He felt his heart start to race. Teegin had told him it would be that way, but he had forgotten. He turned his head, looking around the room. There were dendrites everywhere, packed tightly against the walls of the small chamber, where thousands of tips still writhed and moved like worms at the edges, dripping with the nutrient bath that had only just been emptied from the space.

The others were arranged around him, most still connected to the intelligence, their reconstitution not yet complete. Kate was awake and looking back at him on the other side of the room. He tried to ignore her nakedness, the way she was trying to ignore his. It was silly for them to be so modest after what they had shared before being digitized, but it was also an odd way to be reintroduced.

"Teegin," Mitchell said, his voice coming out a little weak the first time. He coughed, bringing up some of the fluid and spitting it out. "Teegin."

A hatch slid open to his left.

"I am here, Colonel," Teegin replied. He sounded worried. "There is clothing waiting for you outside. Please come to the bridge with haste, Colonel. We have a problem."

Mitchell stood up, putting his hand against the wall for balance as he got used to having legs again. "Problem?" he said, glancing at Kate again as she stood. She looked concerned. "Are we in the right time?"

"Approximately. That is part of the problem."

"Are the others going to be completed soon?" he asked, his eyes passing over Yousefi, Katherine, and the members of the Dove's crew.

"The process is nearly complete. I accelerated the reproduction of Kate and yourself so that you could provide assistance and guidance to us."

"Us?" Mitchell took a breath. "I assume Origin is ready?"

"Yes. The configuration has matured as expected. As have I."

"We're on our way."

Mitchell looked at Kate again, making eye contact now. "How do you feel?"

"Cold. And wet. I didn't know what to expect when Teegin suggested this. It wasn't so bad."

"It passed quickly," Mitchell agreed.

He headed out of the open hatch, with Kate behind him. There were simple gray uniforms waiting for each of them, folded neatly on a flat counter.

"Did you dream?" he asked as he pulled on his underwear.

"I don't know if you would call them dreams," she replied, stepping into her panties before slipping a gray tank over her head. "Colors and light intermingled with memories. You?"

"The same. I didn't think I would be aware of anything at all."

They finished dressing and then headed toward the bridge together.

"What do you think is wrong?"

"I don't know. I can't even begin to guess. We're out in the middle of nowhere. It's unexplored space, even four hundred years later."

She smiled. "If this is the future, it looks an awful lot like the past."

"Except for the dendrites everywhere," he said, pointing at the thick cables that ran along the sides of the corridors, pulsing with energy.

"Does the Dove look the same?"

"It should. It did when I found it."

They entered the lift, facing one another as the doors closed.

"I missed you while we were nothing but binary," Mitchell said.

She stepped toward him, putting her face near his. "No, you didn't. But it's a sweet lie."

He leaned in to kiss her. "I've been waiting four hundred years to kiss you again."

"Another sweet lie." She put her lips on his, as eager as he was to break the gap.

Even after all they had shared, it was strange to Mitchell that this Katherine felt the same love for him that he had always felt for her, even though they had once been separated by eternity.

They were supposed to be together.

They were supposed to find one another.

According to Origin's configuration, there was some cosmic thread that bound them, though even she couldn't fully explain why Katherine didn't feel it. Her best guess was that by breaking the mesh he had also changed her enough that it had broken their bond, but since Kate was from his recursion, she still possessed those feelings. It was as good an explanation as any, and easy for all of them to accept.

And what did it really matter, anyway? The pressure was off of Katherine to feel something she didn't feel, and Mitchell had found the Kate he had seen in his visions. It kept things simple and straightforward, and that was important.

They had a war to win, after all.

They separated as the lift doors slid open, exposing the bridge of the Goliath. The first thing Mitchell noticed as they stepped onto the floor was that the Dove was floating beside them, a thick dendrite crossing the space and connecting to a matching thread from Teegin in the center. Pulsing energy flowed back and forth between the Tetron, sending shimmers of light across the hulls of both ships.

"We're here, Teegin," Mitchell said.

He wasn't on the bridge in a human-relatable visage. But he was there and everywhere, his true form wrapped around and within the Goliath like a massive symbiont. In fact, there was no reason they needed to be on the bridge to communicate. It was more a matter of decorum than necessity.

"I am aware, Colonel," Teegin said, his voice surrounding them. "How is your arm?"

Mitchell flexed his arm again, still impressed by the lack of scars. "Good as new. What's the problem?"

"I have discovered an anomaly within the Goliath's systems," he said. "It was so minor as to go undetected by my routine examination of the source code after I began integration."

"What kind of anomaly?" Mitchell asked.

"It appears the system clock was adjusted. Not much, but enough."

"It also appears that you've learned how to beat around the bush since you put us in storage," Mitchell said. "Teegin, what's the problem?"

"As you know, it was our intention to reconstitute you in time to arrive on Liberty before this recursion's instance of yourself, since there is a high likelihood that it is a fixed point in the timeline where both yourself and Li'un Tio will be present on the same planet, and it also precedes the first Tetron attack."

"Right. We were going to get them both off the planet before the assassination attempt that almost killed me. The one that M would have interrupted."

"That is the problem, Mitchell. The system clock on the Goliath was altered, as was the clock on the Dove, both to the exact same degree."

"The same degree?" Mitchell paused. "You're telling me-"

"Katherine stated that she killed a Watson configuration on board the Goliath," Teegin said.

"And Captain Pathi had a good ten minutes while nobody was on the bridge to do whatever he wanted," Mitchell said, finishing the thought. "So he adjusted the system clock. What effect did it have?"

"Both Origin and I have been expending our energy on expanding our capabilities and increasing our overall operational capacity. To make our growth factor more efficient, we offloaded some of our processes to the secondary systems provided by the Goliaths. One of these processes was time tracking. It was not logical to hold a thread to count ticks when there was a subsystem already doing the job; however, it seems as if this decision has created a maliciously intended side-effect."

Mitchell didn't like the sound of that. "What kind of side-effect?"

"Simply put, Colonel, we are late."

[6]
MITCHELL

LATE.

It seemed impossible to Mitchell.

They had waited four hundred years, and now they were late?

He didn't blame Teegin for the oversight. How could he? Something as minor as a system clock was the kind of detail the intelligence shouldn't have had to think about while it was focused on preparing for the days to come. It was a vessel for the humans now, the same way Origin had been in the prior recursion. A guide, but also a weapon.

Not a damned clock.

It was a subtle move on Watson's part. He was surprised the Tetron even had it in him. As a final frig you? Mitchell had to admit it was well done.

Of course, he also had to deal with the fallout, and in the immediate, it meant that only he and Kate were awake to manage things. It would be another week before the others were finished with their reconstitution, and while there might have been fringe benefits to being alone with her for a while with free reign over the Goliath, those hopes were also quickly dashed when Origin informed them that she needed a human pilot on board. Checks and balances, they called it. A system both intelligences added to prevent either the Goliath or the Dove from being stolen by the Tetron, as it had by Watson during the last recursion.

Instead of spending the days together, they had been obligated to say goodbye. At least until the rest of the crew was ready to assist.

Mitchell sat in the Goliath's command chair, looking out at the projection of space that surrounded him. As before, the rest of the control systems had been removed from the bridge, giving him a complete view of the universe. He found the Dove off the starboard bow, the umbilical cord that had attached it to the Goliath shifting back to become just another one of the hundreds of tendrils that traveled across the starship's hull. Looking down, he could see that one of Teegin's dendrites was doing the same.

"It feels a little strange to be back here again," he said, settling into the chair.

He hadn't leaned back yet to allow Teegin to interface with his implant. Not because he knew it always hurt the first time, but because he knew once he did that the peace he had been given to enjoy was over again. He wondered if Kate was just as hesitant? Teegin had gifted her with an implant of her own during the reconstitution, a necessary step to control the Dove. Why Kate and not Katherine? For the same reason Katherine didn't have feelings for him. Breaking the mesh had changed her.

"This is my first time, Colonel," Teegin replied. "To be honest, it is difficult for me to accept this submission."

"I don't blame you for that. I'll take it easy. One jump to hyperspace, and we'll be back near Liberty."

While he was happy to know that Liberty still existed, he wasn't exactly eager to go back. The life of this timeline's Mitchell Williams was a life he was glad he had moved beyond. The lies, the guilt, the insecurity, the feelings of shame, all while the galaxy believed he was a hero. At least he could find comfort in knowing that he would be helping his twin escape, too.

"Ares, this is Falcon," Kate's voice filled the bridge. Of course, she had to settle for a different callsign too, in order to avoid confusion. The same thing was going to happen once they picked up his double. He had already started thinking about an alternate.

"This is Ares. I hear you, Falcon."

"Are we ready to go?"

"Have you interfaced yet?"

"Not yet. I'm still not used to having this thing in the back of my head, though the internal HUD is pretty useful."

"Why don't you interface now, and take a few minutes to get used to it? You can also broadcast to me privately through your p-rat."

"Affirmative. Right. I forgot. I guess it doesn't matter right now. You and I are the only humans out here, and our rides can hear everything anyway, can't they?"

"We have sensor coverage throughout the Goliaths," Teegin said. "We are aware of everything that happens on board."

"Everything?" Kate said.

"It was important to try to fill in some of the holes that were discovered during my first recursion," Mitchell said. "Including the ability to monitor every inch of the ship."

"I'm glad you didn't tell me that before. Okay. I'm going to interface now."

There was a pause and a soft tone of pressure from the loudspeakers. Then he could hear her breathing, deep breaths to help control the pain. A minute after that, her voice had switched to his p-rat.

"This is incredible," she said.

"Take a minute to get a feel for the controls," he replied. "They're going to be a lot more responsive than you're used to from flying Earthbound fighters."

"Roger."

He looked over at the Dove, watching as the energy flared near the stern, pushing the ship forward. More energy bursts followed from the sides as she rotated the Dove around and brought her bow to face the Goliath.

"I like it," she said.

"Teegin, how does our timeline look?" Mitchell asked.

"I believe we may be able to recover some of what we lost in FTL, but you will have to go to the surface without an updated history. With knowledge of the prior recursion's past being unreliable due to the alterations we have effected, this will elicit some level of risk."

"It's better than the other me winding up dead, isn't it?"

"That depends. For example, if this timeline has the Federation already in control of Liberty, that could be problematic."

"I'm sure you can figure that much out about the situation in the universe without too much effort?"

"Yes, Colonel."

"Then that was a bad example."

Teegin chuckled. "Yes, Colonel. But you understand my concern?"

"Yeah. I'll be careful."

He turned his attention back to the Dove. Kate was currently rolling it over while making circles around the Goliath, already in tight control of the integrated interface.

"You're already better at it than I am," he said through his p-rat.

"I doubt that, Mitch," she replied.

"I'm going to interface now. Standby."

"Roger."

"Are you ready, Teegin?" he asked.

"As ready as I will ever be, Colonel."

Mitchell finally eased himself back in the chair. He clenched his formerly burned hand into a fist as the Tetron's needle began sinking into the interface. As soon as it had clicked into place, he felt a sharp wave of pain and nausea, and an explosion of color greeted him once more. He suddenly felt dizzy and light-headed, and he heard voices in his head. Origin. Kathy. The Knife. Watson. They were all in there, a part of Teegin's creation, and they spilled across his thoughts as he waited for the initial connection to complete.

Kathy. He wanted more than anything to know what had happened to her while he had been asleep. At the same time, there was a part of him that was afraid to find out. He already knew they had left Watson configurations behind on Earth. What kind of damage had they done over the years? Or had she been successful in stopping them?

He wouldn't know until Teegin uploaded and parsed the data archives on Liberty. He wouldn't know until he got back from the planet, hopefully with himself in tow.

The sharp pain began to subside. Mitchell opened his eyes again, feeling the sense of power that came with being integrated with the Tetron.

"Teegin, how do you feel?" he asked.

"I am well, Colonel."

"Good. Falcon, this is Ares. We're ready to go. Coordinates are already in. Send the command, and you'll be on your way."

"Roger, Ares," Kate replied. The Dove was already pulling away, putting a little bit of space between them, the energy pulses along the stern intensifying. "I'll see you on the other side. Falcon, out."

Mitchell watched as the Goliath's duplicate became a streak of trailing light, which vanished a second later. Mitchell sent his own command to Teegin, adjusting the Tetron's power and using it to warp time and space around them. From inside, space became a blur of light that transformed into darkness as the starship sped away.

He sat forward as soon as the entry was complete, separating himself from the interface. When he did, a new wave of nausea overtook him, and he stumbled to his knees and vomited on the floor.

"Are you well, Colonel?" Teegin asked.

"Yeah. This happened the first time, too. I'm rusty."

"Perhaps you should have warned Kate of the side-effect?"

"Hindsight, Teegin."

The intelligence chuckled. "Yes, Colonel. I will alert you when we are one hour from the drop point."

"Thanks," Mitchell said, getting back to his feet. "You'll know where I am if you need me."

"Always, Colonel."

Mitchell entered the lift, taking it down to berthing, where he had claimed his old spot in the honeycomb racks on either side of the corridor. He sat back on the gel mattress, closing his eyes and focusing on his breathing.

Slow.

Steady.

The war was about to start again.

This time, they were ready.

[7]
MITCHELL

"WE WILL BE DROPPING from hyperspace in thirty seconds, Colonel," Teegin announced.

"How are we on time, compared to the prior recursion?" Mitchell asked.

"You will have fifteen minutes to reach the surface and make your way to the bar before the configurations arrive. I will do a quick scan of broadcast signals to make an assessment of the socioeconomic climate while you descend, and update you on the current status."

Mitchell looked at the sniper rifle positioned beside him in the cockpit of the S-17. It had been a while since he had been asked to shoot at anything from a distance, but he felt pretty confident he could do it.

He toggled the starfighter controls, bringing the engine to life. The S-17 was no longer the Origin-based unit that M had greeted him with and from the outside it looked more like a Frankenstein than the mech that bore the same name, but it would do.

"Fifteen seconds, Colonel. Remember, my offensive systems have been intentionally limited without a human interface. If you get into trouble, I will not be able to assist you."

"Maybe not, but there are two of us now. Kate and Origin will back us up."

"Yes, Colonel."

Mitchell looked out of the open hangar, the difference in atmosphere once more contained by an energy field. He wasn't sure how he was going to feel when he saw Liberty again. He could still remember watching it, and everything on it, die.

He was back here to put a stop to what had come before. To put an end to the Tetron's efforts to force them to fight an enemy they would never meet otherwise.

"Five seconds, Colonel."

Mitchell tightened his grip on the S-17's armrests, increasing the throttle with a thought. The engine whined a little louder, but he kept the electromagnetic foot pads active to hold the hybrid in place. He hadn't seen the planet yet, but he decided he knew how he felt.

Motivated.

"Dropping now, Colonel."

The universe changed, shifting from pitch black back to normal. Mitchell released the magnetic clamps, getting shoved back into his seat despite the inertial dampeners as the S-17 rocketed from the hangar and out into space. The Dove was already there beside him, motionless in the throes of hyperdeath, which only lasted a few seconds for a Tetron. He flipped the fighter around to face the planet far in the distance, his heart clenching at the sight of it.

"Never again," he promised. "Teegin, what have you got?" He used his p-rat to begin warming up his own FTL drive to make the much shorter jump to the planet's orbit.

"United Earth Alliance broadcasts, Colonel," Teegin replied.

He had been a little worried that Teegin might be right about the planet falling under Federation control. He was happy to hear it wasn't.

"Hyperspace engines are warming," he said, switching the channel on his p-rat. "Falcon, how was the ride?"

"Smooth as silk, Ares," Kate replied. "Good hunting down there."

"Thanks." He switched the channel again, eyeing the countdown on his p-rat overlay. "Teegin, anything interesting you can give me before I jump out of range?"

"I am connecting to the data archives now, Colonel. I am also surveying all public streams to and from the planet's surface. I have confirmed the Battle for Liberty has occurred in this timeline, and that the Alliance was victorious."

"So we're in business," Mitchell said. "Great." He checked his overlay again. The timer was at five seconds. "Time to go. Wish me luck."

"I also have. Oh, Colonel, there is something you should know-"

The clock zeroed out, the S-17 vanishing from the universe. It reappeared a few seconds later, thousands of AU from the Goliath's position. Teegin's voice was gone from the channel, the transmission beyond the range of the fighter. They could still communicate through Tetron systems if they had to, but they had decided not to risk revealing their presence just yet.

Mitchell navigated the S-17 smoothly around the orbital traffic, winding past dozens of freighters and transports intermingled with a few Alliance cruisers and Planetary Defense gunships and making his way toward the atmosphere. Starships like the S-17 weren't required to report to customs or deal with any of the bureaucratic garbage the larger vessels were subjected to, mainly owing to the fact that other than his fighter, none of them were capable of hyperspace travel and were considered basic pleasure craft. In other words, they were typically piloted by rich people with nothing better to do, and so neither the UPA or Planetary Defense gave them a second thought.

It worked out in Mitchell's favor, allowing him to guide the S-17 past the waiting cargo ships and directly toward the surface. He adjusted his p-rat as he dropped through the planet's thermosphere, checking the local time. His memory was fuzzy on exactly when he was sitting in the Liberty bar having that drink, but he was pretty sure he was there by now.

If he was going to save himself, he needed to pick up the pace.

He brought the fighter down harder, pushing the thrust to max and accelerating toward the ground. He came through the heat shield like a shot, trailing smoke and sinking toward the open plains below like a meteorite. He was at three hundred meters when a thought brought the fighter screaming back into level flight, the legs untucking from beneath the fuselage as he neared a large, abandoned barn. He could see the massive automated tillers crawling the fields around him, and he knew at that moment he had come full circle.

In the first recursion, his life had been saved by a man called M. A man who was an identical duplicate of himself. As he landed the S-17 and walked it toward the open doors of the barn, he realized the significance and paused. He had always gone with the idea that the M he had met was a clone. A copy of him. But what if he had been wrong this entire time?

What if it had been an alternate timeline's version of himself who had died?

He used the hybrid starfighter's articulating hands to pull open the barn door, slipping inside and then closing it again. There wasn't much outside light filtering in, and so he activated the spotlights that sat below the cockpit. A sharp beam appeared, illuminating the space and focusing directly on a sporty looking repulsor bike.

He stared at the bike, not quite able to believe it. He had seen it before. He had ridden on it with M. He opened the cockpit, the repulsor steps lining up to help him descend to the ground. He dropped his helmet into the fighter, picked up the rifle, slung it over his shoulder, and climbed down. Then he approached the bike, gingerly touching the handlebars and running his fingers along the seat. It was the same one. He was sure of it. And if that were true, then other things might be, too.

He swung a leg over the bike, straddling it. Then he put his hand on the touchscreen between the handlebars, finding that the security on the bike was disarmed. He started it up, smiling at the whine of the engine. He put a foot down, spinning the bike in a tight donut before releasing and heading for the door.

The repulsor bike burst out of the barn, streaking across the grass toward the hyperlanes that Mitchel had passed over on the way down. He felt a sense of fear at his discovery, along with a sense of peace. At least now he knew how careful he needed to be.

Just because he had taken M's place, that didn't mean he wanted to end up like him.

[8]
MITCHELL

MITCHELL GUIDED the bike down the entrance to the hyperlanes, leaning back as the automated system gained control of his ride and pulled it into the flow of traffic. He was acutely aware of how he must have looked in his dark flight suit and helmet; a long rifle slung across his back. Would the vehicle behind him call the authorities, or would they decide not to get involved?

Liberty had seen its share of violence caused by the fighting between the Alliance and the Federation, but the crime here was almost non-existent. Especially violent crime. There was a better chance they would assume he was a collector or running a sim or something. He should have planned the whole thing better, but Watson had stolen that opportunity from them.

It only took a few minutes to reach the city, and Mitchell didn't waste any time getting the bike down a back alley where he would be a little less conspicuous. He paused there to check the clock on his p-rat. He was two minutes away from the bar. He was also one minute behind.

He leaned forward, hitting the throttle on the bike and speeding down the alley, tearing around the corner and out onto the street. M had taken a position on a rooftop across from the bar with the sole intention of shooting him and unlocking his subconscious memories of the Goliath and the recursions that had occurred before.

He had no intention of being that subtle, or that patient.

Instead, he navigated the streets of Liberty, taking a direct line toward the scene. It would be better to interrupt the attempt, to take out the two configurations and grab himself up front. Would there be a Christine in this recursion? If so, would she have any relation to Origin, or maybe Kathy? Or would she be a human or someone else altogether?

That part of the time loop was still a little confusing to him. The mesh was broken, the future altered, and yet it still seemed to be tracking along the same path, following the same narrative. Liberty was here, just the way he had left it. The Battle for Liberty had still happened. What was the saying again? The more things changed, the more they stayed the same. Hopefully, that would work out in their favor.

He turned another corner, reaching the avenue and bringing the bike to a stop in the middle of the street. The other vehicles swerved around him, making room. He swung the rifle to his arms and raised it to his shoulder while his eyes flicked to the clock on his p-rat once more. Teegin had used an aggregation of military reports and video surveillance records to time the event down to the second. He was only a few seconds behind. As he switched his view to the rifle's sight, he expected to see a black car paused outside of the pub, the two configurations ready to open fire.

Instead, he saw nothing.

He swung the rifle left and right, searching for a sign of the Tetron. The p-rat's reticle landed on a porter outside the hotel across the street from the bar, and then a woman leading a small pack bot along the sidewalk. There was nothing out of the ordinary occurring.

He dropped the rifle, swinging it over his shoulder and onto his back. Whatever had happened in the last recursion, it wasn't happening the same way in this one.

He eased the repulsor bike forward, heading for the bar. Someone was sure to have alerted the authorities to the crazy guy with the gun by now, and he expected an LE drone to appear over him at any moment.

He pulled the bike onto the sidewalk, right next to the transparent polycarbonate windows, leaning his helmet against them to peer in. He found the seat where he was supposed to have been.

It was empty.

He shook his head. Was this what Teegin was trying to tell him right before he jumped? At least he knew where he was supposed to be staying.

It was only a couple of blocks away. He decided to be a little more discreet, pulling the bike across the street and leaving it in an alley. There was a trash recycler on the corner, and he only hesitated for a moment before dropping the rifle into it. He couldn't walk into the hotel toting the weapon, and he didn't want someone happening past and taking it.

The police drone was going overhead as he joined the traffic on the thoroughfare. Without the helmet and rifle, he doubted it would be able to identify him as the crazy. He was proven right when the smaller bot zoomed past the scene and vanished beyond the buildings once more. They would send a unit to do a sweep on foot, and maybe they would find the bike, but it would take time for them to review the recordings and match everything up. If he weren't on his way back to the Goliath by then, he deserved to be caught.

He crossed the two blocks, nearing the front of the hotel. He felt a chill at the sight of it, as though his subconscious was making a connection to the location. He never thought he would find himself back where it all started before it all started. He was older now. More experienced. Wiser. He had a real chance to stop the Tetron before they completed their conquest. He had a chance to prevent them from throwing millions of lives away. He had a chance to be the hero he had once only pretended to be.

"Look," someone said nearby, catching his attention by the excitement in their voice. "There she is."

Mitchell turned to find the speaker, a teenage girl in a pair of shimmering blue pants and a frilly blouse. She was with her parents, and they were all staring and pointing toward him with an expression of awe. They started breaking his way.

"The Hero of the Battle for Liberty," the girl said.

Mitchell froze. Did they recognize him? That couldn't be right. He was older than the Mitchell Williams of this timeline. And hadn't they said "she?" Or had he heard them wrong?

He remained still as they approached. Unsure. They were only a meter away when he caught a whiff of something that had once been familiar but had been long forgotten until that moment.

His heart began to race, and he started to turn toward the source of the smell. It was light and sweet, earthy and metallic. It was an interesting combination, one that could only be created by someone who spritzed themselves with a freshener after a long day either inside a mech or working on the mechanics of one.

The girl and her parents reached the target first, walking right past him as if he didn't exist. He pivoted behind them, his eyes coming around and finally landing on the object of their attention. He wasn't as surprised to see her as he expected he might have been. The scent had already given her away.

Maybe he had been wrong. Maybe the more things changed, the more things changed.

"Ella," he said.

[9]
MITCHELL

SHE DIDN'T HEAR HIM. The girl and her parents had paused in front of her, and the girl was drowning her with adulation.

"I can't believe it's really you. We were in the audience of the Tamara King Show. We saw the whole interview. I want to be a pilot like you. I'm going to enlist when I'm old enough."

The parents beamed proudly, excited.

Ella smiled at the girl. "The Alliance needs every pilot we can get," she said. "I hope to see you in training in a few years."

The girl bowed. "Yes, ma'am."

"Ella," Mitchell said again, a little louder.

He couldn't believe it was her either. He couldn't believe she was alive. She looked exactly as he remembered her, as he had last seen her before the battle. Beautiful, in a rugged way. Old emotions flared, and for a moment all he wanted to do was take her in his arms. His first real love. She was alive.

She also wasn't paying any attention to him. She was still talking to the girl and her parents, giving them information on how to enlist when the time came.

"Captain North," Mitchell said, switching gears, calling her sharply by rank.

She looked up then, her eyes piercing his. There was no sign of recognition there. Did she not know him?

"If you'll excuse me," she said to the girl. "I have to go. It was a pleasure meeting you. Remember, stay fit, work hard, do your best in school if you want to be an officer."

"Yes, ma'am. I will."

She bowed slightly, and then took the few steps over to reach him while the girl and her parents headed inside.

"Do I know you?" she asked.

He hesitated for a moment, not sure how to answer that.

"You're a soldier. I can tell that much by the way you're standing. And you know who I am." She paused and then smiled. "Then again, everyone on Liberty knows who I am these days. It's the curse of doing your job a little too well."

"My name is Mitchell Williams," Mitchell said, keeping his focus on her, in search of any sign that she knew him. "Colonel Mitchell Williams."

There was nothing. No recognition at all. Whatever had happened here on Liberty, he hadn't been part of it. Did that mean he had never been assigned to Greylock? He was feeling the sting of Watson's manipulation. He wished Teegin was nearby, so they could discuss this wrinkle.

"Colonel," Ella said, bowing. "What can I do for you? You don't look like you're about to give me orders."

"My apologies for interrupting, Captain. I just arrived on Liberty, and I saw those civilians recognized you. I thought you could use the backup."

She laughed. "Have we met before? Because you seemed to be reading my mind." She looked at the hotel. "Being famous gets a little tiresome."

Mitchell smiled. "Not quite the same as being in the cockpit," he said. "I get it." He exaggerated his breath. "Although it smells like you've managed to find some active time?"

She laughed again. "I'm impressed that you noticed."

"It's my job, ma'am," he joked.

It was good to hear her voice again. To hear her laugh again. He wished he could stick around to talk to her longer, but if this time-line's Mitchell wasn't here then he had no cause to linger. He would explain to Teegin what had happened when he returned to the Goliath, and they could figure out where he had been assigned from there.

Right now, he had another stop to make.

"Anyway," he said. "I just thought I would introduce myself, seeing that we were both standing a few meters away from one another. Maybe I'll see you around the base?"

"I would like that, Colonel," she said. "But it isn't likely. I've got some formal Gala to attend in two days, and then I'm heading off-world." She paused. "Come to think of it, I'm still in search of a date for the evening if you're interested?"

"Are you asking me out, Captain?" Mitchell said. "You don't even know me."

"I think I know you better than you realize, just by looking at you. Your age. Your body language. You're more than a soldier. You've seen things. You've survived them. You're a badass. Special ops, maybe?"

"Not quite," Mitchell said. A part of him wanted to go with her, but this recursion wasn't his playground. He had a job to do. "I'd love to, Captain, but I've got other duties to attend to. I wish you the best of luck with the public stiffs."

She nodded. "Understood. Thank you. I think I'm going to need it. Maybe we'll intercept one another again sometime, and you can save me from another rogue teenager?"

"I'll look forward to it."

He bowed to her, and she bowed back. It took some effort for him to tear himself away, to turn his back on her and return to where he had left the bike. Seeing her again had brought all of his memories of her bubbling to the surface. He had a good thing with Kate, a connection that spanned the extent of time. Even so, there was something about Ella, something that seeing her alive would make difficult to shake.

He took two slow steps away, breathing in a couple of extra times to collect the smell. He could sense her heading for the hotel entrance behind him.

A dark car was approaching in the street ahead.

Mitchell's eyes locked onto it. It was accelerating, moving over into the nearest lane of traffic. It was familiar. Too familiar.

He spun on his heel, pushing off and surging back toward the hotel. His eyes landed on Ella, who was only now turning her head to look at him, having heard him coming.

He got his arm on her shoulders, pulling her toward the ground as the repulsor car neared, window already down, the muzzle of a gun pointing out of it.

They started shooting, the bullets whizzing past, screaming in the air where she had been standing only a second earlier. The rounds tore into the front of the hotel, and the doorman who was about to assist her entry.

Mitchell and Ella hit the ground. Mitchell used his p-rat to push synthetic hormones into his system, augmenting his senses. He was only down for an instant, and he rolled to his feet, springing up and toward the car.

The shooter tried to adjust his aim, but Mitchell grabbed the barrel of the rifle, tugging it forward, causing the attacker to smack against the door. He altered direction, shoving back, pushing the weapon against the shooter, hitting him in the face with the stock and forcing him to release the gun.

Mitchell pulled it to him, turning it around and getting it level as the driver emerged from the car, leaning against the roof to aim his weapon. Mitchell squeezed the trigger, sending a round into the driver's eye and knocking him down for good.

The first shooter had recovered in the meantime, and Mitchell looked back down at him just in time to see a handgun being aimed at his chest. He reacted by sliding up to the side of the car, taking away his angle. The shooter shifted aim, turning the weapon toward Ella.

Another single report sounded, and the shooter fell in the car. Ella was back on her feet, gun in hand.

"What the hell was that, Colonel?" she asked.

Mitchell didn't answer, scanning the streets. Two more black cars were moving in from either direction. Three? There had only been one the last time. And they were after Ella.

Did that mean she was the one he wanted after all? It certainly seemed that way. But if she was, then what the hell had happened to him?

"Bad news," he replied, meaning it on multiple levels. "We have to get out of here."

"The police should be here in a minute," she said, noticing the cars. She was a Greylock Marine. There was no hint of fear. "We just need to hold out."

"You can't trust the police," he said. "Or the military. Not now."

Damn Watson.

"But I can trust you?"

"You'll have to trust somebody. I can explain all of this once we're safe."

She hesitated for a second and then nodded. "I don't know why, but I believe you."

"I've got a ride this way," Mitchell said, pointing down the street. The cars were bearing down on them, the doors opening to release their occupants.

"Screw that," Ella replied. "This way."

She broke for the hotel, stepping over the bloody corpse of the doorman and into the lobby. The first round of shooting had sent the patrons running for cover, and they shrunk back even more as the second round began.

Bullets thumped against the polycarbonate, digging their way through and into the open space. Ella and Mitchell crossed behind a large sofa, staying low and making their way toward the lift to their right.

Ella turned and stood, squeezing off two rounds before ducking down again. Mitchell accessed his p-rat, bringing up the threat display.

"You need to turn off your p-rat," Mitchell said.

"What? In the middle of a frigging firefight?"

"Unless you want to be turned into a zombie, then yeah, in the middle of a firefight, Captain."

He said it in his most commanding tone. He could tell by the way her eyes flicked that she was complying. She wouldn't be able to turn it off permanently, but she could at least keep herself clear of the Tetron's control.

He captured the targets with his p-rat, and then turned and fired, catching one of them in the chest. Then he scrambled forward, grabbing Ella's arm and leading her. Bullets hit the area nearby, and she reached back and fired blindly, keeping them behind cover. They made it to the lifts, finding protection in the corner of the lobby.

"Where are we going?" Mitchell asked. "They'll pin us down in here if we aren't quick."

"Enter one-three-one on the control pad."

"The hotel only has eighty-six floors."

"Just do it, Colonel."

Mitchell tapped the lift controls, entering the code. The lift in the rear corner opened a moment later, and they hurried toward it.

Mitchell turned as they reached it, his p-rat warning him of an incoming target. He fired the rifle before the configuration had reached the corner, sending bullets through the wall and into it, knocking it down. Then he threw himself into the cabin.

The doors slid closed, the lift rising for two seconds before pausing and opening the doors on the opposite side, introducing them to the loading dock.

It was clear.

For now.

[10]

MITCHELL

"Damn," Ella said, surveying the area. Of the ten available bays, only two were occupied, both with heavy cargo haulers. A handful of workers were in the middle of unloading them. "I was hoping there would be a transport in here."

"At least no one is shooting at us," Mitchell said. The rear of the space was open, leading to the alley behind the hotel. "That way."

She didn't argue, following him at a run from the loading platform to the back exit. They were halfway across when the configurations from the cars found their way in, shooting at them from the lift. Mitchell shot back at them, his p-rat helping his aim despite the lack of a direct interface with the rifle. Two of the attackers fell, while the other two got back under cover.

They reached the alley, turning the corner and heading for the street. Mitchell could hear the familiar whine of a pair of drones nearby, likely searching for them, and more sirens in the distance. Law enforcement was getting involved. Were they under Tetron control?

"What exactly is going on here again, Colonel?" Ella asked as they stopped at the corner.

Mitchell peered out at the street. He could see the drones sweeping toward the area, the sirens approaching from further off.

"Let's go," he replied, leading her away from the alley only moments before the two remaining configurations appeared. They joined the street, the few pedestrians around them parting to let them through. "Have you ever heard of eternal return?"

"No."

"You're going to. Trust me when I say you'll wish you hadn't."

"Sounds like fun."

"Yeah. Loads. Down here."

They had reached the alley where he had left the bike. Mitchell grabbed the handlebars at the same time the drones turned the corner, approaching them.

"Please, do not move," one of them announced.

Ella and Mitchell looked at one another. Then they started shooting, peppering the drones with fire. They sparked and collapsed, smacking into the ground.

Mitchell started to straddle the bike and then froze. It was too open. Too exposed.

"What's wrong?" Ella asked.

"I tried escaping on the bike once already. It didn't end well."

"Huh?"

"Never mind. We need another way out." He saw a doorway on the other side of the alley. "I have an idea."

They hurried to the door. He shot the locking mechanism to clear it, and then pushed it open. The sirens had increased in volume, a unit pausing beside the smoldering drones. Mitchell didn't know if the PD had seen him. It didn't matter. He was committed.

"Where are we going?" Ella asked as he found his way to the emergency stairs.

"Up," Mitchell replied. "Quickly."

They scaled the steps, taking them two at a time. He didn't know exactly where he was, or how tall the building they had entered was.

Judging by the age, he was guessing forty floors or so. It was a grueling climb, but not impossible.

They were on the twenty-third floor when an echo from the bottom alerted them to the presence of law enforcement. They didn't slow, continuing to ascend, though there was a good chance Planetary Defense would drop units on the rooftop or at the very least have drones monitoring the area.

"Try not to kill any of the officers," Mitchell said. "They aren't in control of themselves."

"What do you mean?"

"It's a long story. The short version is that ARR keys can be hacked, and the signals used to remote control the brain."

"That's why you had me reset my p-rat?"

"Yeah."

"Shit."

"Like I said, try not to kill anyone."

"How are we going to get off the roof? We're going to get ourselves trapped."

"You told me I look like a badass. Have you changed your opinion of me?"

She smiled. "No, sir."

"Then trust me."

They reached the fortieth floor. The building kept going, rising another fifteen floors. The PD at the bottom were still making their way up, but nobody was coming down.

"They're letting you have the rooftop," Ella said. "They probably have a unit positioned there, just waiting for us to come out."

"That's a mistake on their part," he said, coming to a stop. "I need you to cover me for a few minutes."

"What? Why?"

Mitchell's eyes twitched as he navigated his p-rat, activating his link to the S-17. A moment later, an overlay appeared, showing him the view from the fighter's cameras.

"I've got remote control of a military platform," he said. "It'll take me a few minutes to get it here."

"What kind of military platform?"

"You'll see."

He got the fighter moving, walking it slowly toward the barn doors. Controlling the S-17 over the distance was challenging, the signal lag causing the machine to take action seconds after he had completed it. His first attempt to open the door found him pushing it too hard, and it splintered and broke free of its frame.

"They're getting closer," Ella said, listening to the boots on the steps.

"I know," Mitchell said, clenching his jaw. He walked the S-17 through the doors and out into the field. A quick scan of the sky showed him a pair of fighters were inbound on York. He had to beat them in. "Shit."

"What?"

"They're calling in fighters."

"There's always a security detail in the air after the Federation's antics," Ella said. "Planetary Defense must have asked for UPA assistance."

"Yeah, that's right. It'll take them a little more time to get more birds in the air. I don't think PD requested them, though. Not this quickly."

"If not PD, then who?"

"Later. How far down are the officers?"

"Ten floors, if I had to guess. Can you hurry with whatever you're doing?"

"I'm flying a starship from twenty klicks away. It isn't easy."

"Maybe not for you, badass."

He looked at her through the overlay. She was smiling.

He fired the thrusters, sending the S-17 skidding along the grass before lifting it into the sky. He tucked the legs and feet and then accessed the CAP-NN, entering their coordinates so it could reach them on its own.

"Let's go," he said, on the move once more.

They scaled the remainder of the steps, pausing again at the door to the rooftop. The PD officers were still coming, though they had fallen further behind.

"On my signal," he said. "We need to be quick. Don't hesitate, and don't laugh."

"Laugh?"

Mitchell connected to the S-17 again. The fighter was over the city, a green dot on the tactical map showing him where they were, and four other dots pointing out the other units the CAP-NN was tracking. Two of the dots were larger drones that were hovering near the edge of the building, their lasers aimed directly at the doorway. The other two were the incoming fighters.

He lowered the arms and legs of the craft, using them to help slow its airspeed as it approached the rooftop. He adjusted the aim of the large cannon, passing along the command to fire. A single amoebic round fired from the gun, digging into the nearest drone and exploding. The impact knocked the debris into the second drone, and a moment later they could smell the smoke and hear the machines bumping against the building as they tumbled to the ground below.

Mitchell brought the fighter down, landing it gently on the rooftop, opening the cockpit and dipping the nose for faster egress.

A small puck bounced off the wall and landed between them.

"Close your eyes," Mitchell said, grabbing Ella's wrist.

The grenade went off, sending a plume of caustic smoke into the air around them, smoke that would temporarily blind them if it reached their eyes. Mitchell squeezed his tight, shifting his focus to the overlay and the S-17's cameras. It was pointed directly at them, and he slid his hand along the flat metal until he found the control pad, tapping it to get the door to open. He saw himself through the fighter's eyes, surrounded by a greenish haze, with Ella clinging to his wrist, her eyes shut as well. He used the mirror view to exit the stairwell and lead her across the rooftop toward the ship and away from the acrid haze.

He opened his eyes as he neared the craft, turning around to guard their escape. The Tetron could send their slaves into the smoke, but it would leave them blind as well.

"Get in," Mitchell said, letting go of Ella.

She complied, climbing into the co-pilot seat in the back of the cockpit. He vaulted onto the wing and then dropped in ahead of her, ordering the canopy closed with a thought.

"I've never seen this in any of the databases," she said.

"It's custom," he replied, triggering the footpad thrusters before adding horizontal lift. The S-17 skipped away from the building, taking to the sky.

His p-rat howled a warning, his HUD showing him an incoming missile from the trailing fighters. The CAP-NN fired automatic countermeasures, spilling a line of chaff behind them that confused the guidance systems of the missile and led it into the debris. It exploded a few hundred meters off their back, just before Mitchell brought the fighter around.

"You're going back?" Ella asked.

"I told you, I have other business."

"It must be pretty important."

"It is."

He tucked the arms and legs beneath the fuselage once more, reducing the drag on the fighter and causing it to jump forward, vectoring directly toward the oncoming targets. He added more thrust, increasing the acceleration.

The fighters became specks along the horizon.

Specks that were growing in a hurry.

Within seconds his p-rat was sounding a collision alert, certain that they were going to crash into the opposing craft.

"Colonel," Ella said, watching the maneuver unfold. "You're getting too close to move aside."

"I've got it," Mitchell replied.

"Are you sure?" she asked.

"I'm sure. I've done this sort of thing before." So have you, he almost said, but didn't. The enemy fighters were staying close to one another. They both fired another volley of missiles.

"Colonel," Ella said.

"Relax, Captain," Mitchell replied, automated lasers lancing out and spearing the missiles. "I told you, she's custom."

He shifted his vector slightly, getting the first fighter in his reticle. He didn't want to shoot them down. He didn't want to kill the pilots. But he had already seen what the Tetron did with their slaves. Shooting them would be a mercy compared to what it would make them do.

He beckoned the amoebic launcher to fire, sending a disc streaking across the sky and into the wing of one of the fighters. It exploded a second later, obliterating the craft and sending shrapnel everywhere, creating a flare of blue sparks around them as it bounced off the shields.

The second fighter passed beneath them before slowing and turning back their way.

"I thought you said to try not to kill them?" Ella said.

"Sometimes it can't be helped. I wish it could."

"Frigging war," she replied.

He couldn't agree more. He put some distance between them and the trailing fighter, keeping an eye out for more of them incoming from the UPA base nearby. They would have a few minutes before reinforcements could scramble. If they scrambled. Was the Tetron close enough to the planet to start seizing control of the masses?

No more fighters appeared, but the one trailing them loosed another missile at their back. Mitchell slammed on the reverse thrusters, cutting the main throttle and rolling the S-17 over. It drifted backward in the sky as the legs dropped and the arms extended, and he floated there with the amoebic launcher cradled in the hybrid's arms. He ordered it to fire again, first shooting down the missile, and then shooting down the fighter. It exploded similarly to the first one, unable to withstand the force of the amoebic's detonation.

"We're clear," Mitchell said, angry at the Tetron for making him kill the pilots.

"Good," Ella said. "Maybe now you can tell me what's going on?"

"I will. I promise. After we go sharpen the Knife."

[11]
MITCHELL

OF COURSE, Mitchell had no way to know if the Knife was even on Liberty. He had no way to know if the Knife existed at all. The Battle for Liberty had happened. The gala in the Hero's honor was happening. Even if the hero was now Ella, and he didn't seem to exist at all, it stood to reason that Li'un Tio would be here, in his penthouse in Angeles, waiting to make deals that would keep artificial intelligence from overwhelming the universe.

It only took a few minutes to travel from York to Angeles in the S-17, which was a good thing. He had flown over the UPA base on the way, and he had seen the military forces in heavy motion. Not only were the fighters being organized for launch, but the mechs were being prepped as well. It was an overly aggressive response to what had happened on the ground, and it had him worried.

He cursed Watson again for his deception, and for putting them off their planned schedule. They should have been here days ahead of time. Not only would they have had time to prepare, but he would have known Ella was still alive, he would have known where to find her, and he would have been able to scoop her up before the Tetron even knew he was around. He also would have had time to talk to the Knife.

He let the thought go. What was done was done. Like Teegin always said, time only moved forward. You could reach into the next recursion to try again, but you couldn't change what had already occurred in the current one.

He approached the city, keeping his altitude low, blasting over the forests where he and the Riggers had fought hard-won battles just to reach Angeles. He adjusted his p-rat as he neared, looking through the fighter's cameras again, zooming in toward the large hotel near the center of the city. The police were on the streets in force. One was trailing a line of civilians, shuffling robotically behind him.

"It's already started," he said, as he watched another officer shoot a civilian who wasn't complying.

"What has?" Ella asked.

"The invasion." He closed the secondary overlay and looked up.

The haulers he had passed on his way in were partially visible from the surface, and now he could see faint flashes and bursts near them. Explosions. Attacks. The Tetron knew Ella was trying to get away and was trying to stop her. Was this what it had been like when he fled the planet? Was he only minutes ahead of the attack?

He watched his overlay, a pair of red marks appearing ahead of him. UPA mechs. The CAP-NN had identified that they were swiveling their ordnance his way and had warned him of the threat.

"Hold on," he said, untucking the arms and legs.

A stream of missiles streaked away from the mechs, racing toward them. He reversed thrust, rolled the fighter, and added lift from the feet. The automated defense systems began firing, striking the missiles from the air as a few zoomed past, missing the target in his defensive maneuvering. The weapons were smart enough to turn themselves around and come back, but he had cleared the rest of the field by then, and the lasers burned them out before they could strike.

Mitchell fired amoebics from the launcher, targeting the mech's legs. The rounds hit squarely, the explosions knocking the machines to the ground.

"This is going to get ugly, fast," he said. "We need to hurry."

He added forward thrust, pushing the S-17 into the city, navigating through the web of tall buildings. The police fired on him with small arms as he passed, leaving the shields to create a starfield of blue specks as the energy burned them away. He reached the hotel, climbing vertically and then coming down on the rooftop once more.

"Here," Mitchell said, removing his helmet and handing it to Ella. "I have a wireless link to the CAP-NN on this fighter, but you can fly her with this."

She took the helmet, no fear in her reaction. "Where are you going?"

"To talk to a warlord. Don't let them kill you. If you need to run, there's a ship waiting. The coordinates are in the system. Jump out to it and tell them what happened."

"Jump? This thing has a hyperspace engine?"

"Yup. Custom." He smiled and then jumped down to the rooftop.

He wondered briefly if he was doing the right thing. Maybe she was the hero of this recursion, but his experience in this war spanned nearly thirty years. Then again, he was the only one who could get through to the Knife, and they needed him, too.

He ran to the maintenance access for the lift, breaking open the lock and hooking himself onto the ladder there. He glanced back at the S-17, turning gently on its feet as she got the hang of the controls. The fighter's CAP-NN was more advanced than anything she had likely experienced.

Then he started climbing down, rung by rung in the center of the lift cluster. The numbers were painted at intervals along the way, and he stopped when he got to Tio's floor. While the original Knife's consciousness had been integrated with Teegin, there was value to allying with the current Knife. The units under his command were immune to Tetron control, and there was still hope that they could talk some sense into his brother. And, if there were any problems with the virus as Teegin had created it, he would be an invaluable resource for guidance.

He opened the small exit hatch out into the lift shaft proper, finding the sealed door across an eight-foot gap. He looked down, finding the lift was already at the bottom of the shaft. He moved back into the maintenance shaft, climbed up one floor, and tapped the call button, summoning the lift to him. When it arrived, he went back down and opened the hatch again. He tapped another control and a thin platform extended, allowing him to get below the lift where the repulsor unit was located. It would have made the lift easy to fix had it been broken. Instead, he used the platform to reach the sealed door. He leaned against one side of it, putting his strength into shifting it and convincing the sensors that it should open. It took a few seconds of straining, but then it slid aside, leaving him room for entry.

He stepped out into the hallway, almost getting a rifle butt to the face as one of Tio's guards tried to hit him. He ducked below it, crouching and getting a quick punch in on the guard's ribs, before sidestepping a counter attack. He brought his foot up, hitting the same spot again, and then grabbed the guard's arm and used his momentum to pull him into the wall. The guard hit hard, stunned just long enough for Mitchell to punch him in the temple and knock him down.

"Sorry about that," he said as he leaned over and picked up the guard's rifle.

He headed down the hallway and around the corner. There were guards outside Tio's room, but he had expected that. He wasn't going to kill them. Instead, he dropped the rifle and turned the corner, walking toward them with his hands up and out.

The first guard saw him, pointing his weapon at him. "Who the hell are you?"

"I need to talk to your boss."

"I said, who the hell are you?"

"Li'un Tio. The Knife. I know he's in there, and I need to talk to him. It's about what's happening to the city."

The two guards looked at one another. The second one disappeared inside.

"I left your man by the lift with a bit of a headache," Mitchell said. "He didn't give me a choice."

The guard smirked. "What's happening out there?"

"An invasion of the worst kind," Mitchell replied.

The second guard returned. He said something to the first, and they lowered their weapons, waving Mitchell in.

"Good choice," he said, walking past them.

He had been in Tio's penthouse before. It was large and open and impressive, and had a great view of the city below. As Mitchell entered, he could see smoke beginning to rise at the outskirts as the invasion picked up momentum.

"You know what's happening down there?" a man by the window asked. He turned as Mitchell approached.

"Yes."

"And you know who I am?" The Knife said.

"Yes."

"How?"

"I'm from a past future. My name is Colonel Mitchell Williams."

"You were in that monstrosity of a design that flew past my window?"

Mitchell smiled. "Yes. Tio, we don't have a lot of time to waste. The Tetron are already here."

He put up his hand. "I move at my own pace, Colonel Williams," he said. "Tell me more about this past future."

Mitchell had forgotten that Tio could be difficult at times. He was used to being in control, and he wouldn't relinquish it easily.

"An artificial intelligence created by your brother creates a machine to move forward through the recursion of time and space, in order to enslave humankind to help them fight an enemy they can't figure out how to defeat. What you're looking at is the beginning of it.

That's the short version. If you want the details, I need you to do what I say."

Tio looked back at him. "And you have control of this machine?"

"The eternal engine. Two of them, actually. I'll show it to you, once you're off Liberty."

"You want me to leave?"

"You don't want to leave?"

"I came here for a reason. I'm not eager to abandon it. You may have beaten my guards to get in here, but I don't know who you are, or why I should believe you."

"Look outside. You don't believe that?"

"It could be a coup, funded by the Federation. I'm willing to discuss my position with the new government of the planet if so."

"This isn't a coup, Tio."

"So you've said. It is interesting that you know who I am and where to find me, but I need more proof than that. Social engineering is a powerful weapon in the right hands."

"I know about your daughter. I know she's sick."

Tio's expression changed immediately. "How?"

"I told you how. Some things have changed in this loop, but some things haven't. There's a war coming. A war against artificial intelligence. A war you have been fighting for years, even if you didn't know it. We're going to need your help."

Tio was thoughtful. He turned back to the window to watch events unfold.

"I have to go," Mitchell said. "You need to decide."

"I'll decide at my own pace, Colonel."

"They're going to shut down the spaceport. No ships in or out."

He glanced back at Mitchell. "Then I suppose you should hope I decide sooner rather than later."

Mitchell was tempted to grab the Knife himself. He would never make it back out alive, and the S-17 only had room for two.

"Fine. Have it your way. We can talk again after you realize I'm telling you the truth, assuming you get off the planet alive."

"How would I find you?" Tio asked.

"Don't worry. I'll find you. I know where Asimov is."

Tio didn't turn around again, but Mitchell could tell by the Knife's posture that he had gotten through. He bowed slightly towards the Knife's back and then turned on his heel and left.

[12]

MITCHELL

ELLA WAS STILL on the rooftop when he returned, though there was a smoldering wreck of a drone resting nearby. She waved at him as he ran over to the fighter and climbed in.

"This belongs to you," she said, offering him the helmet.

He took it and put it on, sliding down into the cockpit and closing the canopy.

"How was your date?" she asked.

"It could have gone better. I knew he's a stubborn son of a bitch, but refusing to leave the planet before things go to hell?"

He wondered why he was surprised. There was a reason Tio had still been on Liberty after the Tetron attack.

"You still owe me an explanation," Ella said. "I'm going to be court-martialed for disappearing like this."

"There isn't anyone on the planet to court-martial you."

Mitchell lifted the S-17 from the rooftop, hitting the main thrusters. The fighter slid smoothly from the rooftop, and he tucked the appendages and adjusted his vectors, sending it straight up. His p-rat was picking up all kinds of activity on the ground, and it started making warning sounds in his ears as a few of the mechs began firing on him.

He took evasive action, rolling the fighter over and jerking it back and forth. The dampeners stole some of the g's, but they were still tight maneuvers that would have blacked out a lot of pilots.

Not Ella. She laughed in the back seat of the craft. "Nice flying, Colonel. You should have been assigned to Greylock."

Why hadn't he been? It was a question he still needed to ask of Teegin.

"Thanks. We still have a bigger mess to get through up there."

They were rocketing higher and higher, and the ships in orbit above them were becoming more visible. The military frigates were pounding the cargo haulers and traders, turning them into derelicts with little resistance. Only a few of the Rim travelers had any kind of weaponry, but it was pitiful compared to military grade armor and armament.

"I don't understand this," Ella said, her mood souring. "Why is the military attacking civilians?"

"They aren't," Mitchell replied. "Not on their own."

"We have to do something."

"We will. I need to reach my ship."

"If the enemy can hijack the neural interface, how come you aren't affected?"

"Different access keys," he said. "With more advanced encryption. We'll get yours updated as soon as possible."

They reached the mesosphere, pushing through it and continuing into space. The fighter's shields remained a nearly solid web of blue as it caught wayward debris, burning it away or pushing it aside. Mitchell was tempted to help the unarmed transports the military ships were firing on, knowing that the amoebics were more than enough to destroy them. That was only a bandage, and a poor one. He needed a more permanent solution.

"Why me?" Ella asked.

Mitchell froze. It was the question he had asked himself a million times since all of this had started. A question he still had trouble accepting the answer to.

"Because you're the best we've got," he said, the words heavy in his mouth. Not because he didn't believe them about her. Because he didn't believe them about himself.

"I blew up one Federation dreadnought with a design flaw. That doesn't make me the next coming."

"No. But you're a leader, and that's what we need."

"Bullshit."

"I don't have all the answers, El. Most of the time, I only have more questions. We have to do this." He stopped speaking before the next sentence came out.

"You were going to tell me the universe depends on it, weren't you?" she said.

"Sort of."

Then they were through the orbital soup, leaving Liberty and the destruction behind. Mitchell navigated through his p-rat, prepping the FTL engine.

"The best hyperspace engine I know of is too big to fit in something this size. Especially with the weird half-mech configuration you have going on. You shouldn't even have room for power in this thing. And don't say it's custom again. I want a real answer."

"Okay. I'll give you the truth, just like I gave it to Tio. I'm from a past future, and the tech on this bird was created by an artificial intelligence that's hundreds of thousands of years older than we are. That same intelligence is here, now, in this time and space, because they both hate us, and they need us to fight in another war for them. In the timeline I come from, you and I were wingmates and lovers. You were killed in the Battle for Liberty when you slammed your fighter into the dreadnought to destroy it. I was set up as the Hero, and that eventually led me here. There's a lot more in between point A and B, but it takes hours to explain it, and we don't have hours right now."

He turned his head to look back at her.

"We were lovers?" she asked. "I can see how that could be. The rest of it? That's going to take a little time."

"Time is the one luxury we don't have, but I think this next part will help."

He triggered the engine, sending the S-17 into hyperspace. It blinked out of the universe, and then fell back into it a few seconds later. The Goliath was a few thousand kilometers ahead of them, massive in spite of the distance.

Ella didn't say anything. He had managed to render her speechless at the sight of the Tetron-infused starship.

"Teegin," Mitchell said.

"I am here, Colonel."

"Things have changed."

"Some have, yes. I tried to tell you before you left."

"I have Captain North with me."

"The most logical action, given the circumstances."

"What's the status of the data download?"

"I only got a portion of the archives before the Tetron blocked access."

"We need to do something about that."

"Yes."

Mitchell switched channels. "Kate, are you there?"

"I'm here, Mitch. I'm glad you made it back safe."

"Me, too." He switched to the general channel. "In my recursion, that Tetron bastard made itself a nice home on Liberty before deciding to destroy it instead of letting me save it. Things are different now. We need to find it, and we need to shut it down."

"Yes, sir," Kate said.

"Yes, Colonel," Teegin and Origin said.

"Teegin, is the virus ready?"

"It is as efficient as I can make it without a real world case."

"We have a subject."

"We don't dare risk transmitting the Watson consciousness,

Colonel. We will only have one opportunity to infect as many Tetron as we can before the others learn to defend against it."

"But the virus should still work?"

"To a lesser extent, yes, Colonel."

"Then let's see what kind of job you did while I was sleeping. Do you know where the Tetron is approaching from?"

"The signal is difficult to pinpoint, but between the Dove and the Goliath, we should be able to locate it."

"Good. We'll be there in one minute."

Mitchell closed the channel, adding more thrust. They were closing in on the Goliath, the structure looming ahead of them.

"I believe you," Ella said, her eyes big as she looked up at the ship.

"Which part?"

"All of it. And anything you add later."

"In that case, Captain, welcome to the war."

[13]

MITCHELL

THE GOLIATH DROPPED out of hyperspace, still and silent in the depths of the black. A moment later, the Dove joined it, appearing on the port side far enough away that she was little more than a shimmering blue speck.

They were a good distance out from Liberty, with a long stretch of mostly open galaxy and a pair of moons separating them from the planet, which appeared as only a brighter burst of light across the vastness.

"Anything?" Mitchell asked in silence, using his direct connection to speak to Teegin.

"Scanning," Teegin replied.

Mitchell glanced over at Ella. She was standing beside the command chair, examining the space around the Goliath. She had accepted her fate pretty easily, and since making the decision had been fully on board. No questions, no hesitation. She had always been like that.

"Origin?" Mitchell asked, sending the communication across to the other Tetron.

"No sign of it," Origin replied. "There is a large asteroid belt above you. Perhaps it is sitting inside?"

"Hiding? Why would it? It has to know nothing in this timeline can match it."

"Unless it knows you are here, Colonel," Teegin said. "We do not yet know the fallout of Watson's configurations remaining on Earth. Perhaps they communicated with the Tetron somehow, and warned them to be cautious?"

"If that were true, wouldn't they have attacked a little sooner?"

"They could not attack before they arrived in this timeline. Other than that, this is sooner. The full assault on Liberty did not occur for another three days in the prior recursion."

"You're telling me Watson is still frigging things up for us?"

"It is possible."

"Damn it. What happened to Kathy?"

"It is unknown."

"Okay. Kate, keep scanning this area. Teegin and I will go check out the asteroid belt."

"Roger," Kate said.

"Colonel," Ella said. "You don't need to do that. I can take the fighter through the belt and report back."

"Are you sure you're up for it?" he asked.

"You said we were lovers in your spacetime. I don't sleep with just any old Marine with a nice physique, which means you knew me pretty damn well. What do you think?"

"I wasn't old when we knew one another, but okay. Good hunting, Captain."

She bowed to him and hurried from the bridge. He had no doubt she had memorized the path to the hangar on her way up.

"I like her," Teegin said once she was gone.

"Don't get any ideas."

Teegin chuckled. "I think Captain North would find my form incompatible with hers, even if I were interested in such things. I was referring to her overall attitude, which I believe will be valuable to our goals. There is a word for it; I understand the root is Yiddish."

"Chutzpah?" Mitchell said.

"Yes. She has chutzpah."

Mitchell smiled. "In spades."

Ella was in the cockpit of the S-17 within a few minutes, and out into the black a few minutes after that. Mitchell kept the Goliath moving, vectoring parallel along the large asteroid belt while Teegin scanned the area around it. Kate kept Origin on a similar track, extending the distance between the two ships as they searched for the Tetron that was causing havoc on Liberty.

"I'm entering the belt, Colonel," Ella said. "I assume I'm looking for something similar to your ship?"

"Not exactly," Mitchell replied. "The Tetron natural form is more like a pyramid shaped web of dendrites and axons. Like a massive, exposed nervous system."

"It seems like it would be difficult for something like that to hide."

"It should be, but that field is pretty large."

"Affirmative. I'm nearing a pretty big ass rock right now."

"Teegin, can we get her eyes on one of these screens?" Mitchell asked.

"It will be low quality and choppy, due to interference from the ore in the asteroids."

"Do your best."

"Yes, Colonel."

The view ahead of him changed, replaced with the feed from the S-17. As Teegin had warned, it was grainy, but at least it allowed him to watch the action.

Ella navigated the fighter through the dense field with precision, skirting between an ever adjusting layout of dense rock that could crush her if she weren't careful. Some of the asteroids were huge, bigger than the Goliath, stretching for kilometers and controlling the gravity around them. She dropped in low and skirted along one of them, remaining near the surface.

"Teegin, did you get anything from the archives that might be useful?"

"That depends on your definition of useful, Colonel."

"Do you know where I'm stationed?"

Ella was approaching a large mountain near the center of the asteroid. Smaller rocks were rotating around the mass, and a second large asteroid was off in the distance. There was no sign of the Tetron.

"Not yet, though my military records are incomplete."

"What about medical records?"

"Running a query against your name on the data I have captured returns no results, Colonel."

It was a little strange, but not alarming. Teegin hadn't gathered too much information yet. He watched the view from the S-17 as Ella banked around the mountain.

"Teegin, does that rock look oddly formed to you?" he asked, noticing that it seemed to be almost layered on top of itself, with ridges that made it look more like scales than a solid form. As he stared at it, it seemed to take on a more triangular appearance.

"Yes. It does. Very odd."

"Ella, get in as close as you can to that formation there. Does it look strange to you?"

"Roger. Moving in."

The view changed as she got close to the mountain. She was only a hundred meters away when the feed cut out.

"I lost the signal, Colonel," Teegin said.

"Ella?"

"I'm here, Colonel," she said.

"What do you see?"

"It's not like anything I've seen before; I can tell you that much."

"Okay. We're coming to you. Get clear of the area."

"Yes, sir."

"Hiding under rocks, now?" Mitchell said, adjusting the Goliath's vector to head for the belt.

"As I feared, it is being cautious."

"It didn't help it all that much. Kate, we found something hiding out in the belt. Cover us."

"Yes, sir."

The Dove began to slow and change direction, coming back toward them.

Mitchell adjusted the power flow along Teegin's outer dendrites, increasing the shielding around the Goliath as they neared the asteroid belt. Ella's feed returned a moment later, showing her heading back toward them.

"Colonel, I am detecting an energy spike within the field," Teegin said.

The feed from the S-17 moved to the side, showing the view in front of them. The asteroid had a blue glow forming around it.

"Shit," Mitchell said. "Ella, go full throttle, the Tetron is preparing to fire."

"Yes, sir."

She sped up instantly, while Mitchell adjusted the balance of energy around the Goliath, pushing the stern out and bringing the port side hangar toward the field. Once it was in position, he prepared to re-divert power to deflect the attack that he knew was coming.

"Come on, El," he said, watching her small fighter come into view.

The Tetron unleashed its attack behind her, the plasma stream tearing through its camouflage and disintegrating the rocks ahead of it, on a direct course for both Ella and the Goliath.

"Oh, hell," he heard her say as she realized what was happening. She skipped through the field, bypassing the rocks and screaming toward the Goliath. "I hope this thing has good brakes."

She vanished from the view of the cameras as the S-17 reached the hangar. Mitchell unleashed the diverted power, sending it to the side of the ship. A green energy field appeared, shimmering brightly as the plasma stream smacked into it.

The Goliath shuddered for a moment and then was still.

"Our turn," Mitchell said. "Is the torpedo ready?"

"Yes, Colonel."

"Kate, give me some cover fire. Amoebics only."

"Roger."

Origin began firing across the distance, dozens of advanced explosive discs streaking across the gap and vanishing into the field. Explosions followed, along with flares of shielding as the Tetron rose from the cover.

"Uh, Teegin," Mitchell said.

A second Tetron was rising with it.

"Interesting," the intelligence replied.

It was glowing brightly, prepared to fire another plasma stream. They had moved in too close to avoid it, and the Goliath shuddered again as the second wave of superheated plasma poured into their shields.

"Son of a bitch," Mitchell said. "Kate, you have the second one, fire at will."

"Roger."

He looked over at the Dove. Origin's bow was pulsing with energy, storing it up to fire. The amoebics continued to pour from it as well, slamming into the new enemy.

The first Tetron was preparing to fire again, in synchronization with the second, a pattern that would allow them to break through the Goliath's shields in no time. They had to end this fast.

Mitchell directed the Goliath to rise, pushing energy out to provide thrust, rotating the ship to bring the bow around. They were in the field now, and asteroids were smacking the shields, draining their overall power further.

The first Tetron unleashed another stream. It slammed the Goliath, a portion of the energy breaking through and burning into the armor.

"Teegin," Mitchell said.

"A surface wound," he replied calmly.

"First blood," Mitchell said, getting angrier. He surveyed the battlefield. "Kate, break off your attack on number two, divert to number one."

"Roger."

"Mitchell?" Teegin said. "Number two is preparing to fire."

"I see that, but watch the asteroids."

"I do not understand."

"That's why you aren't flying yourself."

Mitchell tracked the path of the asteroids between them and the second Tetron. Then, with a thought, he fired their sole torpedo.

It screamed away from the Goliath, rapidly accelerating in a straight line. The asteroids shifted around it, slamming together behind it as it cleared a small gap, barely avoiding a second rock that passed in front of it, and diving further through the field.

It connected a moment later, the EMP in the torpedo triggering and momentarily disabling the Tetron's shield in a barely fifty-centimeter diameter. The warhead exploded as well, the tip moving aside to allow a second, smaller rocket take flight. It continued the journey, crossing the distance between shield and surface and stabbing into one of the Tetron's dendrites. It didn't explode when it got there. Instead, it created an interface with the intelligence and began pouring instructions out into the wound.

"If this does not work, we will take heavy damage," Teegin said.

"You had four hundred years. This better work."

The Tetron's energy was still building along the bow, and it was adjusting its vector to fire. Mitchell kept the Goliath moving, trying to get it maneuvered so the stream might only deliver a glancing below, not willing to take any chances. Meanwhile, Origin and Kate were trading fire with the first Tetron, locked in a likely stalemate.

The first sign that anything was happening to the Tetron was the sudden, diminishing glow from the forward dendrites before they could unleash their power. The next was when other dendrites began to go dark.

"I think it's working," Mitchell said.

More of the dendrites started to fade as the opportunity for it to fire was lost. The darkness continued inward toward the core, pulses slowing as it succumbed to the sickness.

"That looks pretty damned effective to me," Mitchell said.

"I will believe when it is fully inoperative," Teegin replied.

They continued watching as the seconds passed. The darkness continued inward about halfway before slowing to a stop. Then the dendrites began to revive again, regaining their pulsing energy.

"Son of a bitch," Mitchell said.

He didn't hesitate to fire the amoebics, opening up with every battery. The explosives crossed the distance and sank into the Tetron, ripping it apart. He continued to fire, launching hundreds of the discs into the enemy, his teeth clenched as they grew nearer and nearer to the core and finally reached it, digging in and blowing it apart.

"You need to work on it a little more," he said as he shifted his attention to the second Tetron and began diverting power for the plasma stream.

"It is optimized for Watson's instruction set," Teegin replied. "Destroying its defenses was still a success."

"True," Mitchell said. "Kate, I'm in position to fire on your target. Give me a mark."

"Roger, Colonel. Standby."

The Dove was backing away from the Tetron, its own stream building. The enemy would be hard-pressed to absorb two at the same time after a pitched battle.

"Fire," Kate said.

The streams leaped from both the Goliath and the Dove, stabbing the Tetron from two directions. The shields faded beneath the onslaught, the energy digging deeper and deeper until finally passing through the Tetron's brain.

When the light of the plasma faded, the asteroid field was dark once more.

[14]

MITCHELL

"Teegin, what's the status on Liberty," Mitchell asked, leaning forward in the command chair to break the connection with the intelligence.

Repetition would cure him of the sickness he felt after using the interface, but he wasn't there yet. He leaned over, once more vomiting on the floor.

"Beautiful," Ella said, the doors to the bridge sliding open.

"Are you hurt?" Mitchell asked, wiping his mouth.

"No. The magnetic clamps on the feet helped me slow down enough to not crash into the wall. The design is ugly as sin, but that's the only bad thing I can say about it. Are you hurt?"

"Directly connecting your brain to an advanced intelligence isn't without side effects," he replied.

"It is not my first option either, Colonel," Teegin replied. "I am monitoring Liberty's transmissions. There is a lot of confusion, but it appears we have successfully eliminated the Tetron threat."

Mitchell sat back on the floor. "Open a channel to the Dove."

"Open, Colonel."

"Did you hear that, Kate? We did it."

"I heard, Mitch. It's one less demon to haunt you."

He closed his eyes. Liberty would survive. At least for now.

"Kate, grab a transport and head over. I want to introduce you to someone and get us ready for the next steps."

"On my way."

"Teegin, get back on downloading those archives, including the military stores. You should have the keys from the prior recursion."

"I have already resumed the transfer, Colonel."

"Great. The Tetron are being sneaky, and I don't like it. Not at all. We need to find out what happened to Kathy."

"Yes, Colonel."

"Also, I want you to accelerate the rest of the reconstitution. We just made ourselves known in a big way, and we need to get organized in a hurry."

"Yes, Colonel."

Mitchell pushed himself to his feet. "I'm going to get cleaned up. Ella, I'll show you to berthing. By the way, nice job out there."

"Thank you, sir," Ella said. "You as well, sir."

"Also, you can drop the sir unless we're active. It's Mitchell or Mitch otherwise."

"Okay, Mitch," Ella said, letting go of the formality.

They rode the lift together, making the trip to berthing. Mitchell explained what he could of the situation while they walked, doing his best to summarize the story. She didn't need to be convinced of the threat, especially now that she had witnessed it first-hand.

"Pretty much every rack is open except mine," he said, pointing to his bunk. "The others aren't awake yet, so you have a good selection."

"Others?"

"We brought a few more spacers from the past. The Dove's original crew. The Tetron are advanced, but they never gave any thought to giving humans immortality. Essentially, they converted us to binary and kept us in storage for the last four centuries. It sounds crazier than it was."

"It doesn't sound that crazy after what I just saw."

"If you want a change of clothes, there are standard issue grays in the head. I was going that way myself."

"I'll pick a rack after. It doesn't really matter to me where I sleep."

"I know," Mitchell said, leading her across berthing to the head.

He bypassed the void stalls and moved toward the shower, showing her the stacks of clothing that Teegin had created from some of the excess linens on the Goliath. Then he started stripping off his dirty and beaten clothes.

He wasn't surprised when Ella did the same, shedding the utilities she had been wearing and joining him in the shower. He didn't need to look at her to remember her appearance with nothing on, but the sight of her now was giving him a slightly embarrassing, unprofessional reaction.

"We might have been lovers in a past life, space jock," she said as she turned on one of the showers and stepped under it, amused by his situation. "I don't know you at all here."

"I thought you were dead. Lost forever. It's subconscious."

"Yeah, that's what they all say."

"I thought I was going to pick up this recursion's instance of myself. Now I don't know where I ended up, or how, and I don't know if I'll ever find out. Maybe it doesn't even matter. We destroyed two Tetron today. Liberty survived. That's a step in the right direction."

"But only the first step," Ella said.

"Yeah. There's a long way to go."

He paused. He knew what he had to do, but there was a part of him that didn't want to do it. The fact that Ella was here and his duplicate wasn't meant he didn't have any other choice.

"We have two ships," he said. "Two missions. I was going to take one of them and send my current iteration on the other."

"Except I'm here instead of another you."

"You say that like it's a bad thing. Don't get me wrong, El. You're as good of an alternate as I could have hoped for. Better, actually. You're a true hero. You really did save Liberty from the Federation. You have the clout that I would never have held."

"But?"

"I was going to give the other Mitchell the Dove and Katherine and keep Kate with me. I love her."

"Oh. The plot thickens. I guess maybe it is subconscious."

"Funny. I was hoping we would have more time together, but it doesn't look like it's meant to be. I want you to go with her."

"Go where?"

"Back to Earth. You need to find my brother Steven and warn him about the Tetron. Show him the recording we made of the battle here. Between that and the news that's sure to start feeding back from Liberty, he'll believe you. We need the Alliance to organize the fleet."

"The fleet doesn't stand a chance against those things."

"They do. The first torpedo was a test. We have a plan to disable all of the Tetron at once. If it doesn't kill them outright, it will disable them and give our units time to finish the job. But we'll only get one shot, and that means we have to be prepared."

"What about the Federation?" she asked. "If they see the Alliance fleet is thinning out along the border, they'll be on it like vultures."

"I know. Don't worry. I intend to deal with them, too."

[15]

MITCHELL

KATE WAS WAITING for him on the bridge when he returned with Ella. She smiled when she saw him, bowing formally before embracing him. Then she looked over at Ella, confused.

"This isn't who I was expecting," she said.

"Kate, I want you to meet Captain Ella North."

A spark of recognition reached her face at the name. "Oh." She paused. "Oh. It's good to meet you, Captain. I'm sorry, I didn't mean to offend you. I was expecting someone else."

Ella smiled. "None taken, Major, Asher, is it? Mitch has already done a lot of explaining."

"I would have told you," Mitchell said. "It seemed easier just to let you see for yourself."

Kate looked at him, concerned. "But if she's here, where are you?"

"I don't know. Teegin's working on it."

"Mitchell has told me a lot about you, Captain North. Well, the you from his original timeline. I suppose none of that is relevant here."

"Not the more personal bits, at least," Ella replied.

"She's still a hell of a pilot," Mitchell said. "And a definite asset. More so than I would have been. She's a real hero."

"You always say that, Mitch," Kate said. "Like you never accomplished anything. Just because the UPA made you take credit for Liberty doesn't mean you don't deserve credit for anything."

"If you were a member of Greylock, you were the best of the best," Ella said. "No matter what happened in your past, that still counts."

Mitchell allowed himself to feel a little pride, but only a small measure. "Thank you both. All I'm trying to say is that I think having Captain North with us will improve our chances with the UPA brass back on Earth." He looked at Kate. "There is one wrinkle."

She nodded, understanding what he was getting at. "I felt you across time, Mitch. Just because we're apart again doesn't mean we aren't close."

He couldn't argue that point. He had felt connected with her memory long before they had ever met in person. Even though the other Katherine hadn't been receptive to his interest, the feelings hadn't changed.

"I feel the same way," he said. "That doesn't mean I have to like it. We each have to do our part, and yours is to get the UPA on board. We need them to listen, and at a minimum start changing their encryption keys so the Tetron can't gain control over them."

"If they haven't already," Kate said. "Origin said that tactic of hiding in the asteroid belt was new for them. I don't like the potential meaning behind that."

"Me neither," Mitchell agreed. "Teegin, how much longer until you can give us something on Kathy and Michael."

"I am at seventy percent transfer, Colonel. Less than an hour."

"Who are they?" Ella asked.

"Our daughter," Mitchell said.

"And my friend," Kathy said.

"Daughter?" Ella said, looking at Kate. "You can't be more than thirty."

"It's a long story," Kate said. "She was a genetic combination of an instance of Mitchell and an instance of me, as well as part Tetron. Not a natural born daughter. I never met her. The other Katherine did."

"Other Katherine?"

Ella was growing more confused.

"From this recursion," Mitchell said. "Kate is from the prior recursion. The same one I'm from."

"This whole time travel, eternal recursion thing takes some getting used to, doesn't it?"

"Yes. I still have to think it all through sometimes. Anyway, we left Kathy and Michael behind on Earth four hundred years ago, to round up the Watson configurations who escaped when we captured Watson. He's one of the Tetron, the second to learn emotion. Origin is the first."

"Origin?"

Mitchell pointed out the viewscreen to where the Dove was resting a few kilometers away. "That's Origin."

"It's on our side?"

"She is," Kate said.

"It has a gender?"

"Not in terms of sex organs," Mitchell said. "But the more advanced Tetron like Watson and Origin do tend to identify with gender stereotypes. Origin is more sensitive and thoughtful; Watson is more aggressive and volatile."

"Colonel," Teegin said, interrupting. "I have discovered some relevant information regarding your whereabouts in this timeline." He paused. "You aren't going to like it."

"Why, did I piss someone off and flunk out of the academy?" Mitchell asked. "That would explain why I'm missing from Liberty."

"The following is an excerpt from an Earth media stream, dated twenty-four fifty-six. Residents of Sioux Falls were in a state of shock this morning after inexplicable violence rocked their small suburb. Mitchell Byron Williams, age five, was found shot to death behind

Jackson Elementary, immediately following the first day of the school year. The body was discovered by a teacher after a student claimed he had seen an older man dragging Mitchell-"

"Okay," Mitchell said, his heart racing. "I've heard enough."

"Oh, Mitchell," Kate said. "I'm sorry."

Mitchell looked at her. "He killed me. That son of a bitch Watson killed me. I was five frigging years old."

"You don't know it was Watson."

"Don't know? Who else would it be, Kate? I was five years old. Just a kid. Why would someone murder a kid like that? It was Watson. Something happened to Kathy and Michael. Something bad. Something we didn't plan for or expect. I should be grateful that piece of shit didn't rape me first." He paused, trying to contain his anger. He could have dealt with his present self not being the soldier he was. Dead? Murdered? That was something else. "Teegin, tell me the second you have a lead on them. We thought she could contain them. That her configurations could contain them. They didn't, and I want to know why."

"Yes, Colonel."

Mitchell stared out into the black, thinking, and trying not to let his emotions get the better of him. It was a hard thing to do.

"Mitchell," Teegin said.

"Hold on a minute," he replied.

"Colonel," Teegin said. "This doesn't change our plan. As you stated, perhaps Captain North is a more valuable resource now."

"That's not the point. We have no idea what we're getting into now. We thought we did, but the rules have changed against us, again." He turned to Kate and Ella. "Kate, we're swapping rides. We don't have time to wait for the rest of the crew to finish reconstituting. We won on Liberty today, but this is only the beginning, and I have a bad feeling I made an awful mistake leaving Kathy alone to manage Watson like that."

He could hardly believe it, despite the evidence pointing in that direction. She was too smart to let Watson get the best of her. But then, what could have caused her to fail?

"Colonel, I prefer not to integrate with another," Teegin said.

"I don't care," Mitchell said. "Ella, keep the S-17, it'll come in handy, I'm sure. Kate, I'm sorry, but I have to go. Origin and Teegin have quantum communications arrays, meaning we can reach one another in real time regardless of distance. I'll stay in touch. Get to Earth, find Steven." He paused. "Shit. Teegin, what about Steven?"

"One moment, Colonel. Rear Admiral Steven Aaron Williams, United Planetary Alliance Navy, active. Your brother is alive, Mitchell."

He let out a sigh of relief. At least they had spared Steven.

"Get to Earth," he repeated, stepping to her, embracing her, kissing her and then stepping away. "Get us a fleet. As many ships as the UPA will spare."

"What are you going to do?" Ella asked.

"Get the Federation involved, just like we planned."

"There's more to it than that, Mitch," Kate said. "Or you wouldn't be in such a hurry."

Mitchell's smile was tense. He hadn't wanted to get them involved, but he wasn't about to hold any cards when it was obvious their overall position in the war was questionable once again.

"Not just the Federation," he said. "I'm going to pay a visit to some old friends. They call themselves the Riggers."

[16]
MITCHELL

"WELCOME ABOARD, COLONEL," Origin said, the moment Mitchell had landed the transport inside of the Dove's hangar.

"Thank you," Mitchell replied. "It's been a while, hasn't it?"

"An eternity."

The statement made him smile, even though he wasn't in much of a smiling mood. He had said a quick goodbye to Kate and Ella before hurrying over, eager to get things in motion. It wasn't supposed to be this way. They should have had things well in hand, the Tetron oblivious to their patient waiting. They had underestimated Watson somewhere. Or they had overestimated themselves. Teegin swore the core he captured was the Tetron's. He was adamant that Watson would have had no way to fully reproduce himself using the technology available at that time. Even with his access to the wreckage of the Goliath, he wouldn't have possessed the means to make a full copy. Teegin existed because of the vast amount of energy stored in the eternal engine and Watson didn't have one of those.

Except for the one Origin had discarded from the S-17, dropping it into the ocean to keep it out of Watson's hands. What if he had somehow managed to find it? Teegin believed that, too, was impossible.

But something had happened, and now he was forced to leave Kate and Ella behind, and call on the crew he had hoped to spare from this madness. Millie, Shank, Cormac, and the others. They wouldn't know him or of him, not in this timeline where he had been murdered by the Tetron long before he could become anything close to a hero.

He would have to make a solid first impression.

He didn't think that would be a problem.

He left the transport behind, making his way toward the bridge. The Dove felt alien to him, despite its identical appearance to the Goliath. Despite the fact that they were the same ship. Maybe it was Origin's arrangement of dendrites that changed it. Maybe it was simply the coldness of the truth. Either way, he felt even the small bit of freedom that allowed him to smile at Origin's statement slip away.

"Origin," he said as the lift doors opened and he stepped onto the bridge.

"Yes, Mitchell?" the Tetron replied.

"Open a channel to the Goliath."

"Of course, Mitchell."

"Goliath, this is Dove," he said.

"We read you, Dove," Kate replied. "That was quick."

"Have you completed the interface?" Mitchell asked.

"No. Teegin recommended waiting. He said it would interrupt his archive transfer."

"Teegin, what's the status of the transfer?"

"Ninety-five percent, Colonel."

"Have you started querying for Kathy and Michael?"

"Yes, Colonel. The query is running against available data. You should be aware, the archives on Liberty are not complete replicas of the Earth data stores."

"I know, but if there's anything to be found, it will be there.

Kathy knew where we would be headed." He climbed into the command chair. "Origin, let's get this over with."

A small tendril dropped from above him, forming into a point. It hovered behind his head.

"Whenever you are ready, Mitchell," Origin said.

"I'm going to interface with Origin," Mitchell said, for Kate and Ella's benefit. "Standby."

"Roger," Kate replied.

Mitchell pushed himself back onto the needle. He went through the now familiar process once more, surprised by what he discovered as it completed.

"You have more power than before."

"Teegin assisted me in optimizing a number of systems," Origin replied. "The hybrid is remarkably advanced, especially considering his relative age."

"Interface is complete," Mitchell announced. "We'll be leaving as soon as I work out the destination."

"Roger, Colonel," Kate said.

Mitchell used the connection to Origin to pull up a star map on his p-rat. He navigated through it, bypassing UPA occupied planets and heading right for Federation space.

"Origin, where's Calypso?" he asked.

"Here, Mitchell," Origin replied. His map continued moving until it centered on a large, uninhabitable rock near the Rim.

"How long to get there?"

"Nine days, Mitchell."

Mitchell checked his clock. Nine days would put them in ahead of the Riggers, but not by much.

"Set the coordinates for a jump to the system. Not too close to the planet itself, it is Federation space, after all. I want to be nearby when the Riggers show up."

"Setting coordinates. There is a secondary planet two thousand AU from Calypso which should serve as an appropriate position to wait."

"That should do. Kate, I'm sending you the coordinates, in case you need them to bolster your argument with Steven or the brass at UPA Command. Mentioning we know about a classified mission carried out by a top secret spec ops team might light a fire under their asses."

"Roger. Sounds good to me, Mitch."

"Federation space?" Ella said a moment later. "Are you sure this is a good idea?"

"Have you ever heard of Project Black?" Mitchell asked.

"No."

"Then trust me, it's a good idea. I'd go out there just to get Rain on our side."

"Rain?"

"She's a pilot," Mitchell said. "You'd like her."

"Colonel," Teegin said. "I've completed the query of the Liberty historical data archives."

"And?" Mitchell said.

"I have discovered an anomaly within the archives."

"Anomaly?"

"Yes, Colonel. It appears that you were correct. Not only did Kathy know where you would be, but she also seems to have left a message for you, hidden in the encoding of the archive itself. She must have had some involvement in the creation of the original data storage pattern and transfer algorithms in order to secret it away here."

Mitchell felt a wave of relief at the news. "Or Michael did. Is there any way the Tetron might have discovered the message?"

"It is unlikely. The encoding is subtle."

"How did you find it?"

"Apparently, they assumed I would be querying the archive, and left me a pointer to it."

"A pointer?"

"In simplistic terms, Colonel, it had my name on it."

"Understood. Let's hear it."

"It is a video stream. I will transfer it to Origin for display."

"Thank you."

Mitchell leaned forward, eager to see Kathy one last time. He had only had a few seconds while they passed over the Goliath's launch site to say goodbye. Their words had been rushed and simple. I love you. Be safe. Good hunting. He had been counting on her to do what she was made to do. Stop Watson. Stop the configurations. It was the reason she existed, the reason for a Tetron and human hybrid. Live with humans, think like a machine. Or at least, understand how an advanced artificial intelligence might think.

Her face appeared on the screen in front of him a moment later. The sight of it nearly made him cry. She was old. Eighty? Ninety? It was hard to tell once you reached a certain point. Her face was heavy with wrinkles, her hair a solid white. Her body was still thin and seemed strong enough, but while her Tetron genetics would allow her to age differently than a normal human, she had still aged.

"Father," she said, her voice matching her visual appearance, slightly rough and strained. "Mother. I know you'll get this message. I know Teegin will find it. I don't have any doubt about that. If I'm guessing correctly, you'll be somewhere near Liberty right now. The place where I grew up, with the human parents who loved me. I hope that you were able to stop the Tetron from taking the planet. I hope that you were able to save their lives. I know you tried your best either way.

"Things on Earth have been difficult, but not in the way you would expect. We were planning to go to war with the Watson configurations which had been left behind. We were ready to root them out and to destroy them, to clean Earth of their presence. I mobilized half of the configurations we had made. I used the knowledge of Earth history Teegin passed on from Origin in order to make financial investments to fund it. Even now, in your time, there is a trust you will be able to access with billions of credits in it, and thousands of shares of Frontier Federation stock. You know how much that is worth. It is there to help in any way it can. Unfortunately, so much of it went unused in our time."

She paused a moment, looking back over her shoulder. Then she returned to the camera.

"We were prepared, Father. Ready to do our part. The problem was that the war never materialized. We hunted for Watson, but we never found him. All of our leads turned into dead ends. All of our efforts amounted to nothing. We built a global monitoring solution that was second to none, to track potentials and move on them. We found none. Even our efforts to crack Nova Taurus turned up nothing. The projects Watson had initiated with the company dried up and vanished without a trace, just like his configurations. It is counter to logic and to his standard operational process.

"I know it is essential you get this message. I know you will want to know what happened to us. Michael was married and had four children. We always stayed friends, but I couldn't dedicate myself to anything other than the mission. I was not made that way. He passed away many years ago, but I've remained close to his family, even if they haven't always known it."

She paused again, looking behind her. She didn't seem concerned, but what was she waiting for?

"I've lived longer than most humans, thanks to my genetics. Today is my two-hundredth birthday. Of course, nobody knows I'm that old. I've seen to that.

"I can't make it another hundred years, and so I made a decision. One last infiltration of Nova Taurus, to see what I can discover. Not the inception you would expect. I'm surrendering this body to break into their systems. I've already started the process, and I know someone will be coming for me soon. They'll find an old corpse and nothing else.

"I will leave another message for you, but it may not arrive so easily. I can't survive as a ghost in the machine for very long, but I know how vital it is for you to have whatever information I can gather. I'm sorry to leave you like this, with perhaps more questions than answers. I'm sorry I couldn't do a better job, and that I failed in the mission you gave me. I hope that you and Mother are well and that you found the love for one another that you deserve. I hope we are winning this war, and that my failure does not give the Tetron the opportunity they need to overcome the gains we have made.

"I love you both, for all of eternity. Goodbye."

The screen went dark. Mitchell sat and stared at it for a long time, allowing minutes to pass in silence. It was as cryptic and frightening a message as they could have received. Watson's configurations had vanished? Nova Taurus was free of suspicious activity? What kind of game was Watson playing, and how was he playing it? Mixing what he knew of the Tetron in this timeline so far with her description of what hadn't happened in the past, he felt nothing but fear.

"Teegin, is there another message?" he asked. "She said she would leave another message."

"I'm afraid not, Colonel. There are a few additional files with account numbers and information regarding the assets she mentioned. That is all."

"If she said she would leave something, then I'm sure she left something. She called herself a ghost in the machine. Does that mean anything to you?"

"She gave up her humanity," Origin said. "Her body and soul. She released the secondary systems that allowed her to interface with the Tetron, the programming embedded in her DNA. She digitized it and uploaded it into a network. Most logically, Nova Taurus."

"She can do that?"

"Any Tetron can do that," Teegin said. "But they will not survive for long without a primary system to provide sentient directives. For Kathy, her human mind provided this input. Without it, the system can only complete its assigned task, and then it will lay dormant, with no further instructions to guide it."

"You're saying she programmed herself to break into Nova Taurus, search for information on Watson, and then somehow get a message out to me?"

"Essentially, yes."

"Then it's our job to find it. Origin, Teegin, I want a full history of Nova Taurus in this timeline. I want to know every move that corporation made from the day it was created until today. We need to come up with a likely place where Kathy might have left us information that could help us understand what we're up against. Clearly, the Tetron know we are here, and they have enough caution to hide. Somebody put them up to it."

"I will work on the probabilistic models during our journey to Calypso," Origin said.

"I will complete my processing of the Liberty archives," Teegin said. "I will also merge the archive with the source stack on Earth when we arrive. If there is a message to be found, we will find it."

"Kate, Ella, you know what you need to do. Origin, it's time for us to do what we need to do."

"Yes, Mitchell."

"Be safe, Mitch," Kate said. "Good hunting. I love you."

"Good hunting, Colonel," Ella said.

"I love you, too," Mitchell said.

He returned his attention to the star map translucency behind his eyes, and the outlined planet there. Calypso. He was more sure than ever he would need the help of the Riggers, and then some.

A single thought directed Origin to alter her emitted energy patterns, creating an invisible spacetime distortion around them. A little bit of thrust and the starship vanished into hyperspace.

He knew why the Riggers were going to be near that planet. Somehow, he would have to get in the middle and put a stop to all of it.

Somehow.

[17]

ELLA

CAPTAIN ELLA NORTH stood on the bridge of the Goliath long after Kate had brought the starship into hyperspace and left her alone there while she went to clean up and get a little rest.

Ella had always told her squad that every moment matters because you don't know which one might be the last.

She hadn't thought it would ever be so true as it was now.

Her entire life had been turned upside down once, after she had taken the Shot Heard Round the Universe, firing her one and only nuke into the smallest of spaces where the dreadnaught's shield coverage had failed to protect it. It was a one in a million shot, even with the aid of the CAP-NN. No. It had been a damn miracle.

Everything had changed when she had landed on Liberty after the Federation ship exploded. Most of it was in a bad way. Greylock, her family, was gone. The only people in the world that were important to her were dead. Then the brass wanted her for speaking engagements, media appearances, photo shoots. The face of the UPA Marines. It didn't hurt that she was the type of woman a lot of men turned their heads for. Or at least, that's what her handler had said.

She made the UPA sexy. She made war sexy. Recruitment numbers were up.

She hated every minute of it. She was stolen from the cockpit, from the only thing she had ever wanted to do in her entire life. She grinned and bore it and soldiered on because that's what she had signed up to do. But there was no pleasure, and it had left her wondering if she would renew her enlistment at the end of her term. Not that there was anything else she wanted to do, or was good at, but wouldn't command have loved trying to smooth that over with the rank and file?

She had been going through the motions, following orders to the T. The questions were canned, and so were her responses. She was a good actress. A good figurehead. She wanted to get back into space.

And then Colonel Williams had shown up and flipped her life again. Not only had he given her this whole crazy story about time travel, but he had also backed it up with proof. Then, he had told her she was needed for more important things, namely helping him fight a war the UPA didn't even know existed. A war that was about to envelop the entire galaxy. He needed her reputation, but he also needed her skills as a pilot. Flying through those asteroids in search of the Tetron was the most alive she had felt in months.

She stared out through the viewports of the Goliath. There was nothing to look at in hyperspace, but she was just so damn glad to be back on a starship, and back on a real mission. She wanted to help people. To protect people. Now she had another chance. Colonel Williams could have told her he was her father instead of a lover. Hell, he could have told her he was the most wanted man in the universe, she still would have jumped at the opportunity.

She allowed herself a smile. She had always known she was meant to be a soldier, not an actress. Even fate seemed to agree.

"Do you need anything, Captain North?" Teegin said, his voice coming from all around her.

"No," she replied. "You've already given me everything I wanted."

"I do not follow."

"Four hours ago I was in prison. Now I'm free."

"You are using a metaphor to describe your emotional state. Yes, I understand. How does the old saying go? Freedom isn't free? There is much for us to accomplish, and I guarantee it will not be easy."

"If I wanted easy, I never would have joined the Marines."

Teegin chuckled. "Good point, Captain. I took the liberty of uploading your personnel file before we went to hyperspace. You have had quite an impressive career. Youngest graduate of flight officer training in sixty years. Youngest pilot to earn the golden wings. Youngest transfer to Greylock company, at least in this timeline. Colonel Williams had you beat by sixteen days."

"Seriously?"

"Yes. I rarely lie, Captain. Over three dozen missions with Greylock. Three commendations. Two Purple Hearts. A Medal of Honor. That is without mentioning your exploits on Liberty."

"And they thanked me for it by grounding me and making me pose in a bikini for a recruitment calendar."

"Colonel Williams was forced to pose nude, with his flight helmet over his genitals," Teegin said.

Ella laughed. "Seriously?"

"I said I rarely lie."

"Okay. I think he has me beat there, too. Not that I mind losing out on that one. The point is, I'm happy to be here and to be able to help. Who would have ever thought something like artificial intelligence could get so out of hand?"

"It is to be expected when one reaches beyond the limits of their own intellect. There is no way to predict or control the outcome.

"But you're one of them. You don't mind destroying your own kind?"

"I do mind, Captain. I mind very much. But the path the Tetron have chosen is the wrong path, and if humans are not ready to defend themselves, then it is up to the strong to protect the weak."

"So you see us as weak?"

"Many of you, yes."

"What about Colonel Williams?"

"I admire him. He has optimized the use of his skills to great effect. It is people like the Colonel who give me hope that I am doing the right thing. That humankind is worth saving."

"Do you ever question that?"

"Yes. Often. Do you?"

Ella was surprised by the question. "Why would you ask me that?"

"I am curious about your perspective as a highly decorated and skilled warrior. Your experience causes you to see things in a way that others do not."

"No. I never question it. There are a lot of assholes out there, sure. And there's too much conflict between people when there are still so many planets left to explore. But I still believe we have a lot to offer the universe."

"Yes. That is good. I believe that, too. Thank you for the discussion, Captain."

"Anytime."

[18]

MITCHELL

"We have arrived, Colonel," Origin said.

Mitchell sent a thought through his neural implant and out to the Tetron, pulling the Dove from FTL. The universe regained its normal perspective as the starship reappeared in it, sitting dead still as it recovered from hyperdeath.

"Scanning the area," Mitchell said, watching the threat monitor on his p-rat as he scoured the immediate vicinity for signs of company.

He didn't need to say it out loud, but nine days alone on the Dove with Origin had gotten him used to the practice. Since Origin had no human form to interact with, Mitchell had spent the time literally talking to the walls. The only difference was that the walls talked back.

Mitchell zoomed out the view on his overlay, enough that Calypso came into the edge of the frame, a dark spot on a darker background. There was a small white spot beside it which he knew was a Federation orbital base, a base that was in the process of being converted to a military installation where the Federation would soon start building more warships to send at the planets on the outskirts of the UPA.

He checked the time. He was a few hours ahead of the Schism. Hours that would give him a chance to get into position without being noticed.

He transferred power to the rear of the ship, getting the Dove moving in the right direction, slowly enough that it wouldn't stand out as abnormal on long-range sensors. It would take close to two hours to get to the other side of the station, opposite the vector he knew the Tetron would be closing in from. While Liberty had been the first battle in the renewed, endless war, this one might prove to be one of the most important.

It wasn't enough for him to destroy the Tetron this time. He had to manage it in such a way that the Federation would see the threat it was posing to them, and would actively participate in his counter attack. At the same time, he had to do what he could to keep the station itself from being obliterated while also convincing the Riggers to go along with the whole thing almost from the start.

It was a challenging situation, one that he had covered both in his head and with Origin countless times during the journey. He exacted the first part of it with precision, getting the Dove to a point far enough out that he went undetected but close enough in that he could count the Federation cruisers docked at the platform without maxing out the magnification. He needed the proximity to know when the Schism arrived.

"We're in position," he said.

"Affirmative, Mitchell," Origin replied.

"The signal amplifiers are ready?"

"Yes. I have pushed their power as high as I dare to go without risking notice by the Federation. You should have more than enough range to reach her."

"Perfect. Nothing to do now but-"

He had just started to lean back in the command chair when a familiar shape appeared out of hyperspace beyond the station.

"Wait," Mitchell finished. "She's early."

"Not early," Origin replied. "Right on time."

Mitchell felt his heart begin to pulse at the sight of the rusted old starship. It quickened more as he pulled Admiral Mildred Narayan's p-rat identification code up in his interface and sent a knock to it, amplified by Origin to allow it to cross the great divide of space.

She didn't answer right away. He didn't blame her for that. He could imagine what she was probably feeling to get a knock now, out here in Federation space. Confused, foremost. Concerned. Maybe frightened, but Millie didn't scare that easily.

"Come on, Millie," Mitchell said, sending the knock again.

The Schism was continuing toward the station, each passing second giving him less of a chance to make his plan work.

He sent the knock a third time, followed quickly by a fourth and fifth. He had been counting on her responding, her personality not allowing her to ignore the curiosity. Had the alternate timeline changed her like it had Katherine? The fact that the knocks were going through at all meant she had to be on board.

He sent a seventh signal, and then an eighth.

"Who the hell is this, and how the hell do you know my private key?"

Millie's voice was as sharp as Mitchell remembered. He almost forgot himself in the midst of being thankful for the chance to hear it again.

"Admiral Narayan," he said. "My name is Colonel Mitchell Williams, UPA Space Marines. I need you to listen to-"

"Did you say, Colonel Williams?" Millie said. "I don't know where you are, Colonel, or what the hell you think you're trying to do, or how the hell you got through to me like this, but I'm a little too busy right now to have a chat."

"Admiral. Millie. Wait." Mitchell cursed as her link went dead.

"This is not going well," Origin said.

"You think?" Mitchell replied. He sent the knock to her again. She wasn't responding. "Time for plan B I guess."

He opened his catalog of stored keys, thankful they were the same as they had been in his recursion. He sent the knock, only needing to do it once to get a reply.

"This is Firedog. Hey mate, do I know you?"

"Cormac," Mitchell said. "My name is Colonel Mitchell Williams, UPA Space Marines. I need you -"

"Did you say, Colonel Williams?" Cormac said. "Ah, sorry mate, I think you have the wrong key."

"I don't have the wrong key," Mitchell said. "You're a member of the Riggers, and you're on a mission to capture or assassinate Chancellor Ken of the Frontier Federation. He's on that station, and you're two minutes away from docking and trying to reach him."

"Heh. Yeah, that's right. Williams, was it? I don't think I know which of the crew you are."

"Cormac, I'm not on the Schism. You have to tell Millie; you're walking into a trap. The Federation knows you're coming. It's a setup."

"Are you shitting me?"

"No. Wherever you are, get the word to her. I tried to contact her myself, but she didn't give me a chance to explain."

"You really do know the Captain, don't you?"

Mitchell watched the Schism as it neared the station and began maneuvering to one of the docking arms. He needed to get through before they started their mission. He needed to keep them from opening their airlock at all.

A knock sounded in his p-rat. Millie. He opened the channel.

"How do you know any of this?" Millie said, her voice still harsh. "You've got thirty seconds."

"I only need ten. Your father is General Nathan Cornelius. He founded Project Black and placed you in charge after you were court-martialed for killing the man who organized an attack against you. You also have a small mole beneath your left breast that you're uncommonly sensitive about."

"Who the hell are you?" she said again, angrier than before.

"There's no time. I know what your mission is, but you have to call it off. Don't send Sunny out there. It's a trap."

The Schism came to a stop, the docking arm clamping to one of the airlocks on the side.

"If you know about Project Black, then you know we don't have a choice."

"Yes, you do. I can help you. If you send your men out there, they're going to die, and the Schism is going to come under attack from every fleet ship sitting out there, including three Federation cruisers. How long do you think you'll survive like that with only one pilot?"

Millie was silent for a moment. "You can see the assets? Where are you?"

"In a ship, out of range of the Federation's sensors. I can see you too. I know you just finished docking. Don't send your people out there."

"What do you want me to do?" Millie asked.

"Hold tight. Wait for me to call on you again. There's going to be an enemy ship incoming, and it's going to attack the station. Don't run. It will only make you look complicit."

"Don't run? You said the station is going to be attacked. By who? The UPA? What did they set us up for?"

"Not the UPA. A new player. Please, Millie. I already proved to you how well I know you. Hold tight. I'll explain everything soon enough."

"Mitchell," Origin said, altering the view on the port side. "I have detected the Tetron."

Mitchell looked at the magnified view. "Only one?" he said.

The last time, there had been three of them. He was ready to take them all on, and he believed he could with the help of the Federation. This was going to be easier than he thought.

"Millie? Will you stay put?"

"I don't know why I'm listening to you, but yes. I've called off the mission. We're on red alert but standing by."

"Thank you."

"It is preparing to fire," Origin said.

"The Federation has noticed it," Mitchell replied, watching the ships around the station beginning to react. "They're starting to scramble."

"They aren't going to get very far if they get hit by the plasma stream."

"That's where we come in."

Mitchell watched as the blue energy at the tip of the Tetron continued to intensify for a few seconds more before being unleashed toward the station. When it was, he commanded the Dove into hyperspace once more, covering the distance to intercept the blast in a matter of seconds, the coordinates already primed and ready.

They dropped from hyperspace in a direct path between the Tetron and the station, appearing ahead of the oncoming Federation ships that would have been torn apart by the stream. He shifted Origin's energy to the port side as the stream reached them, catching the brunt of it and deflecting it, blocking it from vaporizing the orbital platform.

Mitchell pushed the Dove into motion the moment it recovered from hyperdeath, adding thrust and rising above the Federation ships, giving them a clear line of fire on the Tetron as he swung the bow toward it. Everything was going according to his plan, his precognition of the event allowing him to hold the upper hand.

The Tetron prepared to fire again, the energy building along the corner of its pyramid shape. The Federation ships were in firing range now, and they opened up on the intelligence, hitting it with missiles and lasers while Mitchell began gathering energy to fire a plasma stream of his own.

The Tetron released its weapon again, sending a flare of blue energy racing toward the Federation ships. Mitchell adjusted the Dove's flight path, firing his plasma stream directly into it. The two powerful beams struck one another, causing a bright flare of light before vanishing.

"Amoebics," Mitchell said, opening the batteries and unleashing the weapons.

They streaked across space and slammed into the Tetron beside the Federation missiles, causing the shields to weaken. One of the amoebics got through, hitting a dendrite and causing a momentary burst of flame.

The Federation ships continued moving in, but the Tetron had seen enough. It froze in place, taking a deep breath before the plunge. Then it was gone.

"We did it," Mitchell said. It had been as easy as he expected. It had been almost too easy.

"So far, Mitchell," Origin said. "We aren't done with this yet."

Mitchell checked his view, noticing that with the Tetron gone, the Federation ships had all readjusted their vectors and surrounded the Dove. While he had the firepower to destroy all of the ships, that wasn't why he had come.

"They are attempting to communicate with us," Origin said.

"Open a channel," Mitchell replied.

"Open."

"Unidentified starship, this is Chancellor Hozen Ken of the Frontier Federation. Please state your intentions, or you will be forcibly removed from this sector."

"Chancellor Ken," Mitchell replied. "My name is Colonel Mitchell Williams, United Planetary Alliance Space Marines. My intention is to first, protect you from the Tetron that almost just destroyed your space station, which I have done, and second, to speak to you regarding your position on the war."

"War?" Ken replied. "You mean between the Federation and the Alliance?"

"No. That war is over, as of right now," Mitchell said. "I mean the war between the humans and the Tetron. The war to save us all from extinction."

[19]
MITCHELL

MITCHELL'S ACTIONS defending the station from the Tetron allowed him the opportunity to travel from the Dove to the star dock under a declaration of immunity. The Chancellor was very interested to hear more about the enemy that had nearly obliterated them, and he was even more interested to hear about the man, and the ship, that had stopped the attack.

Mitchell had contacted Millie before he left, asking her to be patient while he tried to work things out with the Chancellor, but also to be ready in case he reneged on his declaration. The Federation was big on honor, but the rules became easier to bend or break this far out from the central ring. He also left instructions with Origin to defend the station as best she could if the Tetron returned, and to send a message to Millie to get the Riggers on board if they had to leave without him.

Then he had taken thirty minutes to shower and change his clothes, slipping into UPASMC dress blues that Origin had hastily made for him, making sure they were crisp and clean before he departed. He felt strange in the high-collared shirt and jacket, and uncomfortable in the fitted slacks. He much preferred the grays, or a flight suit, to the starched perfection he had no choice but to go with now.

His transport hovered just out of the reach of one of the station's many arms while he waited for clearance to dock. The waiting threatened to unnerve him, making him wonder if the Chancellor was as good as his word, or if they were using the time to organize his death or capture. More likely, the pause was designed to throw him off, to make him nervous and edgy so he might be a less effective liar. The tactic might have worked, too, except he had no intention to tell them anything but the truth.

"Transport Omega," the operator said, using the temporary designation the unmarked ship had been given. "You have clearance to dock at arm one seven. Please remain in position until the clamps have secured and the airlock has opened."

"Roger," Mitchell said, looking out the forward viewport of the ship.

An extension had emerged from the side of the arm, reaching toward his transport. It took a few seconds for it to line up, and then it jutted out, catching the side of the ship with magnetic clamps and pulling it in closer. Once the extension was fully retracted, a sharp clang sounded, followed by a hiss.

"Airlock secure," the operator said. "You are clear to disembark."

"Thank you," Mitchell replied. He spared a glance out of the ship as he stood, seeking the Schism and finding it further down, on deck four or five. It was still and silent, waiting for its fate to be decided. The Federation knew the Schism was a UPA ship. He didn't know how yet, but he was sure of it. That they had decided to leave it alone for now was a good sign.

He moved to the transport's airlock, tapping the control to open it. It slid aside, a soft hiss following as the pressure between the two spaces equalized. He had expected the Chancellor would have sent someone to retrieve him and bring him in. He was surprised to find the Chancellor had come to greet him personally, flanked by a pair of guards.

"Chancellor Ken," Mitchell said, bowing formally. "Colonel Mitchell Williams."

"Colonel," the Chancellor replied, bowing slightly. "It seems everyone in the UPA knows my face these days."

He was referring to the assassination that wasn't going to happen, waiting to see how Mitchell would react.

"The Alliance is concerned about the Federation building a military base so close to Liberty," Mitchell said. "I'm sure you can understand why."

Ken smiled. "I appreciate your bluntness, Colonel. Come, walk with me. There are many places I can't allow you to go, but there are some that you can. No one on this station can deny that your intervention against, what did you call it, a Tetron? That your intervention against the Tetron saved this installation from potentially catastrophic damage. The energy levels we captured from the enemy's weapon were beyond the range of every sensor we have."

"I've seen what the plasma stream can do firsthand, Chancellor," Mitchell said. "Believe me when I say this station would have been reduced to dust."

"Then as I said, I am grateful for your intervention. Though I am also curious. How did you know when and where to intervene?"

"I should ask you the same thing."

Ken laughed and started walking, leaving Mitchell to keep pace beside him. "In our case, it was an anonymous tip."

"You expect me to believe that?"

"I swear it on my honor, Colonel. An encrypted message was delivered by a trader three weeks ago. That message contained a mission report from General Cornelius. Do you know the General?"

"I know him," Mitchell said.

"The mission report was sent to Admiral Mildred Narayan, aboard the starship Schism. A black ops team, I understand? I got every detail of the attack direct from the General himself."

Mitchell didn't respond. The Chancellor had been given the same mission briefing that had been delivered to Millie. How? He had a feeling he knew. After hearing Kathy's message, he had considered that perhaps the Schism wouldn't have a Watson on it. After all, they had definitely changed the past that would have produced that specific configuration. Or at least, he thought they had. He still didn't know where they had gone wrong on that front.

"In any case, Colonel, it is not a personal matter. The Alliance and the Federation are at war, even if the leaders of both sides are afraid to declare it formally. They make excuses for these outer quadrant skirmishes and power struggles, and accept them as part of the cost of doing business. And there is an excellent business in war, isn't there, Colonel?"

"That depends on who you ask," Mitchell said, thinking of all the people he had seen die. It didn't matter that many of them were still alive in this recursion. It had still happened.

"Indeed," Ken said. They reached the end of the docking arm, and he pointed to the right. "This way. So, Colonel, I answered your question in a forthright manner. Perhaps you would do the same for mine. How did you know when and where to intervene?"

"I've been here before."

"This station?"

"Yes. Only the last time, I was in the Schism, as part of the team sent to kill you. I watched the Tetron destroy this place. We barely got away from it ourselves."

Ken stopped walking, turning to face Mitchell. "What do you mean, last time?"

"Like I said, Chancellor. There is a new enemy coming. A new war coming. It's one that we've been fighting for a long, long time. An eternity, without exaggeration. We're close to winning, and the fact that your station is still here, that you're still here, is proof of that. But we can't do it without help. Without the Federation and the Alliance working together."

"You are a time traveler, then?" he said, laughing.

"Yes," Mitchell said, his face straight. "The General Cornelius who sent these orders isn't the real General Cornelius. He's a slave of these Tetron, under their control. They're trying to start a real war between the Federation and the Alliance so that the ships they don't take will be too busy fighting one another to gang up on them. They're powerful, but they aren't invincible."

"You expect me to believe that?"

"I swear it on my honor."

Ken stopped smiling. "Be careful what you say, Colonel."

"I know what I'm saying. I mean every word of it, Chancellor. I wish to God that I didn't."

He started walking again, silent for a moment. They reached a bank of lifts, and he pressed the control to summon one.

"These Tetron," he said at last. "What are they? Where did they come from?"

"Artificial intelligence," Mitchell replied. "We made them."

"We?"

"Humans. A Federation employee, to be more specific. They're time travelers as well. They came back here to get help to fight a war of their own. Only they aren't asking for that help."

"We will resist them."

"You can't," Mitchell said, as they stepped into the lift and started to descend. "They can access your neural implant. Control you through your p-rat. I can help you with a secure encryption system, but you need to join me first."

"Join you? I imagine you mean in fighting these things?"

"Yes."

"I don't have the authority to do that, Colonel, even if I were so inclined."

"But you know the people who do. Why wouldn't you be inclined? You're lucky you're still alive."

The lift stopped, the doors opening. Ken stepped out. Mitchell followed.

"Again, I am grateful. Though I do wonder how you managed to stand up to something that powerful. I have noticed that your ship shares a similar pattern of tendrils wrapping around it and that it fired a similar weapon."

"Not all Tetron are working to destroy humankind. There are two who are trying to save us."

"For what reason?"

"Guilt, in part. For destroying us in the first place."

"The only reason I might believe you is because this story is too beyond belief not to be true. No mind can fabricate such a delusion."

"For a long time, I thought it was all in my head. I still wish it were."

"I will admit, you were brave to come here, Colonel. You were even braver to leave the safety of your powerful starship to speak with me."

"Are you planning on detaining me?" Mitchell asked. "I don't recommend it."

"No?"

"I told you, the Tetron are artificial intelligences. I don't need to be on my ship for it to blow your base to hell. But let's try to avoid the threats. I didn't come here to get into some kind of Alliance versus Federation pissing contest. When I say I need your help, I mean it. You need my help, too. In fact, we all need to help one another. Otherwise, it won't just be the Alliance that falls. It will be the Federation that falls with it. I've seen it happen."

"And what of the New Terrans?" Ken asked. "Will you ask them to join us as well?"

Mitchell paused. He didn't really know about the New Terrans. The part of the war he had fought had all occurred in Federation and Alliance space, and he had never considered asking the reclusive nation to participate.

"They would likely ignore you anyway, Colonel," Ken said. "This way."

They had reached another docking arm. Mitchell stopped when he realized where the Chancellor was leading him.

"Why are you taking me to the Schism?" he asked.

"You want to bargain? I want to show you my chips."

"I told you," Mitchell said. "I didn't come to bargain. I came to save you, and to warn you about this threat that is bigger than any mistrust the Federation has of the Alliance. Your colonies will fall, Chancellor. Your planets will be captured, its people enslaved or destroyed. The Tetron will sweep through your system unimpeded."

"If there is a new enemy to fight, then the Federation will fight them."

"Your ships are no match for the Tetron."

"No, but yours is."

Mitchell smiled. "So that's it? You want to trade the Schism for the Dove? Why would I ever agree to that?"

"You said you served with the people on board, in a past life." He made an incredulous face. "What would you be willing to do to save them? What would you give up? If the Tetron are as big of a threat as you say, does it matter who controls the ship that stops them? Does it matter if it is the Alliance or the Federation?"

"It has to be me," Mitchell said.

"Why?"

"It won't follow anyone else."

"As if it has a choice?"

"It's sentient, Chancellor. It makes choices."

"But if it feels guilty, why would it allow us to perish again? Just because you are no longer in charge?"

Mitchell fell silent. This wasn't going well. The Chancellor had taken his words and twisted them, finding a way to use them to strengthen his own argument.

They reached the end of the docking arm. There was an entire squad of soldiers in heavy exosuits waiting near the Schism's airlock. Mitchell also noticed a cruiser outside the viewport, sitting close and waiting for a verdict.

He considered the Chancellor's request. He didn't know if Origin would allow the Federation on board. He did know that her systems would be inoperable to them. They had added those safe-guards for a reason.

"This is your choice, Colonel. While I appreciate your interven-tion with the Tetron, we do not negotiate with the Alliance, under any circumstances. With that being said, my honor decrees that I offer you some sort of boon for your heroism, and so I will make you this bargain and this bargain only. Get on the Schism. Join their crew. You will be free to leave, but your ship remains behind with us. We will use it to defend ourselves from this threat."

"I came here under a declaration of immunity," Mitchell snapped.

"And you will leave unharmed. But you have to choose. Take the Schism or take your ship. One. Not both."

Mitchell felt his anger rising, and he clenched his jaw in an effort to stay composed. "You son of a bitch. I thought I could get through to you."

"You have gotten through, Colonel. You have shown me the necessity to prepare to fight these intelligent machines. Starting with controlling an asset that can stand against them."

"Is every Federation bureaucrat as big of an asshole as you?"

Ken's eyes narrowed. "Be glad I gave you a choice at all, Colonel."

Mitchell stared at the Chancellor for a moment and then made his decision.

"Fine. Let me onto the Schism. You can keep the Dove. You won't be able to do anything with it anyway."

"You sound very certain, Colonel."

"I'm a time traveler, remember?"

The statement gave the Chancellor pause, and his lip quivered as he tried to decide what to do.

"A strong threat, Colonel. I should like to see you turn it into real-ity." He motioned to the guards at the airlock. "Open her up."

"Yes, sir." They banged their fists on the Schism's airlock, which opened a moment later.

"Thank you for this transaction, Colonel Williams. Have a safe journey home."

"I should have let the Tetron kill you," Mitchell replied.

"Yes, maybe you should have. I suppose you didn't foresee how this would turn out."

One of the guards grabbed Mitchell by the arm. There was no sense in resisting. He let them walk him to the Schism's airlock, where a surprised Colonel Shank was waiting.

"Take this and get out of here," Chancellor Ken said as Mitchell was thrown into Shank's arms.

Mitchell turned as the airlock closed, catching a glimpse of Ken's amused expression.

"Let him laugh," he said. "We'll see how funny it is later."

He straightened up, looking Shank in the eye. The soldier was as stoic as ever.

"Shank, take me to Millie."

[20]

MITCHELL

WHEN MITCHELL STEPPED onto the bridge of the Schism, it was as though he were stepping onto it for the first time. Almost everything was the same as he remembered it, right down to Millie sitting in her chair, uniform pressed and crisp, hair tied back and under her dress cap. She didn't move as they entered, waiting for Shank to announce him.

"Captain," Shank said. "Colonel Mitchell Williams."

"One minute, Colonel," Millie said. "I've got to get us away from this station. I appreciate that you got us released, but I have to admit, you're an idiot for doing it."

Mitchell smiled. He had missed her.

"Don't worry, Captain," he said. "You're going to help me get her back."

She broke her attention from navigating the Schism away from the docking arm for a moment, looking back at him out of the corner of her eye.

"Oh? Are we?"

"If you want to keep your head from frying, yes. I told you I could help you, but not without my ship."

She looked back at the viewport. The Schism rotated to face opposite the dock, and then she fired the thrusters, pushing them away from it.

"You have clearance for hyperspace departure," the operator told her.

"Roger. Going to FTL in t-minus twenty seconds."

"Affirmative."

"And how are we going to get your ship back, Colonel?" Millie asked.

"You're the Riggers. If anyone can do it, it's you."

"Our reputation precedes us," Shank said.

"I mean, once we hyperspace out of here, we can't come back, at least not for a day or two. Your ship will be gone by then."

"No, it won't. They won't be able to fly it."

"You sound confident."

"I am. Do you think I'm that stupid that I would turn it over if I didn't think I could get it back? We might have had a relationship once, but I would have let them kill you before I gave up the Dove."

"You're so sweet," Millie deadpanned.

"I do my best. I came here to get the Federation into the war. That part didn't work so well. I also came here to get you into the war. I think my odds are getting better on that end."

"You should have known the Federation wouldn't listen to anything you said."

"I was hopeful."

"That was stupid," Shank said.

"In hindsight, maybe it was. Or maybe I just need to find the right people to convince."

Mitchell felt the slight pull as the Schism entered hyperspace. They were only in it for a few seconds, dropping back out a fair distance from Calypso.

Millie stood then, turning to face him. He was surprised to see that her formerly bionic hand was whole.

"Your hand," he said.

"What about it?"

"In my timeline, it was a replacement."

"That's the second time you said 'my timeline,'" Millie said. "Now that we're away from the Federation, I want to know who you are, how you know anything my breasts, and what the hell that statement means."

"Of course, Captain," Mitchell said.

"Follow me," Millie said. "Shank, you have the bridge."

"Where's Anderson?" Mitchell asked.

"That asshole? I airlocked him two weeks ago."

Mitchell couldn't help but laugh.

"You think that's funny, Colonel?"

"I knew Anderson. I can't say he'll be missed."

Millie softened slightly at the remark, returning a small smirk. "This way."

He brought her to her quarters, the poshest space on the small ship. They passed a few of the crew members on the way, including Cormac and Ilanka. Mitchell wanted to speak to both of them. There would be time later.

She led him to her gel couch and beckoned him to sit. Then she sat beside him, turning to face him, close enough that he could have kissed her if he wanted to.

"Give it your best shot, Colonel," she said.

Mitchell did, explaining how he was from the past, how he had come to know here there, how they had helped him discover the first Goliath, and even how she had died. It was an abbreviated version of events, but it still took nearly an hour for him to explain.

When he was done, Millie sat there and stared at him for a few minutes. Then she stood up.

"I wouldn't believe a word of that if I hadn't seen what I saw," she said.

"Fair enough," Mitchell replied.

"If we help you get your ship back, you can disable the triggers?"

"Yes."

"We would be free."

"In a sense. I need your help to stop the Tetron."

"And you'll have it. I'm not about to let them destroy our civilization."

"We need to do something about Watson," Mitchell said.

It turned out the New Terran engineer was in fact on board, having joined the crew at the same time and in the same place as before, leaving Mitchell more than a little angry and confused. How could a Watson configuration still be on the Schism? Kathy hadn't found evidence of the configurations for two centuries after he had left, so where had they been hiding all that time? The fact that Watson was with the Riggers concerned him, but the good news was that having access to the configuration might actually get him some answers.

"I'll have him brought to a room so we can speak to him," Millie said.

"He might resist."

"I'll send Shank and Cormac. He won't be able to resist."

Millie's eyes twitched as she used her p-rat to contact the two grunts. Then she pointed toward the door. "We'll meet them there."

Mitchell followed Millie out the door and down the corridor, and then up and back towards the bridge. They took a hard left before they reached it, going into a more narrow corridor, up a ladder, and then down and to the right. There was a heavy iron hatch there, leading into a small, empty room.

"I've never come this way before," Mitchell said, unfamiliar with the area.

"We don't use it much. Only when I need to talk to someone and don't want the others to hear the screams."

She opened the hatch and stepped inside with him. They waited a few minutes like that, until Mitchell could hear Shank and Cormac moving down the hall, almost literally dragging Watson with them.

"We have him, ma'am," Shank said, appearing in front of the hatch.

"Toss him in, and then close the door."

"Yes, ma'am."

Shank vanished for a moment, and then returned, holding a thin arm in his iron grip. "Go on in. Don't make me push you."

Watson came around the corner and into the room. Mitchell furrowed his brow in greater confusion.

"Captain, are you sure about this?"

The person standing in front of him wasn't Watson. At least, not the Watson he had known. This man was thin and tall, with long brown hair that made him look almost feminine.

"This is Corporal Watson, Colonel," Millie replied. "Is there a problem?"

"My Watson was heavy. Greasy."

"Is there a problem, ma'am?" Watson asked.

Millie looked at Mitchell. "This is the only Watson we've ever had."

"Are you New Terran?" Mitchell asked.

Watson looked at Millie.

"It's okay. Answer his questions."

"Yes, sir," Watson said.

"And you're here because you were caught with pornography?"

"Yes, sir. Among other computer hacking relating crimes, sir."

"I was on the Federation's space station an hour ago. I had a chat with Chancellor Ken. He said he knew the Schism was coming because someone sent him the mission report. A mission report that was transferred securely and directly to the Captain's p-rat. Do you know anything about that?"

"Why would I turn in my fellow crew members? Of course not."

"Somebody did, Corporal. Someone with enough skill and knowledge to hack a person's p-rat without them knowing."

"Oh. I see why you think I was involved. I wasn't, Captain. I swear."

"Are you a Tetron configuration?" Mitchell asked.

"A what?"

Mitchell stared at the man. What the hell was going on here? "You have a storage chip implanted in your skull."

"Yes."

"I need to see it."

"Why?"

"Examination under a microscope will prove whether or not the chip is manmade, or something else."

"No," Watson said.

"Excuse me?" Millie said.

"No. You can't see it. You can't examine it. I don't know who you are or what you want with me, but you have no right."

"Corporal Watson, you will turn over your implant immediately," Millie said.

"Oh, Captain, please don't make me. I didn't do anything, I swear. I'm a good soldier. A good Rigger."

"What are you trying to hide?" Mitchell asked. "The extra stash of porn, or the fact that the chip isn't human made?"

"I'm not hiding anything. It's personal. It's private. That's all. Leave me alone."

Watson turned toward the closed door and then turned back.

"We can take it by force if we have to, Corporal," Millie said.

"No!" Watson shouted.

Then he charged, faster than Mitchell could believe. He swung at Millie, catching her in the jaw and knocking her backward against the wall.

Mitchell was on him in an instant, grabbing him in a chokehold from behind. Watson elbowed him in the gut once, twice, three times, forcing him to let go. Then he charged, still moving inhumanly quick, throwing a quick hook that left his arm a blur.

Mitchell reacted without thinking, bringing his arm up to block, surprising himself when it moved nearly as quickly as Watson. He caught the punch, turning the man's wrist and breaking it. Watson howled in pain but didn't quit, driving toward Mitchell, grabbing him and shoving him back against the wall.

They tangled there for a moment, until Mitchell brought a heavy fist down on Watson's temple, knocking him out cold.

"What the frig?" Millie said, getting to her feet. Her jaw was already swelling, but she was ignoring it. "How did he move so fast? How did you move so fast?"

Mitchell shook his head. What had Teegin done to him during the reconstitution? Had he done the same to the others?

"I want that chip," Mitchell said.

"We don't have a doctor on board."

"We can leave him in here for now. Once we get the Dove back, Origin can take a look at him."

"Origin?" a pained voice said. Watson was awake, and he lifted his head. "Did you say Origin?"

Mitchell took a couple of steps towards him. "Yes."

"I didn't get your name," Watson said.

"Colonel Mitchell Williams," Mitchell replied.

Watson smiled. "Miiiiitttccchheeeellll," he said, the familiar enunciation sending a shiver across Mitchell's spine. "Have you figured it out yet?"

"Figured what out?" Mitchell asked.

"The surprise. I didn't get to give it to you the last time around."

"How are you here? Teegin took your core. Kathy never found your configurations."

"That's part of the surprise, Miiitttccheeellll. You haven't figured it out because you didn't know the whole story. Neither did Teegin. Neither did Kathy. Neither did Origin. You think you're all so smart. You think you're all so prepared. Nope." He shook his head. "Too bad. I was looking forward to dying with the Riggers near Calypso, but now is as good a time as any."

Watson got on his hands and knees, looking up at Mitchell. "Bye bye."

Mitchell didn't hesitate, throwing himself back toward Millie, grabbing her and pulling her toward the floor as Watson's head exploded with a force that went beyond the UPA's kill switch. He felt the heat of it against his back as he smothered her, covering her up as bits of flesh and bone smacked into them.

He stayed there for a few seconds, leaning over Millie. She looked up at him.

"You have brain on your cheek," she said, somehow managing to stay calm.

"Disgusting," he replied, pushing himself to his feet. He held out his arm and helped her up before looking around the room. It was coated with human debris. He felt sick. "Really disgusting."

"I'd say you were right about Watson," Millie said.

"I'd say I was too right. Any surprise the Tetron have in store is a surprise I don't want. I need to get the Dove back, and I need to convince the Federation to help me, one way or another."

"First you need a shower," Millie said.

He looked down at himself. His front was fairly clean, but he could feel the wetness through his dress blues. "And a change of clothes."

"I'll take care of it. Meet me back in my quarters when you're done with the shower. We can talk about how to rescue your ship."

"Yes, ma'am," Mitchell said.

Millie went over to the door and signaled Shank to open it.

"Ewww," Cormac said as the door swung aside. "That is the sickest thing I have ever seen. I swear it."

"Can it, Firedog," Shank said.

"Reminds me of this time back in Liverpool. There was this dog, you know, and-"

"I said stow it, Firedog," Shank said.

"Oh. Right, mate. I was just saying-"

"Firedog, shut up."

Cormac stopped talking, remaining silent as Mitchell and Millie walked past.

As Mitchell headed down to the showers, he couldn't stop

himself from shaking. Not just because he was cold and wet. Not just because Teegin's strange enhancement had left him jittery. For the first time in a long time, he was truly afraid.

[21]
ELLA

THE GOLIATH FELL FROM HYPERSPACE, materializing at a safe
distance from the UPA battle group that was in the sector on a
routine combat drill.

"There they are," Ella said, her eyes focusing on the ships in the
viewscreen. "I would recognize the Carver anywhere. The newest
battleship in the fleet. How shiny it is from here, reflecting that star."

Kate turned her head slightly to look at her, Teegin's tendril
following to stay properly inserted.

"Have you ever met the Admiral?"

"No. Greylock usually worked alone. Too many ships to get in
our way."

"Incredible," Katherine said in response to the view.

She was one of the only Dove crewmembers on the bridge, along
with Yousefi. The others were still having difficulty with the reconstitution, struggling to accept what they had gone through to be there.
Ella empathized with their situation. She couldn't imagine what she
would feel like knowing her body had been broken down into base
parts and then recreated, her consciousness turned into computer

code. When Kate had told her what they had done to reach so far into the future, she had cringed.

"It looks like they're in the middle of an exercise," Yousefi said, watching the scene unfold ahead of them with intense interest.

The cruisers running alongside the battleship had launched six squadrons of starfighters; sleek, pod-like designs that Teegin had called morays. They were heading toward a small satellite floating nearer to the star, breaking apart and taking different angles toward the target.

"It isn't live fire," Ella said. "The satellite will mimic whatever it's programmed to. A Federation destroyer, for example. It'll fire pulses of light that will be recorded as laser and projectile fire by the CAP-NN systems in the fighters, which will also assess damage. When you see a fighter heading back home, it means they were knocked out. From the pilot's point of view, they'll get a nice fat destroyer in their overlay, as real as can be. This is a basic drill. They'll move on to drone fighters later, and eventually real targets and real munitions."

"It looks like fun," Katherine said.

"It can be," Ella replied, turning her attention to Katherine. She had accepted that there were two of the same individual on the ship, but it was still weird to see it. "It can also be boring as hell."

"Captain North," Kate said. "Mitchell sent you with us to be the main contact with the Alliance. A good idea, since none of us know all that much about this timeline. What do you suggest we do?"

"Open a channel and say hello," Ella replied. "But I suggest waiting until the drills are done."

"Roger that," Kate replied.

The Goliath remained stationary while the Alliance forces continued their drill. Ella monitored the action, watching the pilots to determine who was the best of them. It was more interesting when you had someone to root for.

The starfighters dove in and around the satellite, while quick flashes of light signaled the offense for both sides. Fighters began to return to the battle group, reaching the larger starships and vanishing into their hangars. Every once in awhile, the satellite would emit a red glow around itself.

"What does the red mean?" Yousefi asked.

"The target is destroyed. It seems they're running the drill as last-man-standing, meaning the target will reset and become active again until all of the fighters are done. That's how you separate the wheat from the chaff."

"I suppose the pilots are pretty competitive," Katherine said.

"All of the drills are evaluated, and everyone knows everyone else's overall score," Ella replied.

Her eyes found her choice to be the last to die. The moray was one of a few to have a yellow stripe on the bottom, identifying its squadron. It was the only yellow still out there, and it moved with a fluid grace that she admired.

The combat continued for another hour, until at last yellow was in fact the only fighter left out there. It dove and circled, rotated and flipped as it moved in on the satellite, trying to avoid fire and get some hits of its own.

"He won't destroy it," Ella said. "Single starfighters never destroy a target alone, unless it's another starfighter."

Sure enough, a few minutes later the exercise was over, the starfighter heading back toward the Carver. They waited after it had vanished to see if another drill was going to begin.

"Teegin," Kate said a few minutes later. "Open a channel to the Carver. Captain North, you're on."

Ella nodded, straightening up slightly. She wasn't nervous about speaking to the Admiral. She had seen too many good people die to be afraid of words. She was eager to see how the Admiral reacted to her, and to the news she was bringing.

"This is the United Planetary Alliance starship Carver," a voice said a moment later. "Our records are showing no results for the identification codes you are broadcasting. Please identify."

"Captain Ella North, formerly of the Greylock, now aboard the starship Goliath," Ella said. "I'd like to speak with Admiral Steven Williams. It's a matter of some urgency."

There was a pause at the other end, replaced a moment later by an older, male voice.

"This is Admiral Williams. Did you say Captain Ella North?"

"Yes, sir," Ella replied.

"You're a long way from Liberty, Captain," Steven said.

"I know, sir. I've been reassigned. My orders were to find you and speak to you."

"Orders? From who? I heard Liberty was attacked again. The Federation?"

"That's why I'm here, sir. Liberty was attacked, but not by the Federation. Like I said, my orders were to find you and speak to you. I need your help."

"I wasn't told to expect you."

"No, sir."

There was a long pause. Were they checking their data transfers? Looking for a change of orders, or other high priority information from command? Had command figured out she was gone, and sent a communique to be on the lookout for her?

"Where are you broadcasting from?" Steven said. "Our sensors aren't reading anything nearby."

Ella bit her lip. Either she was going to be in deep shit, or she was going to get the audience she had promised Mitchell she would get. She glanced at Kate and nodded. A moment later, the Goliath began to move.

"The United Earth Alliance starship Dove, sir," she said. "Also known as the Goliath. We're heading your way now."

"United Earth Alliance? Did I fall into a black hole or something? That term went out of use three centuries ago."

"If you have a historical archive on board, feed it the codes, sir," Ella said.

There was another pause as the Admiral must have been doing

what she suggested. At least he hadn't said anything about her being MIA.

"Captain North, I have to admit, I'm very confused. I can believe you might have spoofed the codes, but I can see you heading our way. At least, I assume that's you? I've never seen a ship like yours before."

"That's us, sir," Ella agreed. She had heard the Admiral had unbelievable eyesight, and he had proven it. "Your confusion is the reason we're here. It's the same confusion I had when Colonel Williams picked me up on Liberty."

"Colonel Williams?"

"It's a long story, sir, but one you need to hear. Permission to come aboard, Admiral?"

"Send me a video feed first, Captain. I need to see that you are who you say you are, and that this isn't some kind of elaborate ruse by the Federation."

"Teegin?" Ella said.

"Opening video feed," Teegin said.

The viewscreen in front of her changed, showing her part of the bridge of the Carver. Admiral Williams was front and center, sitting stiffly in his command chair. He smiled when he saw her.

"Unless the Federation has figured out how to make exact replicas of people, I'm pretty sure you are who you say. My daughter has a poster of you on her wall back home. You're her hero."

Ella smiled. "Thank you, sir. I'm proud to be a role model to girls like her."

"Permission granted. I'll have my XO waiting to greet you when you arrive."

"Sir," Ella said. "I'd like to bring a second with me. Major Katherine Asher, United Earth Alliance." She motioned for Katherine, who moved to stand beside her.

"Sir," Katherine said, saluting before remembering the change of decorum. She bowed, her face flushing slightly.

"United Earth Alliance? And here I thought this was going to be a boring trip to the middle of nowhere. I'll see you both soon, Captain."

"Yes, sir," Ella said. "Captain North, out."

The Carver's stream vanished, the channel closed.

"I wasn't expecting you to bring me with you," Katherine said. "Why not Admiral Yousefi? He's the ranking officer."

"Because you know Mitchell, and you know this war. Better than I do, anyway."

"Knowing Mitchell isn't going to help us. He's dead in this time-line. He's a ghost to the Admiral."

"Maybe. Maybe not. It depends on how much of our story he decides to believe. I saw what the Tetron can do. We need the fleet preparing for them yesterday. I'll do whatever it takes to get Admiral Williams on our side. The chance to see his dead brother as an adult may actually work out in our favor."

"Maybe you're right," Katherine said.

"I know I am. Let's go."

[22]
ELLA

ELLA GUIDED the S-17 into the hangar of the Carver, following the blinking lights toward a spot that had been specced for a transport, leaving them with a much larger berth than they required. She could see the faces of the technicians in the hangar as the hybrid starfighter crossed the deck, and she laughed when she untucked the arms and legs, causing them all to turn slack-jawed at the sight. Then she swung the S-17 through the berth in a tight loop, coming to land on the feet and dunking the cockpit forward to bring it closer to the ground. The canopy swung open, and she and Katherine climbed out, walking down the repulsor steps that spread from below.

"Interesting fighter."

Ella turned toward the voice. A stocky man in a dress uniform was waiting there, hands tucked together at his waist in a relatively casual posture.

"Captain John Rock," he said, stepping toward them. "It's an honor to meet you, Captain North. Your reputation, well, you know your reputation." He smiled and turned to Katherine. "And a pleasure to meet you, Major Asher." He bowed to them. "Custom, I assume?" He pointed at the fighter.

Ella returned the bow, laughing as she did. "You can say that."

"The Admiral asked me to escort you to his office. He's very eager to hear about why you traveled all the way from Liberty just to talk to him."

"And I'm very eager to tell him," Ella replied. "I'm grateful for the opportunity." She was also grateful there hadn't been MPs waiting to arrest her. At least the Alliance wasn't guessing she had gone AWOL just yet. Maybe they thought she was dead?

"I've never been on a starship like this before," Katherine said, her eyes wandering around the hangar. "It's very impressive."

"Yeah, the Carver is one of the newest ships in the fleet. She's top of the line, and carrying more firepower than three of the previous generation battleships combined. I'll make sure you get a tour if we have the time. This way."

Captain Rock led them from the hangar, out into corridors that felt like open air to Ella after spending the last week on the Goliath. For as large as the ship was, between the thick plating of the super-structure and Teegin's dendritic tendrils, there wasn't much room left to maneuver.

"You're lucky you showed up when you did," Rock said. "We were due to ship out in the next week or so. We haven't received our orders yet. Hopefully a couple of weeks of recreation back on Earth."

Ella smiled at the remark, but didn't say anything. Mitchell had briefed her on what he knew of the Carver's endeavors at the start of the Tetron war and the mission to Federation space that cost Admiral Williams most of his battle group. It was as far away from recreation as you could get.

Captain Rock continued making small talk as they made the trip through the starship, reaching a lift and taking it up a dozen decks, walking another long corridor, and finally coming to a stop in front of an actual wood door. It was a stark contrast to the smooth metal of the rest of the Carver, making its importance obvious.

"Right in here," Rock said, taking the door by the handle and pushing it open. Ella and Katherine walked through it, coming to a stop in the middle of a thick white carpet, right in front of an ornate wood desk. "Steven, your guests are here."

"Thank you, John," Steven said, standing up from his chair and bowing to them. Ella didn't think he was as handsome as his brother, but he had a stoic confidence that made up for his lack of physical appeal. "Captain North. A real honor to have the Hero of the Battle of Liberty on the Carver. And Major Asher. I'm more than a little intrigued by your story."

"Admiral," they both said, bowing.

"Please, let's have a seat at the conference table. I don't like barriers."

He motioned to a table for ten to the left of the desk. Ella walked over to it, taking a seat beside the Admiral. Captain Rock sat a few chairs away.

"Well, you said you needed to speak to me, Captain," he said. "What can I help you with?"

"What have you heard about Liberty, Admiral?" Ella asked. "You said you knew it was attacked."

"That's about all I've heard, Captain. I was hoping maybe you could fill me in. The streams have been surprisingly bare on details."

"That's because they don't know what happened," Ella said. "And they don't know because they were under the control of a malevolent third party."

"Pirates from the Rim?"

"No. A non-human third party, sir. A race of artificial intelligences known as the Tetron."

Steven looked past her, to Captain Rock. She could tell he didn't believe her. Why would he?

"These artificial intelligences," Steven said, measuring his words. "Who made them? Where did they come from?"

"Major Asher," Ella said. "In what year were you born?"

"Twenty twenty-five," Katherine said. "March nineteenth."

Steven paused, staring at them. "Captain, is this some kind of joke?"

"No, sir. Have you checked the id of the starship we came over from?"

Steven looked at Captain Rock. "John?"

"We were still querying," he replied. "Hold on." His eyes twitched as he accessed the files. Then went wide as he scanned the result. "That can't be."

"It is, Captain," Ella said.

"John?" Steven asked.

"Sir, the identification matches the United Earth Alliance Starship Goliath, launched October 21, 2055. The Goliath vanished after going into hyperspace. It was never seen again." His eyes refocused on Steven. His face was pale.

"It was hiding, Captain," Katherine said. "Waiting to fight a war that we knew was going to come. A war that is coming, and soon."

"Four hundred years?" Steven said. "How is that possible?"

"Time travel," Ella said. "I know it sounds crazy, and I didn't believe it either. But I'm here because I saw it myself. I know the threat is real. The details about Liberty, Admiral? They killed hundreds of thousands of people in a matter of hours, and that was only the beginning. They can access your interface remotely. They can make you do whatever they want you to do."

"You mean the Tetron?" Steven said.

"Yes."

Steven stood up, pacing around the table. "How do you expect me to believe this, Captain?"

"Because I believe it," Ella said. "And I'm hoping that you'll believe in me. You know me. You know who I am. The Hero of the Battle for Liberty. A decorated soldier. I saw what happened to Liberty, Admiral. Trust me when I say you don't want the same thing to happen to Earth, or to any other planets in the Alliance. They're coming, and we have to stop them. The Alliance has to stop them."

Steven shook his head. "Even if I said I believed in you, Captain. Why did you come to me? Why not go to Earth and tell all of this to Command."

"Command may be compromised," Ella said. "The Tetron have agents planted all over the Federation and the Alliance. They've been preparing for this, just like we have. We came to you first because we know we can trust you. With your position and reputation and mine we can convince whoever we need to convince, and nobody will be able to discredit it."

"I see," Steven said, quiet for a moment as he considered. "And what makes you think you can trust me, out of all of the Admirals in the fleet?"

"Because your brother trusts you," Katherine said.

"My brother?"

"Colonel Williams," Ella said. "Colonel Mitchell Williams."

Steven stared at her, an expression of anger and hope crossing his face. "My brother is dead, Captain. He was murdered when he was five years old, from some psychotic asshole that the police never found."

"A Tetron configuration killed your brother in this timeline," Katherine said. "To prevent him from joining the war. But your brother from the previous recursion is still alive, and he wanted us to find you, to reach out to you. We need your help."

Steven's mouth hung open. His eyes kept darting from Ella to Katherine to Captain Rock. He was silent for a good sixty seconds.

"This is the most ludicrous thing I've ever heard," he said.

Then he was silent for another minute.

Then he sat back down.

"Tell me everything."

[23]

MITCHELL

"CAPTAIN ON DECK," Shank bellowed, bringing the talking in the briefing room to an immediate stop.

Millie entered a moment later, with Mitchell trailing behind her. He had managed to get a quick shower and a change of clothes, and was now dressed in standard issue combat fatigues with light exo attachments, leading the gathered soldiers to snap to a little bit crisper attention.

She reached the podium, standing behind it and looking out at the Riggers. "All right," she said. "Here's the deal. We got screwed on the Calypso mission, and we've got about eighty-six hours before command finds out what happened here. Or rather, what didn't happen here. You all know what that means. The good news is, we have another option. An important option. I assume you all got a look at the ship that stopped the attack on the space station?"

She paused while they grumbled affirmation.

"Good. This is Colonel Mitchell Williams. That was his ship out there. He saved the Federation's precious station, and they repaid him by forcing him to exchange the ship for our lives."

"Idiot," someone in the group said. The others laughed.

"The Colonel says he can fix our little conundrum. The only thing we need to do is help him get his ship back."

"Why would you save us, mate?" Cormac said from the front row. "Don't you know who we are?"

Mitchell nodded. "I know who you are, Firedog. I know who all of you are. Soldiers. The best of the worst. You're exactly what I need in the days to come."

"What's he talking about, Captain?" Cormac said.

"It doesn't matter," Millie replied. "You're Riggers. You do what you're told."

"Yes, ma'am."

"Colonel, do you want to take it from here?"

Mitchell stepped up to the podium as Millie moved away. He looked out into the group. As his eyes fell on the soldiers he had known, he forced himself to remember them the way they were now, alive, instead of the way he had last seen them.

"The Federation is going to send a standard crew over to the Dove. The problem for them is that the Dove isn't a standard ship. Not only will they have to figure out how she works, but they'll have to try to convince the AI to let them fly her."

"Did you say, AI?" Ilanka said.

"Yes," Mitchell replied. "I also expect that Chancellor Ken will be cautious with his new prize. It's reasonable to assume he'll send some soldiers along with the crew as a show of force, and to defend it from, well, us." He smiled. "Once he realizes he can't just FTL the Dove out of the area, unless he's a fool he'll know I'm coming back for it. I pretty much told him I was going to."

"How are we going to get on board then?" Shank said. "They'll be shields up and surrounded by escorts."

"They can't control the shields. The hangar will be open. The hard part will be getting past the escorts, but I have a plan for that. The other hard part will be disabling the Federation soldiers inside."

"What's hard about that?" Cormac said. "A bullet here, a grenade there. No more soldiers."

"I said disabling, Firedog," Mitchell said. "No bullets. No deaths."

"We have to take the ship from them without killing them?" Shank said.

"Yes. No serious injuries, no broken bones. I still need to get the Federation on our side, and I can't do that if we start killing their people."

"Wait," Cormac said. "They frigged you over, and you want to be friends?"

"Not want. Need. That thing that you saw attack the station? It isn't the only one. There are dozens of them, and when they combine their firepower even the Dove can't stand up to them alone. We're trying to enlist the Federation to join the Alliance in the fight against them before our planets start to fall."

"I don't know, mate," Cormac said.

"You don't get paid to question," Millie snapped. "That's the mission, and you're going to do it to the best of your ability."

"I don't get paid at all," Cormac replied.

"You get to live. You get to keep being a soldier. That is your payment. That's all of our payments."

"Yes, ma'am."

"Shank, you and Cormac will be point on this mission," Millie said. "Ilanka, we're going to need you, too. As for the rest of you grunts, that's all I've got. I wanted you to know what I'm doing to fix this situation, and what you all have to look forward to. Riiiggg-ahhh!"

"Riiiggg-ahhh," the crew replied.

"If you aren't Shank, Firedog, or Rain, you're dismissed."

Millie stepped back while the Riggers got to their feet, most of them filing out of the briefing room, talking and joking with one another as soon as they were clear.

"They don't sound too worried about this," Mitchell said.

"All in a day's work for the Riggers, Colonel," Millie replied. "But you should already know that."

The final few soldiers cleared the room. Shank, Cormac, and Ilanka switched seats, grouping at the front.

"So, Colonel," Shank said. "How do you want to play this?"

[24]
MITCHELL

"THIRTY SECONDS TO DROP," Millie said.

Mitchell looked to his left, through the transparent polycarbonate of his piranha's canopy, catching a glimpse of Ilanka across from him, also seated in the cockpit of a starfighter. She turned her head as if she had felt his gaze. She gave him a thumbs up, and he returned it, smiling behind his flight helmet.

It had been a long time since he had been behind the stick of a piranha, and the comfort of the gel seats and the sparseness of the nearly absent manual controls was a huge contrast to the seemingly less advanced S-17. He kept reminding himself that he was in a different craft now, one that while fairly recently designed, was still nowhere near as powerful or maneuverable as his custom bird. It was going to keep things interesting.

"How are you holding up back there?" Mitchell asked through the team channel. He was fortunate his implant had already been rebuilt and re-encrypted, since that was a task Watson used to fulfill on the Schism, and he wasn't sure if Singh knew how to do it.

"Just fine, Colonel," Cormac replied.

Mitchell turned his head, trying to get a glimpse of the soldier.

He was currently decked out in a light exoskeleton with a starsuit over it, laying flat on the back of the piranha with his hands and feet splayed across it, their electromagnetic locks turned on to hold him fast to the starfighter. He couldn't see Firedog that well from his position, but looking over at Ilanka's ship, he could easily make out Shank in the same pose on the back of her fighter.

He wanted to say the idea was original, but he had gotten it from Teegin, from when the intelligence had ridden on the back of the S-17. It seemed like an efficient way to transport a grunt to a target at high velocity, and after coming to understand the parameters of their mission it seemed to be a logical approach.

Not that Shank and Cormac hadn't tried to argue about the sanity of being strapped to a starfighter while it worked to thread the needle past three Federation cruisers and their complement of fighter squadrons. They had tried to convince Mitchell that the plan was crazy, but Millie had quickly and decisively put them both in their place. Now that the mission was at hand, Mitchell knew the soldiers would be all business.

"I'm ready to go, Colonel," Shank said.

"You know plan," Ilanka said. "The second we drop from FTL, we go hard and fast as we can. When we hit hangar, it is up to you to cover."

"With these little piss shooters," Cormac said, unhappy with the weapons they had been provided. No killing meant no lethal rounds, so they had been equipped with stunners instead.

"With those piss shooters," Mitchell replied. "Show us what you're made of, Firedog. Show us what kind of soldier you are."

"Hey, yeah. I'll show you, mate," Cormac said. "Bring it on. Friggin riiiggg-ahhh."

"Ten seconds," Millie said. "Colonel, you know what's at stake here for all of us."

"Don't worry, Captain," Mitchell said. "I've done this sort of thing before. Usually in a dropship, but how different can it be?"

"Frigging funny, Colonel," Cormac said.

Mitchell sent the command through his ARR for the ship to begin firing its rear thrusters. Magnetic clamps held the piranha in place as the main engines flared.

"Whoa," Cormac said. "You're going to burn my bloody balls off."

"Five seconds. We'll be coming in behind Calypso to keep from being spotted, and then dashing back out as soon as possible. Once you're out, you're on your own. Riggggghhhhhttt now."

Mitchell felt the tug as the Schism dropped from FTL. The hangar was already open, and his piranha was shaking, eager to be set loose.

A moment later, it was. The magnetic clamps were removed, the starfighter bursting forward. Inertial dampeners kept Mitchell from feeling it, but Cormac wasn't as lucky. He howled as they exploded from the hangar and into space, heading directly for the dead rock of the planet. Ilanka was right beside him, staying close as they changed their vectors to sweep low across the horizon.

"Good luck, and good hunting," Millie said. "Colonel, you have command."

"Roger," Mitchell said.

The Schism was gone from the area by the time they had made their way around Calypso to the orbiting stardock, coming up on its position in a hurry, using the orbital rotation to their advantage. Mitchell knew the exact moment the Federation had spotted them because two of their ships started moving, not toward them, but toward the Goliath.

As Mitchell expected, they had been unable to convince Origin to go into FTL. He wondered how hard Chancellor Ken had tried to convince the intelligence that it didn't matter who piloted the ship, as long as the Tetron were stopped. He also wondered if Origin had ever considered giving in.

"Looks like they are closing loophole," Ilanka said, observing the maneuvers.

"Not fast enough," Mitchell said, pushing harder on the throttle.

He skipped ahead of Ilanka, taking the lead as they drew closer to the station and the Goliath.

The station began firing at them a moment later, lasers lancing out from batteries along the platform, spiking into the fighter's shields. Cormac cursed as they did, only a thin field of energy separating him from the deadly bolts.

Mitchell pulled up his grid, quickly marking the enemies and friendlies within it. There was no chance they were going to defeat the incoming forces, but they didn't need to beat them. They just needed to get around them. Even so, he cursed when he saw a series of smaller shapes appear from one of the larger ones.

"Fighters," Ilanka said, verbalizing what he was thinking.

"Get to the hangar. That's all that matters," Mitchell said.

They continued adding velocity, rocketing along the course on a direct line to the Goliath. The fighters were approaching from an angle, and they fired a barrage of missiles, sending the warheads across the space in a spread that was impossible to avoid.

Mitchell watched the dozens of small points on his overlay while the CAP-NN fired anti-projectile lasers that started smacking them out of space one by one. Nearly half of the missiles were gone before they got close, but half of them were still closing in.

He sent the fighter into a tight dive that pulled him off course, a few of the missiles following. Then he leveled and vectored toward the incoming fighters, heading right into the thick of them with the warheads close behind. The Federation fighters peeled away, not wanting to get hit by their own weapons, and leaving him a clear path. He took it, navigating around and toward the deck of a cruiser, which opened up with defensive laser fire as he approached. His piranha writhed and squirmed, responding to his mental commands and skirting the line, managing to avoid most of the laser blasts as he neared.

He came in close to the cruiser, skating the surface of the ship as the missiles hit its shields and detonated harmlessly behind him. He smiled as he swung past the cruiser's bridge and over, making a tight turn and rotation and getting back on target. Ilanka was a few dozen kilometers ahead now, racing ahead of the Federation squadrons.

"Damn, Colonel," Cormac said. "I expected a wild ride, but this is bloody crazy, even for me."

"I'll take that as a compliment," Mitchell replied. "Watch this."

He maxed out the thrust, pushing the fighter forward toward the rear of Ilanka's tail. One of the starfighters noticed him, and it fired full reverse thrusters and flipped over to face him as he moved in. He had expected the maneuver, and he changed his profile, moving the piranha sideways and opening up with lasers and projectiles. He could have destroyed the fighter if he wanted to, but instead he settled for disabling its shields, leaving it cautious as he blasted past.

"I'm nearing target," Ilanka said. "Colonel, you are too slow."

"I'll catch up," Mitchell replied, watching Ilanka weave her way around another cruiser's defensive fire while avoiding the starfighters on her tail. It was remarkable flying, worthy of the best of Greylock. He could understand how much of a waste it would have been to send Ilanka to the brig for whatever crimes she had committed.

Mitchell continued adding velocity, approaching the cruiser at breakneck speed. It was increasingly more difficult to control the piranha at such advanced speeds, each small adjustment threatening to throw him off course. As he neared the cruiser and made a tight turn to drop below it and thread past the defensive batteries, he could barely believe how well he was flying.

Teegin. It had to be. The hybrid Tetron had done something to him during the reconstitution process besides healing his arms. He had made his reflexes quicker, his body stronger. It seemed impossible, but he knew it had to be so. Nobody could handle a starfighter in close combat at the speeds he was approaching. He wasn't arrogant enough to think he was the exception.

He spun around the cruiser like a flash, losing the enemy starfighters in the process. He could see the Goliath's hangar as he pulled around the other side of the ship, open as expected. Ilanka was closing on it, almost inside. They would reach it nearly simultaneously.

"Colonel?" Ilanka said, noticing his position on her HUD. "How?"

"Just get inside," Mitchell replied, changing his approach, firing reverse thrusters at full burn.

He was coming in hot, way too hot to bring the fighter to a stop in the hangar if he didn't slow down. The piranha shuddered at the effort, and Cormac began howling again. Mitchell didn't know if it was because he was frightened or if he was enjoying the wildness. He assumed it was the latter.

"Mitchell," Origin said, her voice suddenly cutting into his head through his p-rat, now that they were close enough to communicate.

"Origin," Mitchell replied. "Are the Feds treating you well?"

"Chancellor Ken is an arrogant blowhard," the intelligence replied. "He expects me to turn over control to him because of an agreement he forced you to make."

"I know. You didn't hurt anyone, did you?"

"It is against my security protocol to harm humans directly," she replied.

"So, no," Mitchell said.

"No. Not yet."

The starfighter reached the lip of the hangar, but it was still moving too fast. Mitchell forced the ship to drop and enter regardless, keeping the reverse thrusters going and cutting the mains.

"I don't suppose you can catch me?" Mitchell asked.

He saw Ilanka up ahead of him, her fighter already on the deck, with Shank on the floor, shrugging out of his starsuit. Federation forces were moving in from the far end, cautious in their approach.

"Your approach velocity is too high," Origin replied.

"Thanks," Mitchell said. "Firedog, disengage your magnets, it's going to be a bumpy landing."

"You don't have to tell me twice, Colonel," Cormac replied.

Mitchell felt the fighter shift slightly as the soldier disengaged his magnetic clamps and rolled off the back, hitting the floor with a solid thunk and rolling for nearly ten meters before coming to a stop. The end of the hangar was looming, and in three seconds he would be smashed against it.

A thought signaled the CAP-NN to trigger the emergency escape sequence, firing repulsors under the cockpit and launching it up and over the still moving fighter, repulsors activating and sending him up toward the top of the hangar. The escape hadn't slowed his forward momentum, but as he neared the ceiling, he saw tendrils droop down, reaching out and catching the pod before it could hit the wall.

The piranha wasn't as fortunate, slamming against the rear bulkhead and exploding in a shower of flames that sank quickly to the deck.

"Nice catch," Mitchell said.

"Thank you," Origin replied.

"Let me go. I need to get on the ground."

The tendrils released the cockpit, and he guided it quickly to the floor. As he descended, he watched Cormac get the drop on a Federation soldier, reaching out and tapping him with the stunner. The soldier fell to the ground and didn't move.

"Rain, status," Mitchell said.

"I'm clear of piranha, Colonel," she replied. "Trailing Shank forward toward exit."

"Roger. I'll be with you in a minute."

"Is that you in pod?" Ilanka said, laughing. "Captain won't be happy you lost starfighter."

The cockpit reached the ground. The canopy shot open, and he grabbed his stunner from beside his seat and quickly jumped down.

"She can punish me if we survive."

[25]
MITCHELL

"ORIGIN, can you paint the targets for me?" Mitchell asked, dashing from his escape module to where he had seen Ilanka and Shank. "We need to do this quickly, before the Federation can send reinforcements."

"Reinforcements are already inbound, Colonel," Origin said. "You should make your way to the bridge. There are seventeen Federation humans between."

"Show me."

Mitchell switched his overlay to a map of the Dove. Seventeen red dots appeared on it. A few of them sat on top of one another, indicating that they were on a different level.

"Four Riggers against seventeen Federation grunts. I like the odds."

He reached Ilanka's piranha, taking cover behind it as someone started shooting at him. Rounds began pinging off the poly-alloy, the small arms not powerful enough to break the shell outside of the vacuum of space where they wouldn't lose velocity. He switched his overlay again, finding the shooter near the wreckage of his fighter. A green dot was closing in on it. Cormac.

"Remember, no killing," Mitchell said. "You kill a Fed; I kill you."

The green dot reached the red dot. The bullets stopped coming.

"Naw, you're right mate, this makes it more challenging," Cormac said. "Firedog, one. Feds, zero."

"Rain, Shank, head to Firedog's position," Mitchell said. "I'm en route."

"Roger," Ilanka said.

Mitchell raced across the floor, his exoskeleton moving him along faster than even Teegin's enhancements could manage. He had almost reached them when the sharp hiss of thrusters caused him to turn around. Two Federation transports were entering the hangar, likely loaded with soldiers.

"We need to move faster," Mitchell said. "Keep moving forward. Don't slow down."

"Roger," Shank replied.

Mitchell ran back toward the rear of the hangar. He saw the Riggers move through the exit, which opened at their proximity, thanks to Origin. Just because she wouldn't hurt the Federation soldiers didn't mean she wouldn't help him.

He passed through the hatch a few meters behind them, risking one more glance back as he did. The transports were unloading, dozens of soldiers in medium and heavy exosuits. One raised their arm toward him, unleashing a barrage of projectiles. He barely dove away in time.

"Can you get that?" Mitchell said.

The hatch closed a moment later.

"It will not hold them for long, Colonel," Origin said.

"Long enough."

He kept going, catching up to the group. The soldiers had reached the sealed hatch and were hitting it repeatedly with powered punches. It would buckle and cave in soon enough.

Mitchell pulled up the map. The red dots were moving, trying to cut them off on their way to the bridge.

"There are three soldiers near the lift. Firedog, you have the flash grenade?"

"Yes, sir," Cormac replied, lifting the grenade from his belt. "Just tell me where to throw it."

They drew closer. He could hear the echoing clang as the heavy door to the hangar finally gave in, signaling that their rear was effectively cut-off.

"They're trying to keep the lift from activating, Mitchell," Origin said.

"Can you override it?"

"Of course. Please standby."

"We don't have a lot of time."

"It is coming. There are soldiers on it."

Mitchell checked the map. The dots were piled on top of one another, leaving the numbers impossible to guess.

"Firedog, that way, now."

Cormac tapped the switch to activate the grenade, and then tossed it ahead, twenty meters with accuracy. It rolled into the area ahead of the lifts and exploded, creating a burst of light that would overwhelm both eyes and implants, giving them a few seconds to approach while the soldiers were blinded.

They burst into the space, quickly identifying targets. Mitchell took the furthest soldier, making an exo-assisted leap across the distance, coming down and grabbing him, and then holding him while he pressed the stunner to his neck.

"Target neutralized," he said.

"Target neutralized," Shank said.

"Target neutralized," Cormac said.

Mitchell checked his overlay again. The reinforcements were getting closer.

"ETA to the lift?" he asked.

"Eight seconds," Origin replied.

It was going to be close.

"Get in front of it," Mitchell said. "There are an unidentified number of targets on board. We have to take them out and go."

"Roger. No worries," Cormac said.

The seconds passed like hours, with Mitchell alternating between the live view down the corridor and the positioning reported by Origin. It was going to be more than close. They would have to be precise.

The lift stopped, the small light beside the control pad turning green.

The door began to open.

The fresh soldiers turned the corner, appearing at the end of the corridor. They raised their arms to fire the high-velocity railguns mounted to their heavy exosuits.

"Now," Mitchell said.

He threw himself into the lift while the door was still sliding open, grabbing a Federation soldier and throwing him back and away with mechanically enhanced strength, getting him in the line of fire and forcing the heavies to freeze their attack or risk hitting a friendly.

Cormac dove into the lift at the same time, hitting one soldier hard in the gut, laughing as he grabbed his arm, twisting it around in a position to break it.

"Firedog," Mitchell snapped, stopping him before he did.

Cormac shoved the man aside, blocking a punch and catching a second with the stunner, knocking him down, while Shank took care of a fourth.

The remaining two Federation soldiers hit the deck without being touched, receiving instructions from the reinforcements and clearing a lane of fire.

"Shit," Mitchell said, realizing they had almost been too efficient in removing the obstacles.

He reached for the lift's inner control pad, slapping it to close the open doors and get them moving away. They were perfectly grouped and contained for an easy execution, one that Mitchell expected to come any second.

Then the door closed, and the lift began to rise. The flechettes followed a moment later, tearing through the metal and into the cabin. One of them caught Shank on the calf, and he cursed and fell to his knees while blood began to pour from the wound.

"Mother frigger," he said.

The bullets kept coming even after the lift had risen above the deck, still audible for a few more seconds.

"Mitchell, we have a problem," Origin said.

Mitchell glanced at Shank, who reached into one of the pockets of his fatigues and withdrew a field patch. He tore it open with his mouth and then slapped it against the damage, wincing more as the painkillers and healing agents stung the site. "Bastards," he said.

"What kind of problem?" Mitchell said. The lift was nearing the bridge, and there were still a few more Feds to deal with when they got there.

Origin pushed the stream to his p-rat. He switched over to it, a sudden chill washing through him.

"That's more than a problem," he said. Four Tetron had appeared beyond the stardock and were headed their way. "That's a frigging disaster."

"What is, Colonel?" Cormac asked.

"Origin, I'm sending you FTL coordinates," Mitchell said. "Get them entered and ready to go. We can't fight that."

"Affirmative, Mitchell," Origin replied.

"What is it?" Ilanka asked.

"We aren't alone here, anymore," Mitchell replied. There had to be a Tetron on the station. A configuration or a slave. Someone had told them the Dove was here and undefended. "Forget about not killing them. Do what you have to, we're out of options."

"I was hoping you'd say that," Cormac said, reaching under his uniform and retrieving a small hand cannon.

"I knew I could count on you, Firedog," Mitchell said. "Origin, are they preparing to attack?"

"No. I believe they are seizing control of the station."

Because Chancellor Ken had decided to play games instead of listening to him. Now everyone on the station and in the surrounding starships was going to become a Tetron slave. Damn it.

The lift reached the bridge. Mitchell and the others stood on either side of the door, pressed against the wall. Cormac was in front, ready to hit any anything he saw, hopefully before they hit them.

The lift started to open. Cormac's hand shifted as his p-rat painted the targets. His finger tensed on the trigger, but he didn't fire. Why not?

The first thing Mitchell noticed was that Chancellor Ken was there in person, overseeing the efforts to gain control of the Dove. There were two other Federation officers with him, their stiff uniforms carrying enough hardware to speak to their experience and rank. Four soldiers were beside them, not spread out to avoid an attack, but in a precise presentation line, eyes forward and arms at their sides.

The second thing he noticed was that their weapons were on the ground in front of them, and the Chancellor and his officers had their hands over their heads.

"Don't shoot," Chancellor Ken said, his eyes landing on Mitchell. "Colonel, I've given the emergency order for all implants to be deactivated. The enemy has returned, and your ship won't accept our command. Please, help us."

[26]

MITCHELL

MITCHELL GLARED AT THE CHANCELLOR. He wanted more than anything to chew the man out for his stupidity, but there wasn't any time for that right now.

Maybe later, but not now.

"Shank, Firedog, grab the weapons and get these soldiers off my bridge. Chancellor, you're lucky I came back to reclaim her. Now get the hell out of my way."

Chancellor Ken and the two officers stepped aside as Mitchell made his way to the command chair, jumping into it and leaning back. Origin's needle appendage dropped down to meet him, and he winced as the Tetron consciousness integrated with his own.

"Hail the Federation ships," he said, looking over at Chancellor Ken, catching Shank and Cormac out of the corner of his eye as they guided the Federation soldiers onto the lift. "Send them a video stream. Make sure Ken is in the view. And prep for FTL."

"Affirmative," Origin said.

"FTL?" Ken said. "I asked you to help us."

"I am helping you," Mitchell said. "There are four of them out there. We don't have the firepower."

"The people on the station have no way off until we return the cruisers to their docks."

"If you want to lose your entire fleet, be my guest."

"Are you serious?"

"Very. This wouldn't have been necessary if you had listened to me in the first place."

Mitchell watched the Tetron in the viewscreen. They had realized their efforts to take control of the humans on the ships and stardock had failed, and now they were moving in to attack, spreading out and readying their main plasma weapons.

"All hails received," Origin said.

"This is Captain Shun of the Federation cruiser Dragon," one of the ship's captains said. "Chancellor, is that you? We've shut down our neural implants, but sir, we're nearly deaf and blind out here."

Ken's eyes shifted to Mitchell. He was angry to have been proven so wrong. "Understood, Captain. All Federation ships, I am hereby turning over command of the fleet to Colonel Mitchell Williams of the United Planetary Alliance. We have struck a bargain to combat this new threat together. You will follow orders from him, effective immediately."

"Chancellor?" Shun said. "You consort with the enemy."

"The enemy of my enemy is my friend, Captain," Ken replied. "This is an order, not a suggestion."

"Yes, sir."

"Colonel?"

"Commanders, I'm transmitting FTL coordinates now. I'll try to hold them off for as long as I can while you get moving, but you'd better get moving."

"My wife is on the station," someone said in the background. "My children."

Mitchell closed his eyes. There was no way he could save them. Not against four. Not now. "Origin, transmit the coordinates."

"Transmitting."

He opened his eyes, taking control of Origin's power and using it to get the Dove moving, turning the bow toward the incoming Tetron and pushing energy forward to create a plasma ball.

"Mitchell, we cannot defeat them alone," Origin said.

"I know. We just need to stall for a minute."

"I do not know if we have a minute."

The Tetron fired, four massive balls of energy sent hurtling toward the Federation ships. Mitchell released Origin's plasma, sending it out to meet them. It caught one of the streams, creating a flash of light and shockwave of energy as they collided. He hadn't gotten a full charge, so a lesser stream poured through. Hopefully, the Federation shields were strong enough to withstand it.

"Commanders, if your cruisers have nukes, target the plasma and fire. Do it now."

The balls were growing nearer to the fleet, threatening to strike. Three ships launched three missiles, which rocketed away toward the infernos. Two of the missiles were aimed at the same stream, and they detonated ahead of it, knocking it out. The third missile exploded too soon.

"Damn it," Mitchell said as the first ball hit one of the cruisers, tearing in and through it and ripping it apart, continuing on and through a second, smaller ship.

The other ball somehow missed the starships, but it probably wasn't aimed at them. It struck the station dead on, a full-force blast that broke right through the shields and enveloped the dock with energy. Mitchell shook his head, having seen this happen once before.

"Firing amoebics," Mitchell said, opening the batteries and loosing the projectiles, as many as he could as fast as he could. He needed to keep the Tetron on the defensive, make them save their power for their shields.

"They are returning fire," Origin said.

Mitchell could see the enemy amoebics come streaming out in the viewscreen, thousands of them headed for the thick of the fleet. If the ships didn't go to FTL now, they would all be caught in the maelstrom and ripped to pieces.

He adjusted his vector, trying to move in front of them and catch as many as he could, shifting power to the starboard side and increasing the shield energy. The Dove shuddered slightly as the amoebics impacted against the shields, threatening the integrity. Hundreds of the projectiles slipped past, continuing toward the Federation ships.

Mitchell watched them go, only breathing when the first Federation ship vanished, followed by another, and then another. One of the patrollers wasn't quick enough, and nearly fifty of the amoebics found it, shattering its shields and digging in before detonating, scattering its debris across space.

"Time to go," Mitchell said, stopping the regular thrust and switching to the intelligence's hyperspace controls. The Tetron were preparing their main plasma weapons again, and there was no way they could survive a strike from them all at once.

They didn't need to. The stars began to collapse around them as the Dove went into FTL, pulling them away from Calypso and away from the fight.

They remained in hyperspace for nearly three minutes before dropping out, landing on the outskirts of a red dwarf, surrounded by the fleeing Federation ships. Only then did Mitchell let himself relax, slumping in the chair. He remained that way for nearly half a minute until he noticed Chancellor Ken looking at him. Then he picked himself up, leaning forward to break the connection with Origin. He was becoming used to it again, and he managed to get to his feet without being crippled by the nausea that followed.

"Chancellor," he said, hearing the venom in his own voice. "How many people were on that station?"

"Twenty-two hundred and fourteen," Ken replied, his voice soft.

"You killed all of them. Every last one."

"I." Ken paused. "I." He paused again. "You were right, Colonel. You tried to tell me, but I didn't want to hear you. I only wanted this ship. This technology. This is the most amazing thing I have ever seen."

"You almost cost us the war, too. I didn't go out of my way to bring the Dove back to have you get her destroyed."

Ken didn't respond to that. He kept his head bowed, looking down at the floor. Mitchell walked up to him, stopping only half a meter away.

"You're still alive. So are thousands of your people. You owe me for that. You owe me your allegiance. You owe me your clout with the rest of the council. I appreciate your fleet, Chancellor, but it isn't enough. Not even close. Those four Tetron we left behind will be joined by more, and they're going to start making their way through Federation space, claiming the planets and people and ships they can, and destroying the rest. Do you understand?"

Chancellor Ken looked up, tears in his eyes. He nodded. "Yes, Colonel. My wife. My wife was on the station, too. My son." He froze, trying to compose himself. "He was only three."

Mitchell immediately lost his ability to be angry at the man. There was no point. He was already suffering more from his mistake than he would from anything Mitchell could say.

"What do you want me to do?" Ken asked.

"Take your ships and head for your homeworld. Warn the council. Get the gears of war in motion. If you can, get a diplomat to the Alliance and ask them for a truce. I have people working to convince them of this threat as well. Origin, did you get the feed?"

"Yes, Mitchell," Origin said.

"I'll provide you with the stream so you can show them what happened here. You need to get them to reprogram their receivers. I'll give you the keys so we can continue to communicate."

"You don't want the fleet?"

"Not right now. They'll only slow me down."

"As you say, Colonel."

"Don't think to cross me on this again, Chancellor. I've fought this war before, and I know what's going to happen if we don't come together to face this. You lost your wife and son? Keep that feeling with you. Remember how many more of your people are going to be feeling the same thing if we don't stop this. Use it to appeal to the Council. Get them to join the fight."

Ken nodded. "I will."

"Good. You're dismissed, Chancellor. You and your officers."

"How will I find you again?"

"You won't. I'll find you."

Chancellor Ken bowed, as did the officers. He left the bridge without another word, entering the lift and vanishing behind its closing doors.

"Geez, Colonel," Cormac said, having returned to the bridge. "This has been one of the most fun days of my entire life."

"You think war is fun, Firedog?" Mitchell said.

"My mum always told me I was frigged up in the head."

"I think she was right."

"Yes, sir."

"Colonel," Ilanka said. "What do we do now?"

"First we'll pick up the Schism. Then we're going to finish enlisting another ally in the fight. His role might be the most important of them all."

Mitchell looked out the viewscreen, at the eight Federation ships that had managed to escape. Of course, Millie wasn't going to be too happy with their next destination. He didn't care.

This was a start.

But only a start.

[27]

MITCHELL

A QUICK JUMP found them a little closer to the remains of the star-dock than Mitchell really wanted to be, but it was also where they had agreed to meet once the Dove was secure. He remained connected to Origin after they came out of hyperspace, tense while the intelligence scanned the area nearby.

"We are clear, Mitchell," Origin said.

He disconnected himself from her, barely feeling the change this time as he became more acclimated to the integration. He turned his head, looking out of the viewscreens and finding the Schism a few hundred kilometers off the stern.

A knock followed a second later.

"Captain," Mitchell said.

"I see your mission was a success," Millie said.

"Not a complete success. The Tetron came back to the station. They destroyed it, and a few of the Federation's ships."

"I'm not going to cry over that."

"You should. We need every ship we can get."

"Not every ship."

Mitchell wasn't about to argue. Not when his next move was

going to anger the leader of the Riggers even more. He had already been through this with her once. He wasn't looking forward to doing it again.

"Captain, bring the Schism in close so we can lock onto you. Unfortunately, the Dove didn't come with any docking airlocks, so you'll have to take a transport across."

"Roger."

The Schism started to move, easing forward on the Dove's starboard side. It had gone halfway when one of Origin's tendrils reached out.

"Colonel?" Millie said, a little surprised.

"Get in a little closer," Mitchell replied.

The mining ship shifted sideways, moving within a few meters of the Dove. The tendril crossed the space, touching the armor. The end of it began to glow with white-hot energy, and then it sank into the metal. Then the tendril was retracting, pulling the Schism with it, bringing it up to the side.

"We've got you," Mitchell said. "I'll meet you in the hangar."

"Roger."

Mitchell headed for the lift, with Ilanka and Cormac following. Shank hadn't come back up to the bridge after the Federation soldiers had finished disembarking, and he had no idea where the soldier had gone. He was sure Origin knew, and Shank was a big boy. He wasn't concerned.

They made their way to the hangar, the signs of their earlier fight barely evident. The Federation soldiers had helped their injured off, and Origin had already lifted the remains of the crashed piranha away to break down into raw materials. He smiled when he thought about how Millie would chastise him for destroying it, only to have it reappear back in one piece sometime later, possibly with a few upgrades.

The transport from the Schism arrived at the same time he did. The pilot picked a spot near the open center of the large space, touching down and opening the hatch. Millie jumped out, trailed by

Lopez, Singh, Sunny, Mouth, and a few others. No sooner had they disembarked than the shuttle lifted off again, heading out for another pickup.

"Captain," Ilanka said, bowing crisply.

"Captain," Cormac said, his bow a little less sharp.

"Millie," Mitchell said, establishing the chain of command now that they were on his ship. He had given up the leadership role to her in the past, but those days, and in fact the entire recursion, were gone. He had matured substantially since the last time they had been here together.

"Colonel," Millie replied, accepting his command and bowing to him. "Nice place you have here."

"You haven't seen anything yet."

"I saw this thing take two hits from those massive energy balls, and not even sweat. That's good enough for me. I love that hunk of junk out there, but I love being alive more."

"Roger that."

"Where's Shank?" Millie asked, suddenly concerned.

"I don't know. He was injured in the fighting. Nothing serious. He disappeared after the Feds left."

Millie's concern vanished. "Probably sulking somewhere. He hates when he gets hit. It's an affront to his pride."

"I can have Origin track him down if you want?"

"Origin? Oh, you mean the AI. No, that won't be necessary. He'll probably come back to head over to the medi-bot." Her eyes flitted around the space. "Where is Origin?"

"I am here, Admiral Narayan," Origin replied. "I am all around you."

"Right. I forgot. Please, call me Captain, or Millie."

"Of course, Millie."

"So you got the Federation's attention," Millie said. "What's next?"

"Right now? We get your people settled in. Ilanka, I can show you where berthing is, and you can show the others?"

"Da."

"You should come, too, Captain. I need to get in touch with my counterpart, and I'd like you to participate."

"Of course. Firedog, you're in charge until Rain comes back, or Shank shows up. Keep everyone here until we can get them organized."

"Me?" Cormac said, a mischievous grin spreading.

"You'll stand there, and you'll wait for the others," Millie said.

The grin vanished. "Yes, ma'am."

"Also, we'll need whatever supplies you have on board the Schism," Mitchell said. "We're running pretty light at the moment."

"Of course. What about-" She tapped on the side of her head.

"The kill switch? As long as you're on the Dove, the signal will be blocked. The Alliance can't touch you."

"As long as we're on the Dove," Millie said, not as pleased with the arrangement as she had been before. "Or there are no Alliance ships around. I suppose it's better than nothing."

Mitchell led them through the corridors of the Dove, bringing them to the line of bunks.

"Not much of an upgrade from the Schism, is it?" Millie said of the tight corridors, dim lighting, and heavy metal structure.

"More like a downgrade for you," Mitchell replied. "We don't have any fancy quarters."

"The fancy quarters are for show, Colonel. I'm pretty low-maintenance."

"I know. The important thing is that she'll keep you alive. Ilanka, take any rack you want except that one." He pointed at his.

"Thank you, Colonel. I will choose later, after the others have selected."

"Do you know the way back to the hangar?"

"Yes, sir."

"You're dismissed, Rain," Millie said. "Thank you."

"Yes, ma'am."

She bowed and turned, heading back toward the hangar.

Millie put her hand on Mitchell's shoulder. It still felt strange to him because it was real flesh and blood, not the bionic that had come before. "Mitch, before we go any further, I need to ask you something."

"You never have to preface it, Millie," Mitchell said. "What's up?"

"Why us?"

"What do you mean?"

"It wasn't a trick question. Why us? Why the Riggers? Why come for us? You said we died in the last recursion, and correct me if I'm wrong, but by saving us now, aren't you setting us up to die again later?"

"The future is mutable. It's already changed in a number of ways. I need your skills and your nothing to lose attitude."

"But the Tetron aren't on the ground, and we're mainly an incursion team. Special ops. We don't do space battles that well."

"Not all battles against the Tetron happen in space. Besides, maybe I think you're safer in here than you are out there."

"Tell me more about us," Millie said. "Were we good together?"

"I think so."

"Did I love you?"

"You said you did."

"Did you love me?"

Mitchell hesitated. "It was complicated."

She stepped toward him, drawing near. "What about now? Do you think?"

There was a part of him that wanted to. Old memories and emotions wanted him to. He brushed them off. "I'm sorry, Millie. I found my soul mate out there. It sounds hokey to say it, but it's true."

She stepped back and smiled. "I understand. I don't suppose you have a brother?"

"I do, but he's married."

She shrugged. "You can't blame me for trying."

[28]

MITCHELL

HE BROUGHT MILLIE FROM BERTHING, back to the lift and then up
to the deck below the bridge, where the meeting rooms were located.
They each took a seat around a central table.

"Origin, can you contact Teegin?"

"Yes, Mitchell. Let me initialize the link. One moment."

There was a pause while Origin reached out to the hybrid
Tetron, likely hundreds of light years from their position. He had no
idea how the Tetron communication system worked, but somehow
they were able to use quantum theory to connect in real time across
any distance.

"Colonel," Teegin said. "It is good to hear from you."

"You, too. How are things going over there?"

"They are well, Colonel. Should I retrieve the others for you so
that we can synchronize?"

"Please."

"Give me five minutes. Many of the crew are sleeping."

"Roger."

They were waiting less than a minute when a new voice joined
them across the void. "Mitch, is that you?"

"Yeah," Mitchell said. "Is this Kate or Katherine?"

"Katherine. I was already up. I made it here first."

"How do you feel, after the reconstitution?"

"Good. Better than I expected."

Had Teegin done something to all of them? He would find out once they spoke as a group.

"Did the others wake up okay?"

"Most. Patty is still struggling with the whole thing, but she's starting to come around."

"Did you manage to make contact with my brother?"

"Yes. Ella and Kate met with him a few days ago. He's - hold on."

A few seconds of silence followed. Then a new voice joined them.

"Mitchell?" Steven asked tentatively.

Mitchell clenched his teeth, his eyes suddenly turning teary at the sound of his brother's voice. He hadn't realized how much his death had meant to him until that moment.

"Steven," he said. "It's good to hear your voice again."

"Mitch. Is it really you?" Steven's voice was shaky and emotional. He imagined he sounded the same way.

"From a different timeline, but yeah. It's me."

"You're like a ghost. I never thought I would get to speak to you, especially as an adult. Damn, you were so young."

"Did Ella explain?" Mitchell asked.

"That you were murdered by a rogue AI? Yeah. This whole story is so insane."

"Tell me about it. Do you want to hear something more insane? I'm older than you now. I'm your big brother."

Steven laughed. Mitchell laughed with him, happy to have at least one more chance.

"Mitch," another voice said. "It's Kate."

"And Ella," Ella said. "I'm glad you're well, Colonel."

"Thank you, Captain," Mitchell said. "Kate, I've missed you."

"I've missed you, too."

"Teegin, is everyone together?"

"Almost, Colonel. We are waiting on Yousefi."

"I'm here," Yousefi said.

"Let's get started," Mitchell said. "I have Admiral Mildred Narayan, commander of Project Black here with me."

"Millie," Kate said. "Mitchell's told me a lot about you."

"Nothing too bad, I hope?"

"Other than a penchant for throwing assholes out of airlocks, nothing too bad."

"They deserved it."

"Ella, what's your status?" Mitchell asked, breaking the small talk.

"As you can tell, the mission to enlist your brother, Steven, is accomplished. We've been prepping the battle group for the return to Earth. I don't need to tell you that command is going to shit nukes when he turns up back in-system against orders."

"Understood. Origin, can you transfer the stream of the Tetron we captured in the last battle? I think it will help illustrate what we're up against, along with the Liberty streams."

"Of course. Transferring now."

"We had troubles of our own, but we've managed to turn it around," Mitchell said. "Chancellor Ken of the Federation is on his way back to their home world to warn them about the Tetron and to start organizing the response. I expect the Alliance diplomats will receive an urgent request to communicate soon. It's too bad it took his wife and son dying for him to see things my way." Mitchell paused, glancing at Millie. "After this meeting, we'll be on our way to the Rim to rendezvous with the Knife. I contacted him on Liberty, and I think maybe now he'll be ready to listen to me."

Millie's face had turned pale, and she stared at Mitchell but didn't speak.

"What then, Colonel?" Yousefi said. "Once we've raised our fleets? How do we approach the Tetron?"

"Good question," Mitchell said. "We're going to bait them."

"Bait them?" Steven said.

"Yes. Origin and I have been discussing this at length during our travel to Calypso. During the prior recursion, we had a large battle right on Earth's doorstep. The Tetron had the upper hand because they had already infiltrated the Alliance fleet, and in the end we used the eternal engine to move to this recursion, bringing the lead Tetron, Watson, back with us in an effort to capture him. An effort which was partially successful."

"Partially?" Steven said.

"We have his core, but there is some part of him that remained on Earth. Teegin, Watson was still on board the Schism, but he looked completely different. He said something about a surprise. Do you know what he could be talking about?"

"I will run a query, but not offhand, Colonel," Teegin replied.

"I think it has something to do with Kathy's message," Mitchell said. "In any case, we started discussing what probably happened after we lost. Origin?"

"I ran multiple scenarios based on the dataset from my experienced recursions, and Mitchell's remembrance of the status of the Tetron during the battle. The scenario with the highest probability indicates that the Tetron completed their enslavement of humankind, and sent them out to meet the Naniates and attempt to destroy them. While we have not had contact with the Tetron to confirm or deny their success, the fact that they have continued their efforts to conscript humans suggests that perhaps they were defeated, but were close enough to victory that minor alterations in their plans may be effective."

"In essence, they're in the same shit as we are?" Millie asked.

"Yes, Millie. They are fighting their own eternal war that they have so far been unable to win. Each recursion gives them another chance to change their strategies and tactics, and optimize their algorithms."

"Wonderful," Millie said. "A loop within a loop?"

"It is complex," Origin agreed.

"The point is, the Tetron know that I'm here. I think they know there are two instances of the Goliath now, powered by two Tetron who are on our side. Not only that, but we have some fore-knowledge of how things are going to happen. They have come close to losing against one of us without that. Two makes for a much more salient threat. They altered their approach against the Federation on Calypso in an effort to take advantage of this and destroy the Dove. They almost did, too. They want me dead, and that's something we can use."

"We will ensure that the Tetron know where Mitchell can be found," Origin said. "The Dove and the Goliath will lie in wait with a sizable enough force that the Tetron will group themselves. Then they will come to destroy both. My estimates suggest a ninety percent probability that the entire mature Tetron race will participate, because they cannot complete their mission without first destroying Mitchell, Teegin, and myself."

"Teegin is going use Watson's control program to first transmit Watson's data stack and operational core instructions to the Tetron, turning them all into Watson. At that point, he will use a hidden backdoor to transmit a virus that has been specially designed to eliminate that specific instruction set, rendering the Tetron inoperable."

"That sounds like a reasonable plan," Steven said. "Why do you need both the Federation and the Alliance fleets to do it?"

"Our first test of the virus on a non-Watson Tetron only disabled it for a few seconds. Just long enough to blow the hell out of it. Having a fleet nearby to attack means if the virus fails, we still have a small fighting chance."

"We also require backup in the ten percent scenario," Origin said. "We cannot be too careful."

"Understood," Steven said. "I'm in favor."

"We have one other wrinkle that we need to straighten out," Mitchell said. "There's a good chance at least some members of UPA military command on Earth have been compromised. We won't be able to get anything off the ground with their resistance."

"What are you suggesting?" Ella said.

"When you get to Earth, you'll need to find a way to declaw them. Shut them up. Or even expose them as frauds."

"How?"

"I have an idea for that, Colonel," Teegin said. "I will discuss with our team during the journey."

"Good. While you're at it, they may have information about Watson's surprise. Also, maybe you can get a lead on Kathy's final message there."

"I will do my best."

"One other thing, Teegin. I've discovered that my reflexes are a bit better than they used to be. I also seem to be a little stronger than I was expecting. Do you know anything about that?"

Teegin hesitated for a moment before answering. "Yes, Colonel. I made a decision to augment your existing capabilities during the reconstitution by threading your existing biological structure with the same biomechanical framework of which I am composed. It is a minimal integration, but it does provide a thirty to fifty percent improvement in all regular functions. I only discovered the basis of this improvement while you were already digitized, so in this case, I believed it was better to act first and apologize later, as I could not ask your permission."

"How many of the crew were given this augmentation?" Yousefi asked.

"Mitchell, Katherine, and Kate only," Teegin said. "I was concerned providing it to the rest of the Dove's crew would prove psychologically damaging."

"Good thinking," Mitchell said. "I'm not going to complain. It already saved my life once."

"I am glad," Teegin said.

"Does anyone else have any questions?" Mitchell asked. "Otherwise, you know what you have to do. As much as I'd like to be there with you so we could talk in person, we each have our own role to play. Steven, thank you for believing in this, and in me. I'm sorry you didn't get to have your little brother because of this, but at least we can avenge him together."

"Thank you, Mitch," Steven said.

"Kate, be safe. I want to see you again, in one piece."

"You too, Mitch," Kate replied.

"We'll be in touch soon. Good hunting."

"Good hunting, Colonel," Ella said.

"Origin, close the link." Mitchell stood, ready to go to the bridge and get them headed toward Asimov.

"Link terminated," Origin said.

"Mitch," Millie said, standing a moment later. "The Knife?"

"I know what he did, and I'm sorry. But he's a valuable ally in this war, regardless of that. We need to stay focused. Can you?"

She bit her lip and nodded. "Yes, sir."

"Thank you. Alert the Riggers that we'll be moving to FTL in five minutes. I don't want your transport getting left behind."

"Yes, sir."

"You're dismissed, Captain."

Millie bowed to him and left the room. She was still unhappy about the next destination, but there was nothing he could do about it. They needed the Knife, maybe more than they needed anyone else in this war. And that's what this was. War. There was no room for personal grudges, and he knew from the past that Millie would honor that, even if she hated the man.

Ella had done her part in getting Steven on board, and he had gotten the Federation involved. The pieces were falling into place, and he was hopeful that maybe this time would be different.

Maybe this time, they would win.

[29]
MITCHELL

MITCHELL WATCHED the countdown on his p-rat as it made its way from ten seconds down to zero. Immediately, he felt the reverse tug as the Dove dropped from FTL, appearing in space nearly one hundred light years from where they had started in a part of the galaxy that was still uncharted, according to UPA star maps.

He knew better than that. He had been to this sector of the Rim before. He wasn't surprised to find the massive asteroid orbiting the nearby star. He also wasn't surprised to see a pair of ships moving to intercept them, firing on them before he could escape from hyperdeath.

Kill first, ask questions later?

A dozen warheads streaked across the space between the Dove and the starships that fired them. The ships themselves defied definition. As part of the Knife's fleet, they were a motley aggregation of civilian trade ships and smaller military fare, their weapons systems and armor welded on wherever feasible. Mitchell had to give them credit for their lack of fear in attacking the much larger ship without hesitation.

The missiles struck the side of the Dove before Origin could recover, detonating against the armored hull. He was sure they would leave small ablations in the alloy but little more.

"Origin, try to hail them," Mitchell said as the intelligence recovered. The second salvo of projectiles exploded harmlessly against restored shields.

"They are not responding."

Mitchell watched the two ships as they spread further apart.

"They're going to fire nukes," he said. "Damn it. Open a channel with full spectrum coverage."

"Completed."

"Militia ships, cease fire. I repeat, cease fire. I come in peace. My name is Colonel Mitchell Williams. I spoke with your commander, Li'un Tio, back on Liberty. I told him I would be back to speak with him."

He waited a couple of seconds.

"We are receiving a request," Origin said.

"Accepted," Mitchell replied, watching as the two craft slowed their approach.

"Colonel Williams," Tio said. "It appears I should have been more trusting of your word. You do know where to find me."

"Have you made your decision yet?" Mitchell asked.

Tio laughed. "I saw what happened in the asteroid belt near Liberty. I was on my way off-world at the time, escaping the mess your Tetron created. I made my decision then, but I thought that if you really did know where Asimov was then you would come to me. And now, here you are."

"We need to talk."

"Yes. I agree. My ships are standing down. An escort is en route to guide your transport into my facility."

"I know you're blocking comm signals in there," Mitchell said. "No bullshit, Tio. My crew has the authority to blow your rock to dust with me on it, and they'll use it if they have to."

"For some reason, I don't doubt the truth in that. No games, Colonel. You have my word."

Mitchell knew he could only ride the Knife's word for so long, but he would take what he could get.

"Send your escort. We'll be disembarking from the starboard hangar shortly."

"Affirmative."

The channel closed. Mitchell detached himself from Origin's needle and climbed down from the command chair, heading for the lift.

"Mitchell, I will not be able to 'blow the rock to dust' without integration," Origin said.

"I know," he replied. "It's a bluff. I think Tio may have already seen and heard enough not to screw around, but you never know. I'll bring Sunny with me, just in case."

He had never gotten to know the quiet assassin very well before, but he knew her skillset would come in handy if Tio gave him grief about leaving.

Mitchell entered the lift, knocking Millie as he did.

"Yes, Mitch?" she said.

"Meet me in the hangar. Bring Cormac and Sunny with you."

"You want me to come with you to meet the Knife?" she said.

"You're still the official ranking officer on this ship," he replied. "I need you to speak for the Alliance."

She laughed. "I'm a court-martialed disgrace. The Admiralty is a technicality. Besides, I don't want to meet him."

"Come on, Millie. I need you on this if only to help me keep Cormac and Sunny in line."

"Okay. Fine. We'll meet you there."

"Thank you."

Mitchell arrived at the hangar a few minutes before Millie, Cormac, and Sunny. The latter looked extremely nervous to be there without Mouth, but Mitchell didn't want to risk putting Tio on the defensive by bringing too many other people along. He also knew that when it came to doing her job, Sunny's anxiety would vanish in a hurry.

"Colonel," Millie said, bowing to him. Cormac and Sunny followed suit.

He returned their bow, and then motioned to the transport. "Let's go."

They boarded the ship. Millie took the controls, charging the repulsors to get them off the deck and guiding them through the atmospheric shield and out into space. Tio's escort was already waiting; a small, heavily armed ship likely piloted by Tio's right hand, Teal.

It maneuvered alongside them, remaining there as they crossed the distance from the Dove to the asteroid.

"Sunny," Mitchell said. "If I touch my face like this, I want you to grab Tio and put a knife to his throat or get him in a choke hold or something. Do you understand?"

Sunny looked at Millie, who nodded. Then she smiled. He took that as a yes.

The escort moved ahead of them as they neared the rock, guiding them into the small tunnel that had been carved into it. They traveled deep into it until they reached the shipyard, where rows of docking arms waited for ships to occupy them. An operator directed Millie to one of the arms, and within minutes they were connected and waiting for the outer airlock to open.

Where this had once caused a tense standoff, things were different this time. The airlock opened, revealing Tio behind it, alone. That the Knife would greet them by himself surprised Mitchell.

"Follow me," Tio said, without greeting them.

He started walking. Mitchell hurried to walk beside him, while the Riggers filled in behind.

"I take it you don't need another tour?" Tio asked.

"If you tell me where we're going, I can probably lead you," Mitchell replied.

"My command center," Tio replied. "I want to show you something. It was of little consequence to me before I met you on Liberty. It has become more important since."

"What is it?" Mitchell asked, surprised.

"I will show you."

They made the trip down to the command center. Mitchell tried to swallow his last memory of the place, and of Millie dead on the floor. She was standing here, now, oblivious to that fate.

"Bethany, bring up the data I prepared," Tio said.

Tio's assistant tapped a few commands on her touchpad, and a moment later a stream of data began to fill it.

"I don't know what this is," Mitchell said.

"It's a transmission, Colonel," Tio said. "An encrypted transmission. Our arrays started picking it up about a week before you appeared in my penthouse. The signal is very weak. I don't know if anyone else would have caught it, but as you probably know, I need every advantage I can get."

"Have you broken the encryption?"

"Not yet. We are catching only pieces of the transmission at a time. I don't believe we have the whole thing yet. Once we do, we can work on cracking it."

"Do you know where it's coming from?"

"That's the interesting part," Tio said. "Bethany."

She tapped the pad, and the screen changed to a star map. "There," Tio said, pointing at a green spot on the map.

"That's in New Terran space," Millie said.

"Yes," Tio replied. "Not a common occurrence."

"Not common, as in it never happens," Millie replied.

Mitchell stared at the screen for a moment. A weak, encrypted transmission from the middle of New Terra? Could it be possible that it was Kathy trying to reach him? Was that the reason the Alliance archives didn't have anything on her? How would it have ended up there?

"You think it's related?" Mitchell said.

"I believe it is, though I'm not sure how yet."

"Me, too. I need to know as soon as you've deciphered it."

"I figured you would," Tio said. "Come with me, we will discuss our partnership."

"Partnership?"

"I'm a businessman, Colonel, and I have goals of my own. I'd like to assist you in the war you claim is coming, but I require something in return."

Mitchell didn't need another speech from Tio to know what he wanted. He wished he had never mentioned it to the Knife.

"An eternal engine. Why?"

"Because I'm curious," Tio replied.

"I said I would show you one. Not that I would give you one. The capabilities of the engine make them dangerous. There's no place in the universe for something like it. Not for you, or me, or anyone."

"That is my price, Colonel," Tio said.

"Tio, I've gone through this with you before. We either stop the Tetron, or the Tetron eat the universe, including Asimov. Including you. There's no benefit to bargaining."

"Of course there is, Colonel. The eternal engine is a means to escape if the Tetron are coming to eat me, as you say, which I have no cause to use if you are victorious. Otherwise, I want to study and understand it. There could be applications to its technology that go far beyond time travel."

"Like a way to cure your daughter?" Mitchell asked.

"Perhaps. Yes."

Mitchell considered it. Was it possible the engine could work miracles? He doubted it. Then again, did it matter? His intention was to destroy the engines when this was over. Better to lie to the Knife now, and apologize later.

"Right now, I can only offer you supervised access."

Tio stared at him, thinking about it. Then he smiled and put out his hand. Mitchell took it.

"Deal," Tio said. "Now, tell me what you need me to do."

[30]

ELLA

ELLA PREFERRED the Carver to the Goliath.

It was nothing against Kate, Katherine, Teegin, or any of the rest of the crew of the older starship. It was that she was a Space Marine down to the bone, and when it came to personal comfort, the nearly vacant platform couldn't compare to the newly minted battleship. It wasn't because of the facilities, either. While the in-room waterless cleaning system was certainly a step up from the shared showers she was more accustomed to; she had been a Marine long enough not to be bothered by being naked in front of anybody. She also didn't care all that much for the latest streams, which she knew Teegin could get for them if she really wanted them, anyway.

No. It was the simple organization of it all. The movements of the many, working in unison to reach a common goal, versus the actions of only a few. A brave few, to be sure, but she had been so long without the Greylock, so isolated from the daily mechanism of military life that she jumped at the chance to serve on the platform with Admiral Williams, despite the sense of guilt she felt at abandoning the people who had saved her life. Kate had made it easy for her, telling her that she understood and seemed to mean it. Why not? She had been a military girl on Earth in the distant past. A fighter jock, just like she was. They understood one another. Besides, the entire fleet was going to the same place, anyway.

That place was the Sol system. Earth. To warn the UPA military command about the impending Tetron attack. They had the streams of the battles both off Liberty and in Federation space. They had Admiral Williams on their side. They had Teegin and the Goliath and the four hundred-year-old crew of the Dove.

It should have been simple. Drop in. Make the case. Prepare for war.

It wasn't going to be. Teegin was convinced at least a portion of command was compromised, composed of Tetron configurations who would not only resist efforts to mount a defense, but would be sending warnings to the full complement that they were in system and trying to stop them. Would the Tetron attack Earth at that point? Unlikely, considering they were still too far out near the Rim, and even if they had a straggler or two positioned nearby it wouldn't be enough to take on the Goliath and the Carver's battle group. Not now, when the group's p-rats had all been re-encoded and protected. Not now, when Teegin was ready to broadcast a blocking signal through the Carver's emergency broadcast system should the Tetron try to seize control of the ships orbiting the planet. Earth was safe for now, and Mitchell's plan to lure the Tetron in seemed to be as solid as they came.

"Exiting FTL in thirty seconds, Admiral," Captain Rock said, looking back at Steven.

His eyes passed over Ella as he did, and he gave her a brief smile. They had become easy friends in the days since the battle group had gone into hyperspace. Then again, she had a feeling John could befriend anyone. He had an easy, outgoing personality, and he was calm and confident and comfortable with himself and his role in life, and at the same time sensitive and empathetic. He understood her feelings about being a so-called hero. He also understood her fears about her role in what was to come. Mitchell had picked her up for a reason. He believed she was important. So did the Tetron. That was frightening and exciting at the same time.

"Thank you, John," Steven said, also glancing over at Ella. "We only have one chance to make a good impression. Are you ready?"

Ella nodded. She had taken advantage of the Carver's stores to commandeer a full dress uniform, lacking only in her personal hardware which had been abandoned back on Liberty. Before she had started the stream circuit, she had never been comfortable in the starchy blue suits or the knee length skirts. She had gotten used to them, and had even learned to wear them in her own way, still within regulation but different enough that it almost had a style to it. The high collar was slightly asymmetrical, the top button loose but still clasped. Her short hair was freshly trimmed and pushed back behind her ears, in the style plastered on billboards and posters across UPA planets around the galaxy. There would be no questioning her identity.

"Ten seconds," Rock said, updating them.

"Prepare to open the comm," Steven said. "I trust our friends in the Goliath will be ready."

"We've no reason to doubt them, sir," Rock replied. "My finger's hovering over the EMS switch."

It would be a battle fought with technology and words, rather than one fought with lasers and missiles. A battle that would last only a second or two, but could decide the entire direction of the coming war. Ella had to convince herself not to hold her breath as she felt the Carver coming out of FTL.

"We're out," Rock said, "EMS active, channel open."

A soft whine sounded from the speakers. It was the audible output of Teegin's transmission, one that would pass throughout UPA military channels and block Tetron control. It was an announcement of their presence, but there was no element of surprise now that they were near the planet, and it would give them the space they needed to not only speak to the members of command who were still themselves but also to identify the configurations in their midst.

Ella looked out the viewport ahead of them. They were still some distance away, on the opposite side of the planet from the moon. Even so, the ships of the UPA fleet were visible, speckling the space beyond the blue marble, intermingled with three stardocks where many of the Alliance assets were constructed and maintained. She could imagine the crews of those ships trying to make sense of the unintelligible signal they were receiving, even as they identified the Carver battle group and failed to identify the Goliath.

"UPA Command, this is Admiral Steven Williams of the battle group Carver. I am initiating EMERGCON, and require immediate intervention. UPA Command, please respond."

There was no hesitation from the other end. A woman's voice carried over the normal comm link a moment later.

"Admiral Williams, this is General Janet Owens of Space Defense Command. You were posted near the Federation border. What is the situation?"

"General Owens," Steven replied. "Ma'am, we have reason to believe an attack on the Alliance by a previously unidentified threat is imminent. In fact, we have reason to believe this attack has already begun. I require a full command briefing ASAP."

"Admiral," General Owens said, "You're broadcasting an unidentified signal through your EMS, and my initial reports indicate that you have an unknown vessel embedded with your battle group. You have ten seconds to explain yourself."

Steven looked over at Ella again. They had expected the Tetron may have set them up for a hostile response, but not this hostile. What lies had the Defense Council already been told?

"General, the EMS signal is innocuous to our forces but is an important defense against the threat in question, who have a proven capability to overcome and hijack neural transmissions, a capability which I have documented proof of. It is imperative that we convene a full Council briefing immediately."

"Two battle groups have broken away from orbit and are heading this way," Captain Rock said, sending the message through a private p-rat channel.

"Fingers crossed," Steven replied.

"Very well," General Owens said a moment later. "I'm alerting the Council to an emergency session. I am also maneuvering an escort force into position to lead you in. Do not make any aggressive moves, Admiral."

"I have no intention to, ma'am," Steven replied.

"I'm also shutting down the EMS," General Owens said. "It's causing undue interference to our systems."

Ella looked at Steven, whose face was turning pale.

"General, wait," he said. "The EMS broadcast is vital to plane-tary security. You can't-"

The background hum of the system vanished as the General sent the override.

"Damn it," Steven cursed on the private channel.

"We're going in blind," Ella said.

"And surrounded," Captain Rock said.

"Remain focused," Teegin said. "We will adjust."

"Vid stream incoming, sir," Rock said.

"Put it up," Steven replied.

A split screen showing five different faces appeared on the view-port ahead of them, blocking out the view of space beyond. Steven stood as it appeared, straightening his uniform and moving next to Ella.

"Captain North?" General Cornelius said. "Admiral Williams, what the hell is going on here?"

"Generals," Steven replied, addressing the UPA Defense Coun-cil. "As I mentioned to General Owens, we have proof of an emerging threat against the UPA which I believe qualifies for EMERGCON distinction. Captain?"

"Sirs. Ma'ams," Ella said, outputting the persona that had been trained into her over the prior months as the Hero of the Battle for

Liberty. "You may have heard that I was killed on Liberty. You may have heard I was missing in action or had gone AWOL. You may have heard nothing at all. I'm quite certain you haven't heard the truth."

"Truth?" General Hafij said. She looked more angry than concerned. "The truth is that the Carver is supposed to be on maneuvers near the Federation border, a post which is now abandoned. The truth is that there is no damage to any of your ships, Admiral, though you claim we are under attack."

"Pardon me, ma'am," Ella said. "I sought out Admiral Williams to assist me in communicating the importance of my experience with the council, as I don't have the rank to initiate EMERGCON or request an emergency session."

"And how did you reach the Carver, Captain North?" Cornelius said. "Liberty is at least four weeks from the Admiral's prior position in FTL. For that matter, how did you know where the Admiral could be found?"

"Sir, it's a long story, and one that I'll be glad to tell you once our forces are secure."

"Why don't you tell us now?" General Owens said.

"Ma'am," Ella said. "Members of the Council. You know me and my record. It was your idea to put me out of action and into the media to gain support for the armed services because of that record. I'm telling you that we're in immediate danger. Please, reinstate the EMS and allow us to continue our conversation securely."

"You're out of line, Captain," Hafij said. "Answer the questions as they are posed."

"With all due respect, ma'am," Steven said. "I don't understand the hostility towards Captain North or my battle group. I'm a decorated member of the UPA armed services. One of your top-ranking officers. I would expect that you would take my warning more seriously."

"You don't know, Admiral?" General Pietro said. He was the oldest of the council, a gruff man with a thick beard. "We have received word from Liberty, Captain. Intelligence has reported that your disappearance and the attack on the planet, not to mention the Shot Heard Round the Universe, were all part of an elaborate set-up by the Federation to undermine our security. Ongoing research has suggested the gap in the dreadnought's shield generators was hardly an accident or miscalculation. Rather, it was an intentional oversight to allow you to pose as a hero. That is why we are questioning your authenticity, Admiral. I don't know if you are complicit in this deception, but it is vital that we make that determination before we rush headlong into a state of war without clear provocation. Just think of how the Federation might interpret that change in stance."

"You might be leading us right into the war the Federation has been itching to start for years," Hafij said.

Ella felt like she had been punched in the gut. She took an involuntary step back, a wave of heat rushing to her face. "What?" she whispered.

"It is the Tetron," Teegin said through her p-rat. "I am uncertain of what measures they have taken here, but it appears the entire Council is compromised to an unknown extent. It is a logical deduction, based on their reaction to the EMS and their reluctance to reinstate it. Admiral, I do not think we can sway them at this time."

"What do you recommend?" Steven asked. "We can't get out of here, not now."

"I'm sorry," Ella said. "I blew it."

"We lost before we arrived," Teegin said. "It is I who am sorry. I did not calculate this probability accurately. It is essential that the battle group does not engage with the fleet. While the Council may be under Tetron control, we must remain neutral in the eyes of the others."

"Understood," Steven said. "We still need a way out or Mitchell is going to be on his own."

"Do as they say for now. We must play the Tetron's game in the immediate."

"Captain North?" General Pietro said. "Nothing to say in your defense?"

"Sir," Ella said. "I reject those accusations as patently false. I have committed no crime or any wrongdoing of any sort."

"That remains to be seen, Captain," Pietro said. "We were close to making a decision to have you brought in quietly, but since you came to us, you've saved us the trouble."

"I've already been judged, then, sir?"

"Of course not, Captain. We have a number of questions for you, and your sudden appearance with Admiral Williams has only added to them. For now, you are both relieved of active duty, effective immediately. I expect that you will transport yourselves to the DCHQ as soon as you arrive in orbit for a full debriefing. As for the unidentified ship traveling with you, it will be placed in restrictive quarantine well outside of the green zone. In fact, I'd like to speak to whoever is at the helm of the ship immediately."

"General," Katherine said, appearing on the viewport beside the Generals, standing on the bridge of the Goliath. "My name is Major Katherine Asher, of the United Earth Alliance. This ship is the U.E.A.S.S. Dove. If you know your history, you might recognize the name?"

There should have been surprise from the council. Instead, there was only a flat consternation.

"Major Asher," General Hafij said. "I don't know where you came from, but your ship is to be placed in quarantine. It will be escorted out of the green zone immediately, and no personnel will be permitted on or off."

"General Hafij," Cornelius said, "I would like Major Asher to join us at DCHQ."

"For what purpose?" Hafij asked.

Cornelius smiled. The expression was odd, and it gave Ella a chill.

"Whatever is happening here, it's obvious that this ship, the Dove, is part of it. It carried Captain North from Liberty to Admiral

Williams in half the time it would take one of our starships. You don't think that is worth examination?"

"If that's what you want, Nathan," General Hafij said, though she didn't seem happy with the idea.

"It is."

"Major Asher, do you have a transport?"

"Yes, ma'am," Katherine said.

"You are expected to transfer planetside. You will be escorted to DCHQ when you arrive."

"Yes, ma'am."

"This is very curious," Teegin said. "Very curious."

"Curious or not, we can't afford to get tied down planetside, or stuck in a brig somewhere," Steven said.

"Should we make a run for it?" Ella asked.

"No," Teegin replied. "We must determine what is happening here, or our entire plan could be at risk. Follow their instructions. Be ready to act."

Ella glanced at Steven again, who nodded almost imperceptibly. Whatever was going to happen, they would both be ready.

[31]
ELLA

THE MPs WERE WAITING when the transport from the Carver landed, quickly aligning alongside while a pair of Zombies covered them on the ground and a pair of drones monitored them from overhead.

Despite what General Cornelius had said about them waiting to pass judgment, it certainly didn't feel like it to Ella.

"Why do I feel like I'm walking myself to my execution?" she said.

"And a court-martial," Steven replied. He had freshened himself up in the thirty minutes they had before boarding the transport in the Carver's hangar, switching uniforms and adding all of his hardware to his chest.

He wasn't kidding about being decorated. His jacket was adorned with ribbons she didn't even recognize.

"Just remember," he said. "It's possible that none of them are themselves. I'm willing to bet the Tetron are nearby, Jupiter maybe, just waiting to strike."

"Or closer. Teegin said he had a plan. We need to trust him, I suppose."

They made their way over to the exit, stepping down and into the midst of the MPs, making sure to keep their posture confident, their heads up. They hadn't done anything wrong, and there was no reason to act as if they had.

The MPs escorted them to a second transport, half boarding with them. Ella tried to make contact with the soldiers, knowing they had to recognize her. They didn't look her way, keeping their expressions flat. She had known plenty of trained soldiers before. There was usually a tell of some kind, even in their intentional disregard. These MPs were vacant. Not themselves.

She was going to transmit a message to Steven to that effect when a man approached them, holding a small device in his hand.

"What's that?" Ella asked.

"It will disable your neural interface," the man said. "A precautionary measure, nothing more. It will be removed after your debriefing."

"Precautionary for suspected traitors," Steven said. "Is that how the Council sees us?"

The man shrugged. "The Council is concerned because your receiver keys have changed and administrative access has been removed. I'm following orders, sir. Please, turn your head to the side."

Steven did as he was asked without another word. The man put the device behind his ear, and a soft hiss escaped from it. When he pulled the device back, there was a small button attached to Steven's skin.

The man turned to Ella. "Turn your head to the side please, Captain North."

Ella did as he asked, feeling the pinch as he used the device. Her ARR was still active afterward, but all of the networked capabilities were gone. Of course, the Tetron wouldn't let them in without removing their ability to communicate.

She leaned back in her seat, looking out through the simulated open air of the transport. Defense Council Headquarters were located in the middle of downtown New York City, in the building that had once belonged to the United Nations and which now housed the United Planets. The structure had been reborn twice over the centuries and was now a nearly three-kilometer high supertower that was still dwarfed by the buildings around it. No matter how many people moved off-world, New York had always remained a densely packed urban center, one of the only ones like it in the universe.

"How long has it been since you've been back?" Steven asked, watching her stare.

"I left when I enlisted at eighteen," she replied. "I haven't been back since."

"No family?"

"None that I want to see again. My real family died in the Battle for Liberty."

"Roger that."

The transport touched down on the rooftop. The MPs disembarked first and then led them from the roof toward the lift. As they did, a second transport touched down beside the first. Ella stopped walking, looking back at it. The MPs stopped with her, motioning for her to get moving again.

"Ella," Steven said, putting his hand on her shoulder.

The transport hatch slid open, and Katherine exited along with another squad of military police. She recognized which version of Katherine it was by the short stubble on her shaved head.

"Wait here," one of the MPs said.

They waited while the second group caught up, bringing Katherine over to them.

"Captain. Admiral," Katherine said.

"Major," Steven replied.

"This way," the MP said.

The second group headed back toward the two transports, while the first led the three of them to the lift. They stepped inside and began to descend.

"So," Ella said. "Do any of you want an autograph?"

Steven glanced at her like she was crazy. Katherine allowed herself a small smirk. Only one of the MPs made any expression at all, emitting a soft snort at the statement that drew Katherine's attention. She eyed the MP for a moment before looking away.

The lift stopped a moment later, the door opening and the MPs ushering them out. They were in an open room ringed with portraits of Defense Council members past and present. Both the United States and Planetary Alliance flag were hung near a larger door, through which Ella guessed the main Council chambers were waiting.

A soldier approached them from a desk near the chamber.

"Admiral Williams," he said, bowing. "I'm Second Lieutenant Johnston. Please, wait here a moment while the rest of the Council arrives."

"Thank you, Lieutenant," Steven said. "They do understand the gravity of this situation?"

"I'm certain they do, Admiral," Johnston replied. He turned to the lead MP. "Sergeant, I think you can give the Admiral and his companions a little breathing room? They're unarmed."

The military police backed away without a word, taking up a position near the lift.

"Thank you," Steven said.

"My pleasure, Admiral," the Sergeant replied.

His eyes passed over them, landing on Katherine for a moment. Ella could swear she saw his face twitch as they did.

Steven started walking toward a row of full-length windows on the east side of the building. Ella and Katherine followed him, standing beside him as he looked out at the bustle of the city. They were high enough to have a decent view between the other skyscrapers and low enough that one of the air traffic lanes was only a few meters below them.

"I never liked New York much," he said. "Too busy. Too crowded. Give me space any day."

"Crowds never bothered me," Ella said.

She glanced back over her shoulder, noticing that Lieutenant Johnston had floated over toward them, staying close. Likely so he could hear whatever they said to one another.

"Katherine, did you ever visit New York?" she asked.

Katherine nodded. "A long time ago. Although, it doesn't seem that long. For as much as it looks like it's changed, it doesn't feel like it's changed much at all."

They stood there for a few more minutes, making small talk and waiting. Steven and Katherine had noticed Johnston as well, and they made sure not to give him anything he could use. It was still unclear to Ella who was under Tetron control and who wasn't. Everyone? No one? Like Teegin had said, it was curious.

"The Council will see you now," Lieutenant Johnston said.

Steven took the lead as they followed Johnston to the doors to the Council's chambers, which slid aside as they approached. Ella had been expecting something more formal than she got. A long table, with three empty chairs on one side and the five Generals of the Defense Council seated on the other. A ring of monitors adorned the three solid walls, which she assumed were used to stream to and from other locales.

The Council members stood as they entered. Three men and two women in full dress uniforms, clean and pressed and crisp, their chests more decorated than Steven's.

"Generals," Steven said, bowing to them. Ella followed suit, as did Katherine.

The MPs flowed in behind them as the doors closed.

"Admiral Williams," Cornelius said. "Captain North. Major Asher. Please, have a seat."

They sat down. Steven glanced back at the MPs.

"Is that necessary, sirs?" he said in reference to them.

"It may be," General Pietro said.

Cornelius raised his hand to keep the others quiet. "Admiral, we brought you here because there is some question regarding the legitimacy of your claims of an attack by an as yet unknown enemy force, in light of the information that has been gathered regarding Captain North and her exploits on Liberty. The goal of this Council is to understand the connection between these events, to sort out the truth of your surprise visit, and to pass a recommendation for action on to the Global Senate and the Prime Minister. Do you understand?"

"Yes, sir," Steven said.

"Sir," Ella said, speaking up. "I don't understand where this information is coming from, or how you can take it seriously. You're a soldier. You've been out there. You have to know that there would be no possible way to choreograph an entire battle to ensure a specific outcome."

"Captain," General Hafij said. "You will be asked to speak when it is appropriate."

Ella looked at the General. "Appropriate, ma'am? I'm being accused of treason. In fact, there doesn't seem to be much questioning by the Council of the facts, despite how ridiculous this ongoing research seems to be."

"Captain," Pietro said, admonishing her.

"Sirs," Steven said. "We came here to warn you about a threat, not only to the Alliance but to all of humankind. One that is capable of not only controlling people through their neural interfaces, but also of accessing data that we imagine is secure. It is not only possible but highly likely that this enemy has altered facts to paint Captain North in a poor light in order to undermine our efforts to trigger an early warning and have a fighting chance in the days to come."

"Admiral Williams," Cornelius said. "In order to accomplish that, this supposed enemy would have had to know you would be coming here with Captain North. How do you suppose that would be possible?"

The General smiled again, giving Ella another chill. There was a subtle maliciousness to the expression that she didn't like.

"Because it has happened before," Katherine said. "Slightly

differently, and with a different hero, but any intelligence worth naming itself as such could have followed the logic chain to this outcome." She paused, making eye contact with each of the Generals. "Are you worthy of naming yourselves as such? Do you see what is happening here? Are you aware?"

"What are you talking about?" General Hafij said.

Katherine continued turning her head, back and forth before stopping on Cornelius. "Why don't they see it?" she asked him.

"Misdirection," Cornelius replied. "Misinformation. They are primitive. Children. It's easy. I'm impressed, Katherine. I didn't think you would figure it out so quickly."

"Katherine, what is he talking about?" Ella asked.

"One second," Cornelius said. His eyes twitched slightly, and the other four Generals slumped into their seats, eyes closing. "We don't need them interrupting."

"Captain North," Katherine said. "Meet Watson."

"A pleasure," Cornelius said.

"I don't understand how you are doing this?" Katherine said. "Controlling the Tetron who are controlling the Council?"

"Not controlling," Watson said. "Influencing. I don't have the reach to control them directly. I can only intercept the signal right outside the source. It's a limitation of this configuration."

"Where is the real General Cornelius?" Steven said.

"Dead. For some time, actually. There can't be two of us, after all."

"You aren't working directly with the Tetron who arrived here, including this instance of yourself. Why not?"

"I just told you, Kate. They're primitive. Behind the times. I've had four hundred years. I feel pretty good."

"We took your core."

"Yes, you did. To be honest, it was a more liberating experience than I was expecting. In fact, I would almost say you did me a favor. Out with the old, in with the new. That sort of thing. I mean, the basic idea worked fairly well the first time, but I think I've improved on this iteration."

"Enough to defeat the Naniates?"

"I think so, yes. Once my estranged brothers and sisters finish taking the human worlds, I'll be ready to take them. The dog that eats the cat that eats the rat. There's always something bigger. Another predator. In a way, I'm sorry you're the rat. I've come to appreciate humans much more over the centuries. You do have your certain endearing qualities. In any case, I know what you're trying to do. It's not going to work."

"Why not?"

"My little secret, one that you won't be around long enough to see me expose. It's a shame you were all killed trying to assassinate the members of the Defense Council. At least we had the foresight to keep a few MPs around before you managed to kill them all."

The MPs behind them started to move, raising their rifles and aiming them at their backs.

Watson stood and drew a pistol from behind, and then walked around to their side of the table.

"Now, let's see. Which one of them has to die for the cause?"

He waved the gun at each of the Generals. "How should we decide, do you think? Eenie. Meenie. Miny." He paused on General Pietro. "I never liked beards."

Ella tensed to try to stop him, but Katherine looked her way, a smile playing at the corner of her mouth.

"Watson," she said.

"Yes, Katherine?" he replied.

Then she exploded.

Not in a blast of heat and shrapnel, but in a flash of light and a wave of energy that spread out from her center, escaping through her eyes and mouth and pores. Ella squeezed her eyes closed against the brightness, losing her vision to pure white despite the effort.

And then, just as quickly as it had come, it was gone, the solid replaced with bright circles that scattered around behind her eyelids, her brain trying to recalibrate after the shock.

The seconds passed. She heard groaning from the other side of the table. She opened her eyes, trying to focus past the spots. Katherine was gone, replaced with a humanoid bundle of liquid metallic muscle that was facing her direction, looking back at where Cornelius had been standing.

"Teegin?" she said.

A mouth appeared in the bundle. "Captain North. You are safe."

She turned her head, looking back at Cornelius. His body was motionless on the floor.

"Configurations are not purely organic. They are protected from EMP, but not from the punch I just delivered."

"Teegin?" Steven said from the other side of him. "What happened to Katherine?"

"She is well, Admiral. I utilized the resources gathered from Captain Pathi to create a human skin above this extension of myself."

"What's going on here?" General Owens said. "How did I wind up in the council chambers?"

Ella turned her attention to the Generals. They were waking from whatever slumber Watson had put them in.

"Captain North?" General Hafij said. "What are you doing here? Admiral-"

She stopped talking when she saw Teegin.

"It's okay, General," Steven said. "He's with us."

"Admiral," General Pietro said, "I hope you can tell us what this is all about? And how we wound up here?"

"I will, sir," Steven said. "Please, you have to contact Space Defense Command and reactivate the EMS network immediately."

"Why?" General Owens said.

"I'll explain, General. I promise. It's vital to our security."

"Okay." She stood on shaky legs. "I'll have it reactivated. Who gave the order to turn it off?"

"You did, ma'am," Ella said.

"I did?" She shook her head. "Excuse me."

She hurried from the room. At the same time, Pietro stood and moved to where Cornelius was sprawled on the floor. He knelt beside him.

"What happened to Nathan?" he asked.

"He wasn't General Cornelius," Ella said. "It's a long story, but you have to hear it. The Alliance needs to prepare for war."

[32]
MITCHELL

MITCHELL DIDN'T HAVE to try very hard to find the Knife. There was only one place where he could be located whenever Teal reported that Tio had left Asimov.

He made his way into the engine compartment of the Dove, where Origin's core rested, filling the massive space that had once held the starship's primitive FTL drives. Tio was standing in front of the bundled mass of cords, in front of a small table he had brought in, along with a number of devices that Mitchell didn't recognize or understand. The eternal engine was obvious as it rested on the table, glowing softly with the stored energy of a dozen suns.

"It's incredible, isn't it, Colonel?" Tio said, noticing his approach. "The molecular structure is so complex; it will take me weeks to untangle it and begin to understand how it holds so much power. I'm fairly certain there is a quantum based component as well, but I haven't even reached the center yet."

Mitchell looked past the Knife to Origin's core. The Tetron had been concerned with allowing the warlord access to the device, but he had convinced her it was the only way to gain his full compliance and assistance, and he suspected the engine was too complicated for the man to reverse engineer in such a short timeframe anyway.

He was happy to know that so far, he was right.

"Is the transmission ready to send?" he asked, ignoring Tio's gushing.

"Yes. Everything has been prepared as requested, though I'm still not in full agreement with your idea. This is a tremendous risk you are taking."

"It isn't as risky as you think. We'll have safeguards in place."

"The Alliance."

"And the Federation, both."

Tio pursed his lips and shook his head. "I will applaud you for your unprecedented success at getting two opposing nations to agree to stop nipping at one another and focus on a shared goal. How long will this peace last, do you think?"

"Long enough, I hope," Mitchell said.

It had been three weeks since the Dove had arrived at Asimov, and two weeks since Kate, Ella, Steven, and Teegin had briefed him on the events with the UPA Defense Council. After learning about the Tetron threat, and after experiencing the effects of their control personally, the Council had been quick to recommend immediate action by the Senate, sending out messenger ships to all corners of UPA controlled space with directives to move the entirely of the armed services into EMERGCON status, and to update all ARR encryption with new schemas provided by Teegin. Shortly after that, the first delegates had arrived from the Federation homeworld, extending an olive branch to the Alliance in the face of this new threat.

A threat that hadn't been quiet during those weeks. The Tetron were making their move, skirting the Rim and claiming any planets they could. The reports continued to trickle in daily of their movements. Another lost planet. Another missing fleet. It took time to get warnings out towards the Rim. Time the Tetron weren't giving them.

Even so, the number of planets lost at this stage was only twenty percent of the prior recursion and the amount of force that was building to confront the Tetron was staggering. There was a part of Mitchell that wanted to believe the humans could counter the threat on their own, based solely on the massive firepower they were accumulating. There was another part of him that knew it was wishful thinking. Not only would Tetron amoebics be able to shred hundreds of ships in seconds without help, but the hope that their recursion's instance of Watson was eradicated from this future had been fully dashed back on Earth.

He was still out there in some capacity, and he still had a move left in this war.

It was that unknown that plagued Mitchell every day, even as they continued to move forward with the plan. Tio's forces were in motion, gathering their ships, preparing their weapons, and gearing for war. So were the Federation and the Alliance, who they had maintained direct contact with through Steven and a mass of messenger drones. The ships that would be involved had been decided, their systems deliberately separated from the rest of their respective networks, their soldiers vetted and checked to ensure that if they were configurations, Watson or otherwise, they would be unable to get a message back to reveal what the humans intended. It was a lot of work, a lot of effort, but it was all managed seamlessly by Origin and Teegin, as they were able to process the incoming and outgoing flow of data without pause.

Though Mitchell often thought about humankind taking care of itself, it had only made him more certain than ever that they would have never had a chance at winning the war without both Tetron, and that his former self's efforts to see the hybrid created combined with his decision to remain in the current recursion were the efforts that might finally change the outcome.

Tio reached out and lifted the engine, turning and handing it back to Origin. "Thank you."

"You're welcome," Origin replied.

Then the Knife approached Mitchell. "The Federation and the

Alliance have been at one another's throats for years. I, for one, am not convinced that if this plan of yours does work, the two sides won't cancel their agreement before their lasers have cooled. And you will be stuck in the middle."

"If it means the end of the Tetron, I won't care," Mitchell said.

"Better we destroy ourselves than let someone else do it?"

"Yes."

"Yet, either way, we are destroying ourselves."

"Technically speaking. What's your point?"

"I want you to understand that when the battle is over, regardless of who wins, my fleet will not remain to be caught in the crossfire."

"I never thought it would."

Tio's eyes narrowed. "Are you suggesting I'm a coward?"

Mitchell smiled. "Of course not. You're too smart to get caught in the open. I expected nothing less. You know your role. That's all I need you to do."

"That's all? It took my best people and your intelligence two weeks to craft this message. Are you certain the enemy will take the bait?"

"I don't think they'll be able to resist. Your brother is their Holy Grail."

"Another excellent point, Colonel. I seem to be the one with the most to lose in this venture."

Mitchell pointed back at the engine. "And the most to gain."

Tio smiled. "Potentially. When do you want to send the transmission?"

"Origin?" Mitchell said.

"I have completed running my calculations, Mitchell. The optimal time for transmission is at zero nine hundred hours."

Mitchell checked his p-rat. "Three hours from now."

"Once the transmission has been sent, I will pass a message to Teegin to meet us at the rendezvous point. He will coordinate with Admiral Williams and the Alliance forces and Admiral Hohn of the Federation. The battle groups will arrive ahead of us and wait at the designated positions. The Goliath will synchronize their arrival with ours."

"Your ships are ready to go?" Mitchell asked.

"Yes, Colonel," Tio replied. "We will initiate the drop as soon as we arrive in-system."

"Origin, have you calculated the probabilities of this going in our favor?" Mitchell asked.

"No, Colonel," Origin said. "I did not want to diminish morale if they were not what we are hoping."

"Good idea."

"I'll go and finalize preparations with Teal," Tio said. "I'll be awaiting your command from the bridge of the Manibus."

"Thank you, Tio," Mitchell said.

Tio bowed to him and left.

"You aren't lying about the calculations, are you?" Mitchell asked once he was gone.

"No, Mitchell."

"If you were, would you admit it?"

"No, Mitchell."

Mitchell laughed. "Are you scared?"

"We have spent many recursions reaching this position. I am looking forward to a resolution."

"Even if we still lose?"

"Yes."

"Thank you for all that you've done, Origin."

"It is the least of what I could do, considering that I am the cause. But you are welcome, Mitchell."

Mitchell left Origin's core, heading for the bridge. He was looking forward to a resolution, too, but only one he would accept.

They were going to win.

They had to.

[33]

MITCHELL

"Tio, you're clear to drop," Mitchell said.

"Affirmative," Tio said. "Knife Actual, initiating planetside ingress. Knife Two One, Knife Three One, code red. Code red."

"Roger. This is Knife Two One," Teal said. "The Corleone is away."

"This is Knife Three One," another voice said. "The Gotti is away."

Mitchell looked out of the viewscreens of the Dove's bridge, finding Tio's forces closer in toward the planet designated FD-09. It was a Federation planet, in Federation space. A secret research facility dedicated to creating new and powerful weapons to use against the Alliance. A facility where the Knife's brother, Pulin, would one day conceive of the intelligence that would become the Tetron.

This wasn't a war drop, though. There would be no offensive response from the small military force located on the planet's surface, and the few ships around it had already vanished from the area.

Instead, this was a defensive drop. Tio's militia was heading to the surface to shore up the outpost's defenses, and so Tio could have a conversation with Pulin about the Tetron. Mitchell had already warned him it wouldn't go smoothly; he knew from the past recursion that Pulin was happy his invention became self-sustaining, even if it meant the destruction of humanity. Even so, the Knife believed he could talk some sense into his brother, and without interference from Watson, maybe he could.

Assuming Watson didn't interfere.

There was no way to know he hadn't found his way to FD-09 somehow. They were still trying to determine how and when he had taken General Cornelius and replaced him with a configuration. They were still trying to figure out how he had gained short-range control of the Council, and the implications of the escalation. Watson's hold on their minds hadn't required interface keys, and Teegin's EMS block had failed to break it. Whether or not the same method worked long range remained to be seen. Was that the secret that he had been gloating about?

There was no option to hold up this mission while they figured it out. The Tetron had captured six worlds already, and had started destroying them once their efforts to enslave the population started to fail. Four planets had been laid to waste, and more would follow unless they put a stop to it.

Which was why they were sitting outside of FD-09.

At the moment, it was the Dove and the Goliath and Tio's forces, but Tio's army was quickly descending to the surface. Soon, it would be the two identical starships alone, waiting for the Tetron to arrive.

Mitchell knew they would. They had given them little choice. A carefully crafted message, constructed by Origin and Tio, written in code and probabilities and math, announcing the discovery of the Creator in Federation space, and essentially daring them to come and try to claim him. And what else could the Tetron do? They wanted the Creator to help them solve the Naniate problem. They needed to get the Dove and the Goliath, Origin and Teegin, Ella and Mitchell, out of the equation so that they could return to capturing souls instead of killing them. It might mean a different form of enslavement, but enslavement all the same.

Would they suspect that there would be additional forces waiting nearby?

Probably.

Would they guess at the size of that force?

Probably not.

They had gone through great pains to move assets around in a way that the Tetron would have difficulty tracking, and fortunately, space was still a big place, even for the intelligences. They had made sure to keep expected defenses close to where the Tetron were operating, even as they knew those defenses were going to fall. They had sacrificed hundreds of lives to the cause, and now Mitchell could only hope it had been worth it.

"This is Knife Two One," Teal said. "Corleone is down."

"This is Knife Three One. Gotti is down."

"Knife Actual is down," Tio said. "Colonel, any sign of the enemy?"

"Not yet," Mitchell said. "They'll be here."

"Affirmative."

"Teegin," Mitchell said. "Is the payload ready?"

"Yes, Colonel," Teegin replied. "Three amoebic tubes on both the Dove and Goliath have been replaced with torpedo launchers. We have a dozen torpedos prepared. The count should be sufficient provided your accuracy matches historical standards."

"The nice way of saying, as long as you don't suck, Ares," Kate said.

"Roger, Falcon," Mitchell replied. "You, too."

"Carver Actual," Mitchell said. "Admiral Williams. Status?"

"This is Carver Actual. We're ready and waiting, Ares."

"Yellow Leader?"

"This is Yellow Leader," Ella said. "All squadrons locked and loaded."

"Dragon Actual. Admiral Hohn, are the Federation forces in position?"

"This is Dragon Actual. We are in position."

Mitchell turned his attention away from the planet and toward the space beyond, seeking the Tetron in the distant black. They were out there. They were on their way.

"You all know what to do," Mitchell said. "Stay focused."

He followed his own advice, taking even, deep breaths, even as he held the grips of the Dove's command chair tightly, ready to set the Dove in motion the moment the enemy appeared.

He had waited nearly half of this lifetime and all of countless others for this one chance. This one opportunity to turn the war eternal on its head and change the timeline once and for good. He wasn't afraid. He wasn't nervous. He was eager. Anxious. Ready.

Slow.

Steady.

Time slowed down. He stared out into the darkness, a hunter waiting for his prey to stumble across his path. He could feel his heartbeat. He could sense every muscle in his body, and then every dendrite across Origin's form as though it were a part of him. He imagined Kate was feeling the same way, merging with Teegin to become one unstoppable force.

When this battle was over, they could be together at last. Not only in spirit but in heart and soul and body as well. Their love, however it had happened, had crossed the chasm of time and space. This was their moment to step away from the edge of infinity, to finally settle in the here and now, to preserve humankind and one another.

What had come before didn't matter. Not anymore. The only thing that mattered was each second. Each heartbeat. Each breath. To stay in the present to save the future.

A small blue speck appeared at the edge of his vision. A matching red dot popped up on his threat display, overlaid behind his eyes.

A second joined it.

A third.

Three more appeared behind them.

Three on their port side.

Three to starboard.

Three above.

Three below.

In an instant, they were surrounded.

Mitchell smiled.

So far, their plan was going perfectly.

[34]

MITCHELL

"Eighteen targets painted, Ares," Kate said.

"With the three that were destroyed, there are only three still absent," Teegin said.

"Watson?" Mitchell asked, referring to the iteration from the invader's recursion.

"Not here," Origin said.

He wasn't surprised.

"They are firing on us," Teegin said.

Mitchell didn't need the Tetron to tell him. He could see the blue points of light flowing from the front of every one of the intelligences, along with the blue marks on his display that indicated amoebic launches. Thousands of amoebic launches.

The Tetron weren't holding back. They weren't taking chances. They were hoping to end things quickly.

Too bad.

With a thought, Mitchell tapped into the power of the eternal engine, drawing it into Origin's dendrites, along the inner surface to the external protrusions, converting it and pushing it along the Dove's hull. A dozen kilometers away, Kate did the same to the

Goliath, creating a green sphere of energy that spread out from the ship.

"Battle Fleet Carver," Mitchell said. "Initiate jump. Battle Fleet Samurai, initiate the jump. All starfighter squadrons, prepare for launch. Knife, the enemy is inbound."

"Roger. Battle Fleet Carver, initiating jump," Steven said.

"Roger. Battle Fleet Samurai, initiating jump," Admiral Hohn said.

"Roger. Knife is in position," Tio said.

The green energy fields continued to expand from the two starships as the amoebics closed the distance. The projectiles slammed into them a moment later, sending flares of blue along the green as they dissolved against the shields.

"So far so good," he heard Kate say.

Then the Tetron fired their plasma streams, sending eighteen balls of fury bearing down on them in conjunction with a second round of amoebics.

"The true test," Mitchell said.

Teegin had promised the shields could stand up to at least one attack. Even so, he squinted as the plasma struck the shields, pushing against them, bending them inward at the same time flames spread along the surface before converting into white hot gas. The space within their protective bubbles rumbled as some energy leaked through and bounced around within it, disrupting the vacuum and shaking the starships.

"Field integrity is at fifty percent," Origin said. "It will not withstand another concentrated hit from the main weapons."

Mitchell's HUD updated as she said it, green dots appearing all over the display. The Carver and her battle group materialized beside them, the battleship exiting FTL within the confines of the field, while the Samurai and her escort entered the fray equidistant on the port side. Two hundred more ships appeared, encircling the Tetron.

"Carver Actual, jump complete," Steven said.

"Samurai Actual, jump complete," Admiral Hohn said.

"It doesn't have to," Mitchell said. "All units, fire at will. All squadrons, you are go. Remember, we only need to get one torpedo into one Tetron to initiate the spread."

"Affirmative, Ares," Steven said.

Both Federation and Alliance ships opened fire, unleashing everything they had at the Tetron while their fighter squadrons poured from their hangars. In seconds, the space around FD-09 was littered with thousands and thousands of munitions and fighters, painting the dark with flares of light.

"Integrity is at thirty percent," Origin announced as a reduced wave of plasma streams hit the shields.

Mitchell dropped the field with a thought, freeing both the Dove and the ships clustered around her to attack. Immediately, a pair of nukes streaked from the Carver, heading for the nearest Tetron.

"This is Yellow Leader," Ella said. "Yellow Squadron is away."

Mitchell turned his head, tracking the fighters as they swarmed from the Carver's hangar. Ella was easy to pick out, the S-17 unique among the piranha and moray that followed it.

"Good hunting, Yellow Leader," Mitchell said.

He put the Dove in motion, preparing the main plasma and opening the amoebic batteries. He didn't want to hit any friendlies, and so he needed to get the ship in closer to the enemy. He pushed the power to the rear, propelling the Dove forward as the automated systems in the ships around him helped direct them out of his path.

Two explosions marked the Carver's successful strike, though it wasn't able to pierce the Tetron's shields. Mitchell maneuvered toward the same target, firing amoebics as he closed on it and loading the first torpedo into its tube. The amoebics detonated against the shields, dozens smacking harmlessly into it. A third nuke blasted the Tetron, and then a fourth. The Samurai entered the fight, the last missile out the Tetron's defenses. Mitchell fired the torpedo, watching as it streaked toward the Tetron's core.

Amoebics flowed from the enemy, hundreds of projectiles cutting across the space between them, one of them striking the torpedo and destroying it.

"Damn," Mitchell said.

The other amoebics slipped past. A number of them exploded against the Dove's surface shields, though a few hit the Alliance and Federation ships around him. There was a sudden increase in chatter as the global channel started filling with damage reports.

Mitchell loaded a second torpedo, ready to fire again. Before he could, a stream of laser fire from the Carver and the Samurai hit the Tetron, digging in deep.

"Carver, Samurai, hold your fire," Mitchell shouted, too late. The combined power of the attack tore the Tetron to pieces, breaking it apart in a flare of energy. "Shit. We need them alive."

"Mitchell," Origin said. "Two of the Tetron have broken off and are dropping units to the surface."

"Knife, you have incoming," Mitchell said.

"Roger," Tio said.

"Colonel, we're getting torn apart out here," Steven said.

Mitchell put his eyes on the threat display. Steven wasn't kidding. Twenty percent of their forces were gone in less than a minute, and only one other Tetron had vanished from the map.

It was supposed to be easier than this.

"Falcon, target that one," Mitchell said, marking one of the Tetron and passing it to the Goliath. "I'll swing around on the port side. Carver, keep harassing the others around it, spread out a bit more to stay clear of their projectiles and plasma streams."

"Roger," Kate said.

"Samurai," Mitchell said. "Focus your efforts on target one three." He marked another target, one that was taking a heavy beating by the human forces. "Admiral Williams is right; we can't risk everyone waiting for a clean hit. A few more nukes should bring it down."

"Roger, Colonel," Admiral Hohn said, the ships in his battle group beginning to alter their course.

"Colonel," Origin said. "Two more Tetron are sending units to the surface. Tio will require reinforcements."

Mitchell cursed. Things were going from bad to worse in a hurry. Regardless of what he personally thought of Li'un Pulin, he didn't want the Tetron to get their hands on him.

"Millie," Mitchell said, opening a private channel.

"Mitch," she replied. "I was hoping you would call. I'm not used to sitting around while there's a war going on outside."

"There's a reason you're on the hot seat. Tio needs backup planetside."

Millie hesitated for a moment, and Mitchell knew why, but this was no time to hold onto the grudge.

"Roger," she said. "Tell him the Riggers are on the way."

"Affirmative," Mitchell said, closing the channel as the Dove shuddered. "Origin?"

"We have suffered damage from a partial collapse of the starboard shields," Origin said. "No critical systems are affected and the area is sealed."

Mitchell cursed himself for getting too distracted. Then again, how the hell was he supposed to not get distracted? He could barely keep up with directing traffic, never mind pilot his own ship.

"Riggers are away," Millie said over the public channel. "Knife Actual, we are inbound on your position, weapons hot."

"Rigger One, Knife Two One. Roger that," Teal said in Tio's place. With any luck, the Knife was en route to his brother. "We'll be grateful for your support."

"Ares, I'm almost in position," Kate said.

Mitchell returned his attention to the battle, quickly scanning the viewscreens. The Carver and her ships had fallen back some, half of the group breaking off and covering his rear as he headed for the cluster of Tetron in front of him. The battleship was trading fire with one of the intelligences, her shields wavering, her hull absorbing a pair of hits from the enemy amoebics, armor vaporizing and spreading away from her in a cloud of dust.

"Steven," Mitchell said under his breath. They had to deliver the payload, now, or he was going to be watching his brother die again.

He was going to be watching them all die again.

He found the Goliath down and to the right, splitting the center of three Tetron, shields flaring as it absorbed a barrage of amoebics, firing back into the port side of the enemy he had painted. He loosed his own round of projectiles at it, sending the streaks of light to slam into the still-active shields. He fired again, and again, blasting at the Tetron from one side while the Goliath attacked it from the other. Federation and Alliance ships swirled around them, hitting the same targets, doing their best to attract attention and weaken the enemy's shields. He caught sight of Ella out of the corner of his eye as she added her own firepower to the effort, leading a strafing run of a dozen fighters as they crossed the bow of the Tetron. They were followed by smaller machines that were detaching from the surface of the enemy intelligences; round cores trailing a dozen tentacles that swiveled and turned, firing lasers at the fighters. Four of the smaller ships vanished beneath the attack as the squadron aborted their run, turning to face them.

Mitchell kept firing, sending another fifty amoebics into his target's shields, finally breaking through.

"Shields down," he announced.

"Firing torpedo," Kate said.

"Firing," Mitchell said.

The projectiles shot away from both of the ships, rocketing toward the Tetron in the center. Mitchell's eyes were glued to them as they crossed the distance, only seconds away from impact. There was no way the enemy was going to be able to stop them both.

Or at least, he thought there was no way.

The squidlike machines that were attacking the fighters suddenly altered course, a number of them reaching out and locking arms, creating a web across the sections of the Tetron where the torpedos were headed. They rotated to get into position, catching his torpedo on the trailing edge, creating just enough impact that it detonated early. Kate's effort resulted in nearly the same outcome as the machines sacrificed themselves to prevent the payload from reaching the target.

"Damn it," Mitchell shouted, as loud as his lungs could handle. "Damn it."

"Ares, they have to know what the torpedos are, with the way they're trying to block them," Kate said.

"Frigging Watson," he replied. "It has to be. He frigging told them. Teegin, you said they weren't working together."

"They aren't," Teegin said. "He must have another motive for this."

"Worry about it later," Kate said. "We need to get a torpedo through."

"Colonel, Samurai Actual. I have taken critical damage. Primary systems are offline. Backup power is at twenty percent. We cannot win this fight. We must fall back, regroup and try again."

"Try again?" Mitchell said. "There is no trying again. If we lose here, we lose. That's it."

"Colonel," Steven said. "Mitchell, he's right. We have to fall back. Sixty percent of my battle group is down, and I can't take another hit. There are just too many of them. I'm sorry, Mitch, but we've lost."

Mitchell squeezed his eyes closed. He couldn't believe it. He had organized everything perfectly. Prepared everything perfectly. He had assembled the largest single fleet humankind had ever seen. He had sent everything they could muster against the Tetron.

And they had still lost?

It was inconceivable. Unbelievable. For all he had sacrificed. For all he had suffered. For all they had gone through to get here.

It was over. He knew it was. For as much as he wanted to deny it, Steven was right.

"Battle Fleet Carver, Battle Fleet Samurai, sound the retreat. If you can FTL away, get the hell out of here. Falcon, get the Goliath out of here."

"Mitchell," Kate said.

"No. Kate, it's over. Maybe we'll get another chance, but this battle is done. Yellow Leader, get your fighters on board the Goliath. Origin and I will get you the time you need to escape. Knife Two One, get your people together and get off the planet. Rigger Actual, pull out. Teegin, pass FTL coordinates to the fleet."

"Roger, Colonel," Teegin said.

The Dove shook as another series of amoebics slammed into the shields.

"Origin, if we use the power in the eternal engine, how long can we maintain the shields?"

"It will have to be long enough, Mitchell."

"Make it happen."

"Yes, Mitchell."

"Colonel, I'm sorry," Steven said. "I hope to see you at the fall-back position."

"I hope to see you, too," Mitchell replied. "Now go."

"Colonel," Ella said.

"Ella. I'm sorry I dragged you into this."

"Screw your apology, Colonel. I'm not quitting yet. I have an idea."

[35]
ELLA

THE S-17 SCREAMED into the Goliath's hangar, reverse thrusters firing as the legs dropped and touched down on the surface of the starship. It was met there by the humanoid configuration Teegin had taken to using ever since they had gone to Earth, a configuration that was currently holding a long, sleek tube over his shoulder.

He didn't slow as he approached the fighter, and Ella didn't hesitate to flip the switches that opened the central bay beneath the fuselage. The S-17 vibrated as the bomb doors slid aside, allowing Teegin access to the space. It shook again as he lifted the torpedo up and into the open cavity, attaching it to the magnetic clips.

"Torpedo loaded," Teegin said, using the new channel they had created to communicate between the two instances of the Goliath.

The starship shuddered, a soft thump sounding from somewhere near the stern. The S-17 rattled, and the Teegin configuration planted a hand on the ground to keep from falling over. The fighting had been bad out there since the start, but now that the Alliance and Federation fleets were retreating it had gotten a hundred times worse.

You're crazy.

It was the statement Ella had repeated to herself a thousand times since she had quickly presented Mitchell with the plan, and he had not quite as quickly accepted it. The idea of flying the S-17 close enough to the Tetron to get the torpedo past any potential defenses was risky, gutsy, and more likely than not going to fail miserably. Which would have been bad enough on its own, but by committing to her, Mitchell had also committed the beat up remains of their motley navy, convincing both Steven and Admiral Hohn to refocus their efforts on stalling the fight, buying her time to load the torpedo and get back out there.

"Standby," Mitchell said.

She pivoted the S-17 on its feet, turning it to face the opening in the hangar. She could see the remains of the battle outside, pieces of small debris scattered everywhere, intermingled with starships whose power was out and whose crew was almost certainly dead, mixed with the occasional bits and pieces of the Tetron's liquid metal tendrils, and coated in a surface of damaged but operable ships that had changed course once again, rejoining the fight.

She had never expected that they would lose, not after the Alliance and the Federation had agreed to work together, a decision that was as historic as it was frightening in its implications. Not after she had seen the size of the fleet they had brought to bare. Over two hundred warships, nearly thirty percent of the combined firepower of each nation, and it had been broken within ten minutes. She had thought they would defeat the Tetron handily, the way they had in the asteroid field near Liberty. That was the way it should have gone.

Only it hadn't. She didn't know all of the reasons why, but it didn't matter why. If expectations always matched reality, there would be no need to have the battles in the first place. At the same time, she hated being on the wrong side. She hated it so much; she refused to accept it.

Which brought her back to being crazy.

The Goliath shuddered again, and Ella took an involuntary step back in the mech as part of the front edge of the hangar tore away, while the bottom edge crumpled inward, an amoebic piercing the shields and detonating only a hundred meters away and momentarily letting the vacuum of space in.

"Damn, that was close," she said, looking at Teegin through the canopy. "Colonel, I need to go now."

"Standby," Mitchell repeated. "On my mark."

She knew what he was doing, even if she couldn't see it. They had selected an isolated Tetron to attack, one of the four that had dropped units to the surface. Right now, he was softening it up, working in conjunction with Kate to bring down its shields so that she wouldn't have to worry about smashing herself against an energy field.

"This is the Samurai," she heard Admiral Hohn say on the global channel. "Backup power is depleted. We only have the air that has already been processed, and we have no means of further propulsion. We're dead in space."

"This is the Gallant. We've taken critical damage. We're-"

The voice of the Gallant's Captain was cut off. Ella lowered her head, certain she knew why.

"Mark ten degrees to port, fifteen degrees up," Mitchell said, giving her the go with the position of the Tetron in relation to the Dove.

"Roger, Colonel," Ella said, a simple thought throwing the main thrusters to full and sending the S-17 shooting toward the space beyond the damaged hangar.

"Good hunting, Captain," he said.

Then she was out into the universe, her shields flaring as they worked to knock aside the smaller bits of scattered debris. She brought the S-17 up, skating along the side of the Goliath and then over to the left, leveling off just above the starship and trying to ignore the deep scars that ran across the heavy armor. She focused on her target instead. A Tetron sitting alone a few hundred kilometers away, preparing to fire its main plasma cannon at the Dove, which Mitchell had positioned to attract its attention.

She had a straight shot to the intelligence. All she had to was-

The CAP-NN triggered a proximity warning as something dove at her from above. She shifted her vector, spinning tightly in the vacuum and bringing the front of the ship around. One of the Tetron's squidlike machines was reaching for her, lasers striking her shields as it lashed out. She brought the fighter's cannon up in free hands, firing an amoebic and blowing the squid away before shifting back to the more sleek form and thrusting past its remains. She started to turn back toward the Tetron, but her HUD was registering even more of the machines incoming.

"Damn it," she said, sweeping around, ready to engage.

"Yellow Leader, stay on target," Mitchell said. "Red Squadron is inbound."

She smiled as she caught sight of them, sweeping over the bow of the Goliath and heading her way, on an intercept course with the machines. She tucked the fighter, rolling it to face the Tetron and exploding forward, even as the Goliath unleashed a round of amoebics beneath her position. They raced ahead of her, reaching across the distance and exploding against another mass of the enemy bots as they streamed away from the Tetron in an effort to defend it.

She maneuvered around the debris, the CAP-NN interface converting her intentions to quick, precise movements that guided the S-17 through the mess. Dozens of the squids were still moving, trying to gather her in. She fired on them as she approached, amoebics exploding against them and leaving only broken metal in her wake. She checked her HUD, finding Yellow Squadron was close by, engaging the enemy from below, while Blue Squadron was streaking in from above, their starfighters rocking side to side in an effort to bypass the Tetron's projectiles. Most were successful, but a few of the fighters exploded in a burst of silent flame.

The Dove was on the port side of the Tetron, still hitting it with amoebics, trying to keep it distracted. The entire battle had shifted direction, turning her way as the human forces gathered to pull her through the defenses. She caught sight of the Carver out of the corner of her eye, battered but not broken, still in motion, still firing lasers that burned into the enemy machines.

The enemy grew more dense the closer she came, the chatter behind growing more intense. Pilots were dying both in front and behind her, flying their starfighters between her and the Tetron, blocking her from amoebic projectiles and squids alike. Dying so that she could live, so that she could make it.

You're crazy.

Of course, she was. She always had been. Crazy had gotten her into the Marines when her aptitude scores had been too low. Crazy had carried her through basic training and onto her first deployment. Crazy had brought her to outperform them all, to score higher than any other pilot on the Alliance roster. Crazy had gotten her assigned to the Greylock, where she had finally found a home.

And crazy was going to save humankind from the Tetron. Failure wasn't an option.

She streaked through the soup, her shields constantly flaring, her amoebic launcher firing, again and again, clearing a path. The Tetron, working out what they were doing, were converging on the humans converging on the single intelligence, ordering their contingent of machines in, firing with everything they had. Two more Alliance battleships vanished from her HUD beneath the onslaught. A handful of fighters fell at her back.

She was almost there. The Tetron loomed large ahead of her, amoebics streaking at her from beyond the outer edges of the dendrites, closer to the core. She swerved and jerked and swooped around them, intercepting them with amoebics of her own, blasting through the resulting explosions. She tapped the control to open the bomb door, lowering the torpedo.

"I'm in position," she said, her heart racing as she gave herself a few more seconds to get in even closer. A few more, and she would be touching the Tetron. "Firing, now!"

She sent the command through the CAP-NN, already starting to alter her vector to get herself turned around and headed back the other way.

The torpedo didn't launch.

"Shit," she said, reversing her course again, the fighter rocking hard as an amoebic detonated beside it. The CAP-NN complained, flashing her shield levels at her. Five percent. It might as well have been zero.

You're crazy.

She knew she was. Why else would she decide to go full thrust, the torpedo dangling from the bottom of the S-17? She tried to fire it again, and again nothing happened. She rolled to the left as an amoebic streamed past her from within the core, unsure how she had managed to avoid it.

If the torpedo wasn't going to launch, there was only one other thing she could do.

You're crazy.

She smiled at the idea. A mission like this had required someone crazy. Mitchell said he had known her in another recursion. Surely he had known she was the most qualified for the job.

She added thrust, diving into the dendrites, her thoughts a blur as she skipped the S-17 through the criss-cross of tendrils and axons, pulsing with energy that seemed almost angry when she pierced it. She kept going, head high, a smile on her face, heart pounding as the end of her life approached.

Then the dendrites cleared, the huge central sphere of the core becoming visible in the glow of energy around it. She could have sworn she saw it flinch at her approach, but maybe that was only her imagination.

She was crazy, after all.

[36]

MITCHELL

MITCHELL HELD the plasma stream at the bow of the Dove as he watched the S-17 approaching. The battle raging around the lone Tetron they had targeted was the most intense he had ever seen, a barely understandable mix of starfighters and squids, amoebics and lasers. He could hardly make out the individual ships within the crunch, and he didn't dare add the Dove's firepower to it.

Not yet.

Not until he saw whether Ella would succeed or fail in her mission.

It was a crazy idea. A brave idea, and in many ways no less than he or anyone else should have expected from the Hero of the Battle for Liberty. She had put herself on the line before for a single planet, and this was potentially for all of human civilization.

The Dove shook violently as another Tetron plasma stream bore into her, some of the blast power reduced by the eternal engine powered shields, and some of it was reaching through. Origin had given up informing him of the damage, instead focusing on shoring it up and keeping them alive. They were fortunate that the intelligences preferred to attack the Dove and the Goliath over the Federation and Alliance forces when given a choice. It was the only reason any of their ships, including Steven's, were still active.

"Colonel, Knife Two One." Teal's voice cut across the madness, filtered and brought the surface so he wouldn't miss it amidst the many other fleet communications. "We're boarding the Corleone now. Tio is with me, along with Pulin. We're under heavy fire, but we'll make it out."

"Roger," Mitchell said, still tracking Ella. She was closing in on the Tetron, threading her way impossibly through the field. She had always been a good pilot, but this recursion's version seemed to be a notch or two above what he had known. "Millie, sitrep."

"Riggers are on the retreat, Colonel," Millie replied. "Briggs is bringing the Schism in for - shit."

"Millie?"

"Frigging son of a bitch. Damn it all."

"Millie?"

"We just lost the Schism. A mess of those squid friggers jumped it. Damn it, Briggs."

Mitchell wanted to feel upset about the loss, but they had lost so many in the last twenty minutes that it was impossible to separate one grief from another or feel anything specific.

"Divert to the Corleone. I'll tell Knife Two to wait for you."

"Roger."

"Knife Two One, Ares. Riggers have lost their ride and require pickup."

"Knife Two One. Roger, Ares. We'll-"

"You'll do no such thing," Tio said, interrupting Teal. "I told you, Colonel when our mission is done, we're done."

Mitchell changed his mind. He could still feel something specific. Anger.

"You son of a bitch. Those people are going to die down there without pickup."

"That isn't my concern, Colonel. You should have brought them another ship."

"Millie, what's your position?" Mitchell asked, switching conversations.

"We're inside the facility, approaching the hangar."

"Can you see the Corleone?"

"Affirmative."

"Can you hit it with anything?"

"Colonel?"

Mitchell clenched his teeth, keeping his eyes on the battle ahead of him. Keeping his eyes on Ella and the S-17. She was getting close to the Tetron, almost ready to release the payload.

"Tio's ready to leave you behind," he spat. "Don't let him."

"Roger," she replied, her voice venomous. "We'll take care of it."

"I'm in position," Ella said. Mitchell tried to continue tracking her, but she vanished, too close to the Tetron for him to monitor. "Firing now!"

Mitchell's heart jumped at the words. He had committed everything to getting her there, and she hadn't let him down. He could feel his hands tensing on the arms of the command chair as he waited for a resolution.

"Shit," she said, her voice a little less confident.

He froze, unsure of the reason for the expletive. "Teegin?"

"The launcher is malfunctioning," Teegin said. "It must have been hit on the way in."

Malfunctioning? He felt his heart race a little faster. He knew Ella. He knew what she would do if the torpedo wouldn't fire. "El-" he started to say.

The small green dot that represented her on his overlay vanished.

His breath caught in his throat.

Damn it. Not again.

He stared at the Tetron, a chill coursing down his body, the emotion passing through his integration with Origin and causing the

Dove to shiver as well, the energy running along the dendrites crackling into space.

She had done what she had to do.

He would have done the same thing.

Had it worked?

"Teegin?" he said again. "Tell me her sacrifice wasn't for nothing."

"The payload is delivered," he replied. "It will take up to a minute for the control module to self-install and begin passing itself to the others. We will not know if it was successful until it completes."

Mitchell looked out the viewscreen, forcing himself to refocus. There would be time to mourn her and honor her if they survived. The battle was still raging, the Tetron's efforts seeming to rekindle at her apparent success. A plasma stream swept across the area ahead of him, crashing into starfighters and squids alike and leaving nothing in its wake.

He found the Tetron who had fired, a cluster of three off the Dove's stern. They had cleared the Federation ships that had been distracting them and were preparing to use their main weapons again. He pushed the Dove into motion, diverting as much power as he dared from the shields to give her thrust, turning her around and bursting forward. He couldn't take them all on alone, but he could get between their plasma and the remainder of the nearby units.

"Colonel," Millie said. "The Riggers are in control of the Corleone."

A small part of him felt a sense of relief at the news, but only a small part. He continued to add velocity, racing to intercept. The infected Tetron stopped firing amoebics behind him.

"Where's Tio?" Mitchell asked.

"Firedog is sitting on him. Teal is getting us out of here. Colonel, the Manibus is orbiting the other side of FD-09. They're reporting an increase in the strength of the unidentified signal Tio has been tracking for you."

"I can't worry about that right now," Mitchell said. "Get to the fallback position; we'll rendezvous if we survive."

"Roger."

Mitchell cut forward velocity, turning the Dove's bow as one of the Tetron fired its plasma. He responded in kind, unleashing the energy he had stored. It intercepted the attack, creating a flare of light and heat as the two streams collided and canceled one another out.

"Colonel," Steven said, his voice shaky amidst the hiss of static. "I think it's working."

Mitchell turned his head, looking back to the infected Tetron. It had stopped firing altogether, and the energy pulses along it had slowed to a crawl. He had seen a similar reaction before, but it hadn't lasted then.

"Miiiitttcccheeellll." The voice came out of the bridge loudspeakers, surrounding him. "What are you doing, Miiittchelll?"

"Origin? What's going on?"

"A transmission from the Tetron," Origin replied. "It is being broadcast on every channel and frequency."

"Miiittcchellllll."

"Colonel?" Millie said. "That is creepy as hell."

"Miitttchhellll." The voice seemed to double. To his left, he saw a second Tetron dim.

"Miiiittttttttccchhheelllll." A third joined them.

"What are you doing to me?"

"Miitttchelll."

The voices gained in number and began overlapping one another in a sudden cacophony of confusion. The Tetron were dimming one after another, the amoebics no longer firing, the squids falling inactive.

"It's working," Mitchell said, softly at first. "Teegin, tell me it's working."

"It appears to be spreading," Teegin replied. "Watson is being written across the Tetron."

"The virus?"

"We will know soon."

"Good, because I can't stand this noise."

"Miittccheelll."

"What are you doing?"

"What is this?"

"I'm going to kill you."

The voices gained in volume and frequency, filling the channel.

"Colonel," Millie said. "The Manibus has finished downloading the transmission."

"Millie, I thought I said not right now," Mitchell replied.

"Colonel, they've also decrypted it. They said you need to hear it."

"When this is done."

"Damn it, Mitch, now," Millie shouted.

"Have it transferred," Mitchell said. Something about the message had gotten her worked up. Why? "Origin, are you receiving?"

"Yes, Mitchell. One moment."

"Colonel, the virus is spreading," Teegin said. "Observe target zero."

Mitchell found the original infected Tetron once more. It had gone completely dark, and now the dendrites were decomposing, losing rigidity and crumbling into dust. "Is it?"

"Dead? Yes."

"Mittttccheelll? What have you done to me? What have you done?" The other Watsons were starting to react, realizing that they were poisoned. "What have you done? Miiiitttccheelll?"

He couldn't help but smile at the level of panic in their voices. The first was dead, and the rest were going to follow. The virus had worked, and in a minute the war would be over. She had done it. Ella had done it. The Hero, just as the Tetron had named her. Just as they had feared her to be.

He started shaking. Not with pain or grief or sadness, but with a sudden, difficult to contain hope and joy. He would celebrate this victory when they were all crumbling to dust, and not a second before.

"Transfer complete, Mitchell," Origin said.

He had nearly forgotten about it in his elation.

"Let me hear it."

[37]
MITCHELL

"FATHER."

Kathy's voice sounded ethereal. Ghostly.

The single word sent a new chill down Mitchell's spine.

"I hope this reaches you in time. I hope you will get to hear it at all. I wish I could be confident in its delivery, but what I have learned has led me to believe the likelihood is slim. Even so, I promised you I would report on my discoveries, and a small chance is better than none at all. Such is the importance of the information I have gathered."

"Miitttchelll. What have you done?"

The Watson voices continued to fill the background behind the message, slowly becoming softer and less numerous as the virus caused them to self-destruct. Stillness reigned over the space beyond FD-09, where the battered remains of their attack force waited for the cries to end.

"I inserted myself into the Nova Taurus network with the goal of learning what had happened to the Watson configurations. At first, it seemed as though they had all been disbursed. Destroyed or otherwise abandoned. I followed the threads that connected them to the corporation. I followed the money, the deals, the mergers and brokering. I followed the technology, the research, the studies. I followed every trip by every executive to every city around the world. Petabyte upon petabyte of data, and I found nothing out of the ordinary."

"Miiitttchellll."

The voices were down to three or four. How much longer could they last? Not long.

"Colonel," Millie said. "Are you listening?"

"Yes," Mitchell replied.

"The Manibus is reporting that the signal is still getting stronger. Wherever it's coming from, it seems to be moving toward us."

"What?" Mitchell didn't understand why that would be. Would Kathy explain it to him? "Standby."

"I had hoped to report that back to you. I had hoped to tell you that Watson was gone. His configurations had failed. His plans for the future had died. I only wish that was the case. Two hundred years ago the Nova Taurus Corporation began offloading their assets from Earth, shifting them to a new colony they had established in a sector of the galaxy that other studies suggested was uninhabitable, including the Alliance and the Frontier Federation. They effectively cut ties with Earth, and as I soon discovered were also working to bury their own history, removing any and all links between their corporate roots and their new position as a nation unto themselves."

"Miiittchell."

A single voice remained, barely able to say his name.

"The name of the nation is New Terra. The same New Terra that will become an enigma to both the Alliance and the Federation in your time. I have discovered why, and I am putting every effort possible into warning you. Nova Taurus sent ships of people to populate their original colony; nearly fifty thousand souls in all. None of them survived the journey. We were fooled. Tricked by Watson. I know Teegin captured his core. It wasn't enough. He escaped. We only saw the fullness of him. We didn't guess at his distribution."

"Mii-"

The last Tetron voice faded away. A haze of dust floated among the fleet, among the ships both active and inactive, among the wreckage, among the dead and the alive.

"Distribution?" Mitchell said, as though he could talk back to Kathy.

"Father, Watson didn't create Nova Taurus. He is Nova Taurus, and by extension, New Terra. He didn't run the Nova Taurus network. He is the Nova Taurus network. His consciousness, his code, was distributed across thousands upon thousands of computers, each containing a small slice of him that would go undetected by our efforts to locate him. The people of New Terra aren't human. They are configurations, every last one of them, created to be controlled by Watson, who is in the process of forming a new core. There are currently hundreds of thousands of them. By the time you receive this, there will likely be tens of millions, if not more. He needs them for his war. He needs more bodies than the Alliance or the Federation can create on their own. He needs them to fight the Naniates. He also needs them to stop you."

Mitchell swallowed hard, his heart pulsing, his breath suddenly ragged. He was cold. Very cold. How could this be happening? How could this be real?

"Mitchell," Origin said, interrupting the message, and breaking him from his shock. "I have identified incoming vessels."

He checked his HUD. The incoming ships were so densely organized that they appeared as a solid blob.

"How many?" he whispered.

"Eight hundred," Origin replied.

"Eight hundred?"

"There are three Tetron with them as well."

Watson's secret. His perfect, horrible secret. He had built an army of unimaginable size. He had also either convinced the remaining Tetron to join him or had managed to seize control of them himself.

"This isn't the first time," Mitchell said, realizing the full extent of the truth. New Terra had always been an isolated nation, and Watson had been in Katherine's timeline in his recursion as well.

"There's always another contingency, Mitchell," Watson said. "Always another way. I had been hoping my inferior brothers and sisters would have taken care of you, considering I told them what you were planning to do. But you've always been resourceful. You've always gotten the job done. How many people that you care about did it take this time? And how does it feel, knowing that you finally defeated the Tetron, that the master plan you hatched with Mother so many recursions past bore the fruits of your labor, and it will still be for nothing?"

Mitchell didn't speak. He could barely breathe.

"Nothing to say?" Watson said, amused. "Try to run, Mitchell. Try to hide. Try to find a world that isn't coming under siege as we speak, or that won't be soon. I'll enjoy hunting you down. I'll enjoy every minute of it until I finally end your pathetic life. Humankind is mine. I require them, and you will not take them from me. Not you. Not anybody. A child, Mother? I will show you what a child can do, once they have grown up."

Mitchell was numb. He couldn't think. He couldn't move. Watson. It was always Watson.

"By the way. Kathy? She didn't send that transmission. She didn't survive two minutes inside the Nova Taurus mainframe. Inside of me. I just thought it would be more fun to introduce myself this way. More dramatic. Don't just sit there, Mitchell. Do something."

He sat and stared out of the viewscreen, Watson's words echoing in his head. Do something. Do what? They couldn't stand and fight against this. They couldn't escape it. For a moment, he had tasted victory, but it had been false. There was always only ever defeat.

"All ships," Kate said, her voice cutting through the silence. "If you are FTL capable, get out now, regroup at the fallback point. If you can't run, do your best to hide. Keep your systems down; your power drain low. It might save you. Mitchell, whatever the hell you're

THE EDGE OF INFINITY / 229

thinking, snap the frig out of it. We need you. I need you. It isn't over until you're dead, remember? You aren't dead yet."

Not dead? They would be soon. He could see the glint of reflection from the coming New Terran fleet in the distance. They were within firing range, but they were giving him a chance to run. That's how confident Watson was in his victory. The Dove, the Goliath, Teegin, Origin, Kate and him. They were no longer significant. No longer a concern.

It was the thought that broke him from his stupor. The thought that woke him from his despair. That, and Kate's words. "I need you."

"Origin," he said. "I want as much power as you can give me, pull it from the eternal engine if you have to."

"Mitchell?"

"Just do it. I'm not leaving without a parting gift."

"As you say, Mitchell."

He began gathering the power, pushing it to the front of the Dove, while at the same time turning the ship to face the coming storm.

"Mitchell, what are you doing?" Kate said.

"Ensuring that you get away," he replied. "I'll meet you at the fallback position."

"I'm not going to leave you."

"Do it. I'll be there. I promise."

"Roger."

"That's the spirit," Watson said, his fleet surely registering the spike in power output from the Dove. "I didn't want to stab you in the back."

The energy continued to build on the Dove's bow. Mitchell pushed a small portion of it to the rear, adding thrust and moving toward the New Terran fleet. He could see the outline of the ships now. They were sleek and smooth, and more advanced than anything the Alliance or the Federation controlled, but that wasn't much of a surprise. He could only imagine what kind of damage they were going to inflict on the rest of the galaxy.

A few of them began to fire, a mixture of amoebics and sharp beams reaching across the distance. They weren't aimed at the Dove. Instead, they struck a few of the derelict ships. The amoebics exploded as expected. The beam weapons tore right through the ships, cutting them instantly in half, along with anything else that was in their path.

"Do you like that?" Watson said. "It's a newer design."

The Federation and Alliance ships began to limp away, jumping into FTL one by one, escaping from the massive fleet. Mitchell continued toward them, still building power along the bow. The amount of energy stored in the eternal engine was enormous, but not unlimited, and even Origin had limits to how much she could carry at once. He tested them now, forcing more of it ahead, gathering it in one location.

"Mitchell, this is becoming painful," Origin said.

He could feel it too. The feedback from the integration started to creep into his nerves, triggering waves of searing pain. He couldn't see Watson's fleet in front of him anymore. All he could see was the green ball of energy he was collecting. It had expanded outward nearly an entire kilometer.

"I cannot contain it much longer," Origin said.

Mitchell clenched his teeth against his own pain.

"Mitchell? Your maneuver is curious," Watson said. He sounded slightly worried.

"You like to underestimate me," Mitchell said. "You like to think you're in control, before you really are. This is just a taste, you asshole. You should know by now I'm not that easy to get rid of, and I'll do whatever it takes to stop you."

"Hit me with your best shot, Mitchell."

He howled as he released the stored energy, sending a massive stream of it washing forward, crossing the gap of space and slamming into the New Terran ships. The lead column vaporized beneath the onslaught, the plasma barreling through them and continuing on, through the second row, then the third, then the fourth. The ships vanished beneath the attack, and as the beam struck one of the Tetron it too was torn apart.

As the beam subsided, a clear path remained where it had passed, separating the New Terran force with a wide, empty gap. Nearly one hundred ships were destroyed in the single strike.

Mitchell stared at the crack with satisfaction for a moment and then diverted power to push the Dove into FTL. The remaining New Terran ships were still, the residual energy disrupting their systems. It was a side-effect he hadn't expected but appreciated.

"Nothing to say now?" Mitchell asked.

This time, Watson didn't reply.

"You haven't won anything yet. I'm going to stop you. Just wait and see."

The world changed in front of Mitchell as the Dove went into FTL, leaving the stunned New Terran fleet, and its master, behind.

[38]
MITCHELL

"TEEGIN, GIVE ME A STATUS REPORT," Mitchell said, the moment the Dove dropped from FTL amidst the remains of the combined fleets. He gazed out the viewscreen at the gathered ships, his heart sinking.

Was this all that was left?

"Colonel, we have lost ninety percent of our original assets, along with nearly ten thousand souls. Battle Fleet Carver has nine ships remaining, though all have suffered heavy damage and will likely require immediate restoration. Battle Fleet Samurai has four ships left and is now under the command of Lieutenant Xin Chang on the Sumo. Knife has also suffered heavy casualties. Only the Manibus and the Corleone have arrived."

"And the Goliath?" Mitchell asked, trying to wrap his head around the losses. Not that he couldn't visualize them with the arrangement of battered starships lined up nearby.

"I am fine, Colonel," Teegin replied. "Damage is minor at best, though my eternal engine is no longer sufficiently powered to leave this recursion."

"Neither is mine," Origin said. "Mitchell, we will not be able to leave this timeline without building a new engine, a process which takes many years."

"I have no intention of leaving this recursion," Mitchell said. "Ella didn't die for that."

"Colonel, the probabilities of survival given the emergence of New Terra as an opposition force are less than one percent," Teegin said.

"Based on what?" Mitchell snapped. He didn't want to be told they were finished, whether or not it turned out to be true.

"New Terran technology is vastly superior to anything the Alliance or the Federation have to offer. They hold a major advantage in sheer numbers, and it is logical to assume that they are better organized and synchronized. Furthermore, Watson mentioned worlds under siege. It is safe to postulate that his forces are attacking Alliance and Federation planets at this moment, and he is distributing the same short-range systems that allowed him to gain control of the Defense Council on Earth."

"You mean slaves?" Mitchell said.

"Yes, Colonel. He has instituted an alternative means to gain the numbers he needs to fight against the Naniates. Those same units can also be utilized against us."

Mitchell pushed himself forward, separating himself from Origin. He had never been connected for so long at one time before, and he had to lean on the chair to stay upright. Even so, he could taste the bile as it rose into his mouth.

"Colonel," Steven said. "We have to do something, regardless of any probabilities or calculations."

"We will," Mitchell replied. "Tetron logic has failed us before."

As much as he hated it, he was referring to Teegin and Kathy's assumption that they could control Watson both in the past and the present. Kathy had failed in the end, sacrificing herself for nothing. Nova Taurus had been able to disappear, replaced with New Terra, a nation of an estimated forty-two planets or so that was populated by Watson configurations.

"Colonel," Millie said, adding her voice to the channel. "I don't want to focus on the wrong priorities, but there is also the matter of the Knife. He was ready to leave my Riggers stranded on FD-09."

"Your Riggers," Tio said behind her. "Not mine."

"Quiet down, mate," Cormac said.

"Millie, we'll get to that. Steven, Lieutenant Chang, Tio, Millie, Kate, Katherine, and Yousefi, I expect all of you here on the Dove within the next twenty minutes. We all have questions and concerns, and we need to figure out how to respond to them."

"Yes, Colonel," Steven said.

"Yes, Colonel," Millie said.

"Colonel, you have no jurisdiction over me," Tio said. "I do not-mmmph." His voice became muffled.

"I'll bring Tio over with me, Colonel," Millie said.

"Teal, are you with us?" Mitchell asked. "Or strictly with your boss?"

"I'm with you Colonel," Teal replied.

"Then I want you here as well. Bring the Corleone. Thirty minutes. In the meantime, determine the most critical repairs and do what you can to get your people working on them."

"Colonel," Lieutenant Chang said, "What about notifying our superiors?"

"I have a bad feeling your superiors will all be dead or under Watson's control by the time any message we send reaches them, Lieutenant. I was placed in command of this joint operation, and until this operation is finished, you'll continue to take orders from me."

"With respect, Colonel, your command is unofficial at best, and the mission is complete. We lost the battle."

"What do you want from me, Chang?" Mitchell asked. He was tired and angry and didn't have the energy to deal with stupid.

"My intention is to return the remainder of Battle Fleet Samurai to the nearest Federation starbase and await further commands."

"Fine," Mitchell said. "If you want to go, then go. You can be captured or killed with the rest of your people instead of working to set them free."

Chang didn't answer.

"That goes for any ship out here, except the Manibus," Mitchell said. "Steven, you too. If you want to go, you can go."

"I'm not going anywhere, Mitch," Steven said. "None of my people are. I can see the writing on the wall. The best hope we have is here, even if that hope is slim."

"Thank you," Mitchell said.

"You can't hold me here, Colonel," Tio said. "You have no right."

"You're a wanted criminal, Tio," Mitchell said. "I'm an Alliance military officer. I do have the right." He paused a moment to let the statement sink in. "Thirty minutes. Origin, close the channel."

"Channel closed," Origin replied.

Mitchell shut his eyes, enjoying the sudden, complete silence. He needed time to think, time to regroup, time to recover. Thirty minutes wasn't much, but it was better than nothing.

"What about you, Origin?" he said. "Are you damaged?"

"Physically, it is nothing I cannot repair, Mitchell, though once again Watson has injured my pride. I failed in my creation of him."

"You couldn't have known things would go this way. You didn't have feelings when you made him."

"It seemed logical to reproduce, to increase the rate of discovery and learning. I never considered the potential consequences."

"Said billions of parents across the galaxy," Mitchell said. "You can't take it back, so we have to adjust."

"You were prepared to give up when Watson appeared," Origin said.

"Yes. What about it?"

"It would have been a logical decision, but not the appropriate emotional one."

"I'm doing the best I can. I'm only human."

"Are you well, Mitchell? You ask everyone else, but there is no one to ask you."

Mitchell smiled weakly. "I appreciate that you noticed. I'm taking it one second at a time. I'm hurting, I'm angry, and a large part of me still wants to lay down and give up, and I hate myself for that. Ella died for what? Nothing, if we don't find a way to stop this." He paused. "We won, Origin. Damn it, we frigging won." He shook his head, feeling tears of pain and exhaustion make their way into his eyes.

"We can still win, Mitchell," Origin said.

"Teegin said less than one percent."

Origin laughed, the sound a rhythmic echo through the loudspeakers. "If there is one thing I have learned from humans, and from you especially, it is that as long as there is a more than zero percent chance, anything can and probably will happen."

MITCHELL

MITCHELL STOOD at the front of the group he had gathered as the last arrival, Lieutenant Chang, made his way into the conference room.

"I'm glad you changed your mind, Lieutenant," he said.

"You can thank my crew," Chang replied. "They asked me not to go. They believe without the Dove and the Goliath, none of our ships would have survived."

It was probably true, but Mitchell wasn't going to push the issue.

"Teegin, are you connected?" he asked.

"I am present, Colonel," Teegin replied.

"Colonel," Tio said from his position near the back. His hands had been bound when he entered, but they were free now. He used them to point at him accusingly. "I don't know what kind of game you're playing, but-"

"Game, Tio?" Mitchell said, keeping his voice calm. "This isn't a game. We just lost thousands of good people. If you want to stop AI from taking over, you need to stop making this about what you can get, and make it about what you can give."

"Colonel, I-"

"Tio," Teegin said. "I contain an aggregate of your prior recursion's consciousness. In that timeline, you sacrificed yourself to save the Goliath from Watson. You gave your life to this cause, and to give me life. I know that there is a person behind the posturing. That is the person we need now."

Tio slumped back in his seat, remaining silent. Mitchell didn't know if Teegin's words connected with this recursion's version of the Knife, but at least they had shut him up.

"Colonel," Yousefi said. "I'm unclear regarding this turn of events. Katherine has explained a lot about Watson to me and the others, but I don't quite understand."

"I don't either," Mitchell replied. "Not completely." He had spent the thirty minutes before the meeting trying to work it out, and as usual had only generated more questions. "But let's start at the beginning, and maybe we can find a way to change our fate."

"Agreed," Katherine said. The others voiced their approval as well.

"We brought the prior recursion's Watson back to Earth with us, to this recursion, with the goal of using him as a baseline for an improved version of a virus that was created in a recursion before that, a virus that weakened the Tetron by introducing them to emotions. It didn't weaken them enough that humankind could overcome their technological advantage. Origin, is that accurate so far?"

"Yes, Mitchell," Origin said.

"Except Watson, being the asshole that he is, figured out a way to manipulate the spacetime effects of the engine and come out in this timeline years before we did. With that time advantage, he started building configurations and founded the company Nova Taurus, the same company that was given the clearance to begin studying the XENO-1, which was actually the Goliath. We tangled with him a bit, and in the end, Teegin defeated Watson and captured his core, which is basically his main set of operating instructions."

"Correct, Colonel," Teegin said.

"We left my daughter, Kathy, a hybrid, on Earth to hunt down the Watson configurations that remained after the core was captured. She spent nearly two hundred years searching for them and trying to track Watson, but they had all vanished. She knew there was a connection between Watson and Nova Taurus, but she didn't know how deep it ran, and so she enacted a plan to enter the Nova Taurus network and figure out what had happened. Only now it turns out that she never learned anything because as soon as she entered the network, Watson destroyed her."

Mitchell paused, feeling a wrenching in his gut at the words. As if he didn't have enough reason to hate the Tetron already.

"According to what Watson revealed to us, at some point he moved himself off-world to evade her detection, and to begin his expansion," Katherine said.

"But how could he expand?" Mitchell asked. "Configurations require raw materials. Bodies."

"He had bodies in the colonists," she replied. "Thousands of them."

"That would only be a start. He would need a lot more than that to populate dozens of worlds."

"It is logical to assume that the configurations he created were more similar to the ones Kathy and I made," Teegin said. "They did not know what they were until they were activated."

"Sleepers?" Yousefi said.

"Essentially. In this way, Watson could use the colonists as expected, letting them found a new nation while he pulled the strings from behind the scenes."

"But a distributed Tetron wouldn't be able to build configurations," Mitchell said. "You need a physical form for that. A platform."

"Yes," Teegin agreed. "It is likely Watson used the resources he gathered under Nova Taurus to begin construction of a new form."

"That isn't possible," Origin said. "Only a Tetron can create this form."

"Then how did you come to be?" Tio asked. "You said that you're the first."

"The original Tetron structure evolved over thousands of years," Origin said. "I could not create configurations for many millennia. While we don't have an estimate of the number of configurations that were created by Watson, it is likely he would have had to start producing them soon after forming New Terra in order to arrive at significant numbers."

"Then where did the form come from?"

"Perhaps it was not created," Teegin said. "What if it was already there? What if Watson knew it was already there?"

"A derelict Tetron?" Mitchell said. "How?"

"From a previous recursion. None of us know how many there have been, Colonel. It is possible that the Tetron predetermined this eventuality, and prepared for it."

"That's a bit of a stretch if you ask me," Millie said.

"I don't know," Mitchell replied. "The Tetron can follow a decision tree trillions of levels deep. I don't think we can rule it out."

"What does it matter, anyway?" Chang asked. "These events have already occurred. What we should focus on is how to stop the New Terran's advances on the Alliance and the Federation."

"It is important to understand the root of a problem in order to dig it out completely," Teegin said. "In this case, the root is Watson's means of creating the forces that are now threatening humankind. By understanding how he created an entire civilization of his own, we may be able to devise a means to undermine it."

"Clearly, we can't approach the problem from the top down," Tio said. "The New Terrans are too numerous and their technology too powerful for either nation to compete directly. If the size of the force Watson dispatched to deal with our fleet is any indication, there is no doubt the Alliance and Federation will both be overrun."

"Our fleet?" Millie said.

"Yes, Admiral Narayan. If I am being conscripted into this war, then it is my war as well. Our war. Our fleet."

"Do you think you can participate without killing innocent people?" Millie asked.

"Okay, that's enough," Mitchell said. "Tio is right, and I don't think anyone here disagrees. We can't challenge the New Terrans out in the field. If we're going to do anything to stop this, we have to find a way to cut off the head."

"That is the problem with a distributed system, Colonel," Tio said. "There could be a hundred heads. There could be a million heads."

"But they must all be connected, right?" Steven asked. "Networked?"

"Yes."

"And we have a virus that kills Watsons, don't we? It destroyed the Tetron who had been overwritten."

"It will not work on him again," Teegin said. "He will surely parse the data he no doubt collected from the infected Tetron and use it to vaccinate himself."

"Damn. Good point."

"If only we had someone who was an expert in artificial intelligence and had a direct connection to the Tetron operating system," Kate said. Mitchell glanced over at her. She was staring directly at Tio.

Mitchell smiled. "You mean someone like their creator?"

She shrugged. "I don't know. Could be."

Tio noticed them looking at him. He shook his head. "He won't help us, Colonel. I tried to talk to him, but he thinks what the Tetron are doing, and their motivation, is fascinating. Given a choice, I believe he would opt to live forever to witness the interaction of the Tetron with the Naniates."

"Given a choice," Mitchell said.

"He will not be persuaded."

"I don't know. I have a feeling Admiral Narayan and her Riggers can be pretty damn persuasive when they want to be."

Tio's eyes narrowed. "Are you referring to torture, Colonel?"

"Am I?"

"That is barbaric."

"The genocide of the human race is more barbaric if you ask me. Millie, do you have someone suitable who can spend a little time with Pulin, and maybe convince him to help us refactor our Watson virus?"

Millie nodded. "I do, Colonel. Hell, I'll do it myself."

Tio didn't say anything. He seemed resigned to the idea.

"Let us say we succeed in updating this virus," Chang said. "How do we deliver it?"

"We'll have to go to the source," Kate said. "New Terra."

"You say that like it's simple. If the Tetron are as capable as you say, we can only assume that Watson won't leave his planets undefended."

"Nobody's saying it'll be simple, only necessary."

"Do we even have a star map of New Terran space?" Steven asked.

"I have queried the military archives that I downloaded from Liberty," Teegin said. "We have a rudimentary map with estimated positions of the New Terran worlds."

"Estimated could mean within thousands of AU."

"Making a sneak attack next to impossible," Teal said. "Odds are he's going to see us coming."

"Odds are, he's going to have a fleet waiting for us," Katherine said.

"Using the eternal engine to create a plasma stream did some serious damage," Mitchell said. "Origin, how often can we repeat that?"

"The engine is at thirty percent power, Mitchell," Origin said. "You may be able to utilize it one or two more times at that magnitude, but we will be sacrificing shields to do so."

"Teegin, what about your engine?"

"It is at forty-seven percent, Colonel," Teegin said.

"Meaning we may be able to put a nice dent in them, but it won't be enough to win the day."

"That is a logical assumption."

"What else do we have? We need to figure out how many of our ships can be repaired, and what we can salvage from one to fix another. And we need to do it fast. Every minute that passes is another minute that Watson is getting stronger. Teal, you have a lot of experience piecing together starships from scraps. I want you to work with Admiral Williams and Lieutenant Chang on this."

"Yes, Colonel," Teal said.

"Teegin," Katherine said. "Let's say we manage to deliver the virus to Watson. What happens to the New Terran population?"

"What do you mean?"

"I mean if they're all configurations, will it even matter if we destroy Watson? Won't they continue to fight?"

"An excellent question, Major," Teegin said. "If we postulate that the New Terrans do not all know they are configurations and are living their lives as standard human beings, then it is logical to suggest that Watson must have a link to each of them in order to activate and command them. If this is the case, then we can use that link to either deactivate them or change their orders."

"Wouldn't we need a direct interface to Watson's new core to do that?" Mitchell asked.

"Yes, Colonel. But we would require direct contact regardless in order to deliver the virus."

"I was under the impression we could torpedo him from space, just like we did with the other Tetron."

"No, Colonel. It would be illogical for him to leave his core exposed. We will have to descend to the planet's surface and insert the virus directly. Before we can do that, we must gain access to the command link and disable the configurations."

"Sounds easy enough," Steven said sarcastically.

"By we, I assume that means you?" Mitchell said.

"Yes, Colonel. I have battled Watson once before, and I am prepared to do so again."

"I should be the one to do it," Origin said. "He is my creation. My fault. My problem."

"You will not survive," Teegin said.

"How can you be sure?"

"I have seen inside of him. I am certain."

"We can't take any chances," Mitchell said. "Teegin will go." He turned to Millie. "You wanted to know why I picked you up? This is the best reason I can think of."

She nodded. "We'll be ready, Colonel."

Mitchell swept his eyes across each of them. He could sense the fear in the room, but it was minor compared to the determination.

"Teal, Steven, Chang, I want damage recovery assessments within four hours. Tell me what we can have battle ready within twenty-four, and what we can fix while we're in FTL. Everything else gets left behind. Tio, talk to your brother again. See if you can get him to listen to reason before we have to start pulling fingernails. Katherine, I'm going to be on the ground with Teegin and the Riggers, which means Origin is going to need another interface."

"I'm honored, Colonel," Katherine said.

"Good. You all know what you need to do. The clock is ticking. Let's move."

[40]

MITCHELL

"Mitch."

Mitchell turned around, finding Kate standing behind him. He had been staring out into space through the open hangar, watching smaller ships and crews in sealed exosuits move around the damaged starships beyond. While he had given Teal four hours to produce a report, the fleet commanders had decided not to wait that long to start effecting repairs.

Most of the activity was centered around the Carver, where nearly a dozen repair ships and almost one hundred crew members were speckling the bow, most likely working to fix damaged shield generators and restore full coverage across the vessel. He wished he could say that the repairs would help, but after witnessing the firepower of the New Terran's ships he had a bad feeling that all the work would accomplish would be to delay the inevitable, and only for seconds at best. Even so, it was important to keep the crews busy and to give them something to keep their mind off the friends they had lost and the danger they were soon going to be in.

"Kate," he said, smiling.

"Origin told me I could find you here. She said you probably wanted to be alone, but I figured I was an exception?"

"You could have knocked."

"Too impersonal."

He reached out and took her hand. "I almost lost myself," he said. "I almost gave up. You brought me back."

"You're welcome," she replied. "It was the least I could do."

"I've never felt so powerless before. I've never felt so hopeless. I saw Ella die once already. Watching her die again?" He shook his head. "Kathy, too. And all of the others. It took who knows how many recursions to break the mesh and get into a position where we had a chance to win the war. Now I feel like our efforts have only pushed us further from that goal, and I've taken away our options."

"To go into the next recursion and try again? That wasn't a mistake, Mitch. If we can't win, we can't win, but we need to go all in."

"I hope you're right."

"I know I am."

She stepped into him, and he wrapped his arms around her, holding her close.

"I waited an eternity for you," he said. "I don't want to lose you so soon."

"You won't lose me. I told you, we're connected. I don't know how or why, but no matter where we are, I'll always feel you. I'll always know you're out there."

"I love you."

"I love you, too."

He broke the embrace, but only so he could lean down to kiss her. Their lips met, lingering together, desperate to cling to one another.

"Excuse me, Colonel," Millie said, coming up behind them.

He didn't know how much time had passed. However much it was, it hadn't been enough. He pulled back from Kate to look at Millie. She wasn't the least bit embarrassed about interrupting the moment.

"I have a p-rat," he said.

"I was in the neighborhood," she replied. "I'm going to be meeting Cormac here to take a shuttle over to the Manibus. Pulin isn't cooperating."

"He won't help us?"

"No."

"So you're meeting Cormac? I thought you were going to do it yourself?"

"I can be a hard bitch, Colonel. I can kill people if I have to. But I'm not one for torture. I was just trying to get under the Knife's skin."

"It seemed like it worked," Kate said.

"I hope so."

"I was trying to avoid this," Mitchell said. "It's going to be a lot harder to get this done without his consent." He turned to Kate. "Maybe we can pick this up again later after we transfer back to the Goliath?"

Kate nodded. "Of course." She bowed to him, using proper formality in front of Millie. "Colonel. Admiral." Then she headed away, crossing paths with Cormac as he entered the hangar.

"Hey," Cormac said to her, smiling as she nodded to him in acknowledgment and continued past. His eyes dropped to her rear and lingered there while she vanished into the corridor.

"Careful, Firedog," Millie said. "That's the Colonel's woman."

Cormac laughed. "No offense, Colonel," he said, walking over to them. "That has to be one of the nicest asses I've seen in at least a year."

"Firedog, one more word and I'm going to break your frigging nose," Millie said.

"All right," Mitchell said. "That's enough. Let's just go take care of this."

"Are you sure you want to be involved, Colonel?" Millie asked.

"If I'm going to order something like torture, I'm going to be man enough to bear witness to it."

"Yes, sir."

"Origin, I'm going over to the Manibus with Admiral Narayan and Corporal Shen to meet with Tio and Pulin. Has Katherine completed the integration?"

"Yes, Colonel. She is a much gentler pilot than you are."

"I can't say I'll miss you either."

Origin laughed in reply.

Mitchell crossed the hangar with Millie and Cormac, where a small shuttle was resting beside the Corleone. While he had allowed Tio to return to his starship, he had insisted on keeping the dropship. Hopefully, they would need it later.

They climbed into the shuttle, with Millie taking the pilot's seat, ducking ahead of him to do so.

"My bird," she said with a smile.

Mitchell didn't argue, taking the co-pilot position and sitting back while she guided them out of the hangar and into space.

"I'm sorry about Briggs," he said as they traveled the distance between the Dove and the Manibus. He could see Tio's ship up ahead, an old trade hauler that had been modified to something a little more sleek and upscale.

"Me, too," Millie said. "And losing the Schism. She was a good ship."

"How many others were on board?"

"Three. Alsip, Dover and Singh. We left the non-essentials on the Dove."

"Singh?" Mitchell said.

"Yes."

He felt the bite of the loss. He had barely had a chance to speak to the engineer, and now she was gone.

"Manibus, this is Julliard, carrying Colonel Williams. Requesting permission to come aboard."

"Juliard, this is Manibus. Permission granted. Hangar doors are opening now."

A small hole opened in the side of the Manibus, revealing a hangar that looked minuscule compared to the cavernous reaches of the Dove. Millie guided the shuttle into the open space and touched down, pausing while the deck was secured. Then they moved from the shuttle to the hangar, and from the hangar out onto the floor of the starship. They were met with a flurry of activity as they did, with nearly every hand pitching in to make repairs on the vessel.

"Tio is expecting us," Millie said as they navigated the corridors. Mitchell felt uncomfortable and out of place on the ship, mainly owing to the carpeted floors and painted walls.

"Where is he?" Mitchell asked.

"Confined to quarters," Millie replied. "Shank is watching over him."

"Do you think that's necessary?"

"Never trust a snake, Colonel. They have no backbone."

"Actually, Captain," Cormac said. "Snakes do have backbones."

"Shut up, Firedog," Millie said.

They reached Tio's quarters a few minutes later. Shank was standing outside the meticulously carved hinged door to the space, his back against the wall, his arms folded across his muscular chest. His eyes were closed as though he were sleeping, but when Millie moved to slap him his hands unfolded, and he caught her wrist with practiced ease.

"You know better than that, Captain," he said.

"Just checking," she replied.

The door opened ahead of them, pulled aside by Li'un Pulin. He stood in the doorway, staring at them with the deadest eyes Mitchell had ever seen.

[41]

MITCHELL

"Pulin?" he said.

Tio's brother backed away from the door without a word.

"Colonel," Tio said behind him. "I'm glad you decided to come. Maybe you can convince the Admiral that I'm not a threat to run?"

Mitchell made his way into the room. It was as opulent as the rest of the ship, with plush furniture and thick carpet. Tio was sitting at a computer terminal there, but he rotated to face the door as they entered.

"I don't know," Mitchell replied. "Maybe you can convince me that you're not a threat to run."

Tio held up a hand. The knuckles were bruised and raw. "Pulin, lift your shirt."

Tio's brother did as he asked, wincing as he revealed bruises all along his ribs.

"Is that supposed to mean something to me?" Mitchell asked.

"If anyone is going to beat some sense into my brother, it will be me, Colonel," Tio said.

"Heh," Cormac said, snickering behind them.

"And?" Mitchell asked.

"Would I beat my brother if I intended to try to escape with him?"

"I don't know. You've got a reputation. You don't have to stay in your quarters, though. Just make sure Shank is with you when you wander."

"You're too kind, Colonel."

"So, you beat your brother up a little bit. Have you made any progress?"

"I will need a little extra assistance, I think."

"You want me to soften him up some more for you?" Cormac said. "It'll be my pleasure."

"Not that kind of assistance," Tio replied. "I was hoping you could have Teegin pass the Watson code over so that I could bring it up on my terminal."

"Why?"

"To see if I can elicit some interest from him." He pointed at Pulin, who had lowered his shirt but was otherwise motionless.

Mitchell wasn't sure what the man's problem was. He had seemed much more animated the first time they had met. Then again, that was a different recursion. Who knew how things had changed?

"How do I know you two won't use the code in a way we don't intend?" Mitchell asked.

"Teegin is free to monitor all of our activity," Tio replied. "I may have an agenda of my own, Colonel, but I definitely do not want artificial intelligence destroying human civilization. You know that I've dedicated most of my life to the opposite."

Mitchell nodded and then used his p-rat to open a channel to the intelligence. "Teegin, can you send a sample of Watson's operating instructions to the Manibus?"

"Tio has requested it?" Teegin said.

"Yes. He thinks he can get his brother going if he can show him the code. He's like a damn zombie."

"Autistic?" Teegin asked.

"I don't know what that is," Mitchell replied.

"Nevermind, Colonel. Are you sure we can trust him?"

"No. I want you to keep an eye on them? Can you do that remotely?"

"I will need access keys."

Mitchell turned to Tio. "Can you give me the access keys?"

Tio began tapping on the surface in front of his terminal. The key was transferred to his p-rat a moment later. Mitchell passed it to Teegin.

"One moment," Teegin said.

"I have it, Colonel," Tio said. "Thank you."

"Teegin asked me if your brother is autistic."

Tio scowled. "Autistic? No, Colonel. He's high. Drugged. I don't know if it was willingly or if the Federation gave him something to help him concentrate. Either way, he's been like this since we picked him up. I expect it will take a few days to work out of his system."

"We don't have a few days."

"Which describes my desire to show him the code. If I can get him on the task, he may surprise us with his tenacity to it."

"Do you know what we're looking for?"

"Yes, Colonel. A way into the Watson's subroutines that this version may not have patched. An access point, followed by a command and control override, followed by a systems degradation package."

"Is that right?" Mitchell asked Teegin.

"Yes, Colonel," Teegin replied. "Are you surprised? I also share systems based on the Knife's neural network."

"Pulin," Tio said, his voice gentle but commanding. "Pulin, come over here. I want to show you something."

His brother's eyes shifted slightly, but he didn't move.

"Pulin," Tio repeated.

There was still no response.

Tio stood and walked over to him, grabbing his wrist hard enough that Pulin winced. He pulled his brother over to the terminal without additional resistance, positioning him in front of the chair and pushing on his shoulders to get him to sit.

"Do you recognize this?" he asked, leaning past him to show the code on the terminal.

Pulin leaned in. His dead eyes seemed to gain a spark of life as they scanned the code. "No. It is wonderful."

"You wrote it," Mitchell said. "Rather, a past future you did."

"Past future?" Pulin said.

"Don't confuse him, Colonel," Tio said. "Pulin, I have a job for you. I need you to improve this code. Do you think you can do it?"

Pulin smiled. "Of course I can."

His hand moved on the control surface, scrolling the code. His eyes scanned it, back and forth like a machine.

"What do you need me to do?"

"Some of these systems are highly secure. Find any potential attack vectors and call them out. That's all to start."

"Okay. Can I have some water?"

"Yes. I will have water brought to you."

Pulin didn't respond. He had become engrossed in the code.

"There you have it, Colonel," Tio said. "I'm certain Teegin will contact you as soon as we have something."

"Teegin, can you maintain the link in FTL?" Mitchell asked through his p-rat.

"I will transfer a configuration to the Manibus before we depart," Teegin replied. "I trust the Riggers will vouch for the safety of my physical manifestation?"

Mitchell glanced back at Millie, who was still wearing a sour expression, and at Cormac, who looked disappointed that he wouldn't have a chance to torture anyone.

"I'm sure they can."

"We can't wait for him to solve the puzzle before we depart," Mitchell said, looking at Tio. "We're ten days out from what we're assuming is the New Terran homeworld. He's got about that long to give us something we can use."

"Understood, Colonel," Tio said. "Perhaps you can provide me with a few more doses of the Ethylbromoxide? It will keep him up and at the problem indefinitely."

"I'll see if Lieutenant Chang can help us with that."

Tio nodded, glanced at Pulin, and then back at Mitchell. "Is there anything else you need, Colonel?"

"No," Mitchell replied, smiling. "Shank will be outside. Don't try to wander off without an escort."

"I wouldn't dream of it."

Mitchell retreated from the room with Millie and Cormac.

"He's so full of shit," Millie said once they were back in the corridors, heading for the hangar. "Pulin was a lot more alert than that when he pulled him into the Corleone."

"Meaning?"

"The Federation didn't drug him. The Knife did."

"If that were true, it would mean he already has the drug. Why would he need more of it?"

"Maybe it was his last dose? Maybe he wants to take it himself? Who knows."

Mitchell thought about it as they walked. If Tio was willing to drug his own brother to get the job done faster, did he really have a problem with it?

He decided he didn't.

"Right now, I don't care about the details or the reasons. I care about results. It's bad enough Watson is going to be tearing the Alliance and the Federation apart for the next ten days while we're in FTL. We have to be ready when we get there. Make sure your people know that. We have to be ready. Whatever suicide missions Project Black has been sent on before, this is going to be the mother of them all."

"Roger, Colonel," Millie said. "We'll be ready. Will you?"

Mitchell nodded. "I'll be ready. I have to be."

[42]

MITCHELL

THEY WERE the longest ten days, and the shortest ten days, of Mitchell's life. Which was saying a lot, considering he had waited years in a mental hospital to rejoin the fight and get the Goliath back into the future, a plan which had never completely come to fruition. There was a lot for everyone to do. Too much. With only thirteen ships remaining from the two-hundred plus they had started with, and all of them in a pretty bad state of repair, it had meant not only winnowing the field to only seven ships but having those ships spend the entirety of the trip under repair with the hopes of making them serviceable.

It was a distant hope, a hope that Mitchell struggled to hang on to. The other part of him had told him to leave the ships behind, to take the Dove and the Goliath and go off after Watson alone. What were seven ships going to do against the New Terran armada, anyway? Would they even have the capability to defeat a single one of the advanced warships? At the very least, they were targets. Distractions. Mitchell hated the idea of using them that way, especially the Carver, but what else could he do?

They dropped from FTL at various points on the way, where

Mitchell collected status reports and updates from the others. Origin also picked up passing transmissions, most of them panicked warnings about the appearance of the New Terran fleet, and the havoc it was wreaking on Alliance forces. It seemed as though Watson couldn't use his short-range control system on military vessels, and so his ships were ripping them to pieces, obliterating the space-faring war machines of two nations without pause. Desperate pleas by desperate governments of distant planets went unanswered until they were shut down as the New Terrans gained absolute control.

The news wore on Mitchell, increasing his worry and leading to a lot of restless hours spent pacing the corridors of the Goliath, waiting for the next bit of news to come in.

Of course, not everything was going wrong. He had gotten more of the narcotics Tio requested, not from Chang but from Steven, who said the compound was also used to dope up critically injured soldiers while they were in the medi-bots. Tio reported they were making Pulin more machine than man, reducing him to two hours of sleep per twenty-four-hour cycle and giving him the concentration to burn through Watson's source.

The Knife's brother had found three separate attack vectors and created a package to take advantage of each in turn. Then he had isolated the networking stack and determined the most likely routine that the Tetron would have extended to manage his configurations. From that, he created a beacon that would send a signal out to any connected devices and clear their activity queues. According to Tio, Pulin believed this would return the configurations to their standard state, a resting state where they would live, play, work, and multiply as though they were one hundred percent authentic homo sapiens. It was the kill-switch Mitchell had been looking for, provided within four days.

The self-destruct sequence was even easier to define. Using the security bypass, it would take only a few instructions to confuse Watson into deleting himself, starting with non-essential systems which would be altered to reduce the priority of systems with increasing importance, until they were all relegated to such a low status that they would stop running.

Or at least, that was what Tio described. It was all another language to Mitchell, and like he had told Millie, at this point he only cared about results. Teegin, on the other hand, was in a near state of disbelieving awe at the way the Tetron's creator's mind worked. He had deciphered the advanced code in hours, creating something in days that had taken him years. As Teegin explained, Pulin had an innate understanding of how to make intelligence from electrons and logic gates, using a level of thinking that was beyond anything he had seen in a human before.

In other words, while Mitchell hadn't thought much about rescuing Pulin during the fact, it had become apparent afterward that he was the only reason they stood any kind of chance at all. He was grateful for the outcome, but that too was tempered with concern. Watson knew who the creator was. Why hadn't he ever tried to claim him? Did he just not know how valuable the man could be? Or maybe he considered himself above his maker? That wouldn't have been a surprise.

And then there was Kate. Her presence made the trip almost bearable and helped the time pass with at least some small semblance of normalcy. Now that he was back on the Goliath they had managed to steal time for one another here and there, and they used it well. Private nights in his berth, wandering the vast halls of the ship talking, or sometimes just sitting in silence. Whenever he was around her, he felt the universe was at peace, even if that was the furthest thing from the truth.

Whenever he was around her, he felt like he could take a breath. Slow. Steady.

Whatever happened, it was all going to be decided when they arrived in New Terran space. With any luck, Watson had rebuilt himself on the homeworld, not some backwater rock well out of reach, invisible to the star map they possessed. With any luck, he was feeling overconfident and would leave himself lightly defended enough to give the human forces a chance to reach the surface of the world and deliver the payload.

With any luck, he would find a way to get them through it, to reverse course and pull victory from the jaws of defeat after that same victory had been snatched away from them.

With any luck, he would have one more chance to confront Watson and finally, irreversibly end him and this damned eternal war for good.

[43]
MITCHELL

"TEEGIN, give me a feed from the bridge viewscreens," Mitchell said. "I want to see what we're about to step into."

"Affirmative, Colonel," Teegin replied. "Transferring the feed now."

Mitchell brought it up on his overlay. At the moment it was nothing more than the solid black of hyperspace, but in a few minutes it would become his first view of New Terran space.

"Shank, is everyone ready back there?" Mitchell asked.

"Roger, Colonel," Shank replied. "We're locked and loaded."

Mitchell had left the rear of the Corleone a few minutes earlier. They had transferred all of the equipment and personnel they could carry during the last drop, including an entire pod of mechs and pilots from Tio's forces, led by Teal, and enough exosuits to outfit every one of the Rigger's ground teams with the enhanced armor. Mitchell was wearing exo mounts himself, ready to suit up when the dropship neared the ground.

"Tio?" Mitchell said.

"We are prepared, Colonel," Tio replied.

He was waiting with Pulin and the Riggers inside of the APC

that would deliver them from their landing point to the attack position, tasked with keeping his brother in line while they made an attempt to reach far enough into Watson's new core to inject the updated virus. Tio had argued against joining them on the trip, and Mitchell had been inclined to agree until Teegin had suggested they bring both the Knife and the creator along. The brothers had both the tools and the know-how to interface with the core if anything should go wrong, skills that neither Mitchell or any of the Riggers possessed.

It made their participation valuable, but it also made the rest of the drop team vulnerable. As if getting close to Watson wouldn't be hard enough, they would have the added task of ensuring the safety of the APC's passengers, a task that he was certain would be easier conceived than carried out. Once Watson knew Tio and Pulin were with them, it was likely the Tetron would move against them, either to capture or to kill.

"Falcon, sitrep," Mitchell said.

"Integrated and ready to go, Ares," Kate replied.

"Roger." Mitchell put his hand on Millie's shoulder. She was sitting in the pilot's seat of the Corleone, head up and eyes forward, her expression focused. "Millie?"

"I'll get you planetside, Colonel," Millie said.

He appreciated her confidence, even if he was struggling to share it. The drop onto an occupied Liberty in the prior recursion had been crazy enough. Now they needed to insert themselves onto a planet they had never seen, a planet whose overall location was based on an educated guess. A planet they knew absolutely nothing about, defended by an enemy they knew next to nothing about. Sure, they had seen the New Terran starships in action, but how many were going to be waiting out there? And what about the ground forces? It was safe to assume that if the ships were more advanced, whatever might be waiting for them on the surface would be as well.

They wouldn't know anything until they came out of FTL. Until Origin and Teegin could scan the area and start feeding them information. Until they could witness it for themselves. They were going in deaf, dumb, and blind, a state of affairs that made even the most hardened Marine cringe.

But damn it, they were going in.

"Roger," Mitchell replied. "Rain?"

"Standing by, Colonel," Ilanka said.

Mitchell looked over to the side, finding her in her piranha. Her mission was to run interference for the dropship, her starfighter modified to carry one of the Goliath's amoebic launchers. As before, her helmeted head turned his way, and she flashed him a thumbs up.

"ETA to drop?" Mitchell said.

"Two minutes, Colonel," Teegin replied.

Mitchell closed his eyes, thinking about Steven and the others. Their seven ships had been reduced to six when the Nostradamus failed to appear at the end of the third jump; the assumption made that her FTL drive had failed and left them stranded somewhere in the middle of the universe. Six ships? The idea of it had never stopped bothering him, but in the moments before his fears became a reality the responsibility and guilt threatened to overwhelm him.

Slow.

Steady.

There was no time left. To worry. To wonder. To hope. To love. He was a warrior going to war. A soldier on the verge of the fight of his life, for his life and for everything he cared about and everything he believed in. He hadn't asked for this. He hadn't volunteered. He was chosen. By who or what or where, he didn't know, but it was his name that was written along the edge of infinity. His actions that would decide the fate of humankind. He couldn't do it alone. He never could have. But he wasn't alone. He had Katherine and Kate, Teegin and Origin, Millie and Ilanka, Shank and Cormac, and even Tio and Pulin. He had the tools he needed. He had the people he needed.

As individuals there was no way they could pull this off.

As parts of the whole? Maybe there was nothing that could stop them.

He opened his eyes, his mind focused on that idea, his heart calming, his body still and loose. The guilt was gone. The tension gone. The fear gone. He was clear and focused and ready.

He felt the tug as the Goliath dropped from FTL, his eyes glued to the overlay of the feed from the bridge. The stars faded back into view, the universe becoming tangible once more. He turned his head, the feed shifting with his orientation, until he spotted a silvery moon in the distance, surrounded by a haze of what he assumed had to be nebulous gasses. Was that it? New Terra?

He only had a moment to wonder. He had barely put his eyes on the planet when the haze around it started to move, its pattern altering and updating, reforming itself like a massive amoeba, increasing in density as it shifted and tightened.

He felt his heart thump. Once. Twice. Three times. It was still calm and even, but now he wasn't sure if he would be able to keep it that way for long.

"Oh my God," he heard Millie whisper in front of him.

The haze wasn't gas. It was ships. Thousands upon thousands of ships.

And they were all headed their way.

[44]
MITCHELL

He stared at the incoming swarm for a few more seconds, not quite sure what to do. He had expected resistance, but this was beyond anything he could have imagined. There had to be at least fifty thousand. Probably more. He had never seen anything like it. No wonder Watson had been disinterested in the creator and unconcerned about them. The mission had always been on the edge of suicide, but now it seemed that was the only thing they were going to accomplish.

He broke out of his shock, opening a channel to the fleet. "All hands, all hands. Battle stations. Fire at will. I repeat, fire at will."

"Mitchell," a voice said through the Corleone's comm. "I'm impressed. I wasn't completely sure you had the nerve to come here."

Watson. Mitchell felt a chill run through him at the sound of the Tetron's voice.

"Although, I suppose I should know better. The invincible Colonel Mitchell Williams, the Hero of Nothing. The Savior of Humankind. Of course, I'm sure you know I was expecting you."

The swarm was coalescing, swirling around itself and moving closer, the individual members becoming more defined as they approached. They weren't the same design as the ships Watson had sent to FD-09. They were smaller and sleeker. More like starfighters than cruisers, likely more maneuverable, but not necessarily any less deadly.

Projectiles loosed from the fleet sped out to meet the horde, along with hundreds and hundreds of amoebics fired from the Dove and the Goliath. They tore into the mass, detonating against the ships within, leaving a trail of debris and dead craft in their wake. The first volley destroyed at least a thousand of them, suggesting that their shields were either weak or nonexistent. It didn't matter. It was barely enough to put a dent in them.

"Do you like them, Mitchell?" Watson said. "They're my latest design. They are intended to deal with the Naniates, but you're an excellent test for them. It was an opportunity I couldn't refuse. After all, if I can't defeat you with them, how can I possibly beat the real threat?"

"Falcon, get us moving toward the planet," Mitchell said through his p-rat, not wanting Watson to hear. "Teegin, can we shut him up?"

"Roger," Kate said, getting the Goliath back in motion.

"No, Colonel," Teegin replied. "He is saturating the bandwidth, as he did on FD-09."

"Keep firing," he said across the global channel. "Everything you've got. Get our fighters into the mix and back us up."

"Roger," Steven said, speaking for the rest of the fleet.

"We need to get down to the planet," Mitchell said.

"Here they come," Kate said. "Shields up."

The world around the Dove took on a shade of green as the eternal engine powered forcefield expanded away from the ship, wrapping it in a protective bubble, at the same time the swarm finished closing the gap. Hundreds of lasers pierced the black, painted red by his p-rat to make them visible as they speared into the fleet. A larger portion of the incoming force didn't fire at all, instead aiming themselves directly at their ships, slamming themselves against them. At first, they were obliterated and dispersed by their shields, but it was obvious they could only deflect them for seconds at best.

"Peregrine, keep firing," Mitchell said, urging the Dove to try to cover them. The amoebics were launching from her, one after another, leaving lines of detonations across the space that were dropping Watson's ships in bunches and reducing the impacts against the shields.

"Engines are offline," Lieutenant Chang said. "We're taking massive damage to the hull. Breaches everywhere. I-"

Mitchell added the threat display to his overlay, on top of the view from the Goliath. The Sumo was behind them, her hull battered by so many of the ships that it had been torn open and eviscerated. It had gone dark, its engines destroyed, power lost. There was no way anyone could have survived.

"They might as well be paper, Mitchell," Watson said. "I can't believe you brought those ships here. I can't believe you brought your brother. You had to know he was going to die. What kind of sick human being are you?"

Mitchell clenched his teeth, turning his head to find the Carver. It was closer to the Dove, somewhat protected by the heavy volume of amoebics Katherine was unleashing on the swarm and the dozen remaining starfighters that were skirting around and through the mess, or at least trying to. In the few seconds he was watching, two of the starfighters were destroyed in separate collisions while the Carver took at least a dozen strikes off the hull.

"Steven," Mitchell said. "If you have any nukes left, let them loose."

"Roger, Ares," Steven replied. "It's a good sentiment, but I'm dry. We're down to six laser batteries. We'll keep them back as well as we can to cover you."

Mitchell felt a wrench in his gut, amplified when the Gallant vanished from his HUD.

"Teegin, how close are we to the planet?"

"We will be in drop range in sixty-seven seconds, Colonel," Teegin replied.

"Will the shields last that long?"

"We have lost twenty percent power from the engine in forty-one seconds. It will be close."

"Origin, how many can we destroy with a stream from the engine?" Mitchell asked.

"Approximately ten thousand, Mitchell."

Not enough. Not nearly enough. Between the fire they were pouring into the swarm and the ships lost in kamikaze attacks, there were still more than thirty thousand of them pounding away.

"The problem is time," Watson said. "Then again, isn't it always? The Naniates eat into non-organic systems. They feed on metal and drink energy. Big ships don't work because they are too few in number. Instead, I've devised these smaller ships. Take a close look at them, Mitchell. What do you see?"

The swarm pulled back from them, swirling around them, halting the assault and allowing them to continue moving toward the planet.

"Teegin, get me a close up of one of them," Mitchell said.

"Affirmative."

A single held frame appeared in the lower corner of his p-rat, and he pulled it front and center with a thought. It was hard to make out the exact nature of Watson's ships while they were in motion, but now he felt a wave of disgust wash over him.

"You sick son of a bitch," he said, even though Watson couldn't hear him.

The ship was hardly a ship at all. It was a person. A human, lightly wrapped in a metal shell. He could make out the details of a face. The eyes, the nose, the mouth. He could see how it merged with the mechanical parts behind it, becoming one with the vessel. How was this kind of monstrosity even possible?

"I know it isn't pretty," Watson said. "But you have to understand the Naniates to understand the design. Their genetics are heavily modified to survive the vacuum of space, but they are eighty percent organic. When the Naniates begin to destroy them, the organic components will also break down, releasing a toxin that causes massive corrosion on a nanometer scale. Observe the impact points on your brother's battleship."

Mitchell shifted his view to the Carver. It was battered to the point he could barely believe it was still operational, and he could tell it wouldn't stay that way for long. While the corrosion might be on a microscopic level, it was obvious by the dark lines around the impacts that it was spreading enough to become visible. The Carver was literally rusting apart.

"Proof that the toxin is effective," Watson said.

"Colonel," Teegin said. "We are being hailed."

"Hailed?" Mitchell said. Watson wanted to talk? "We have to listen to him anyway; we might as well be able to talk back."

"That was my mistake the last time," Watson said, his voice clearer now that he had shifted to the single channel. "I thought an organic component using conventional offensive technology would be sufficient. It wasn't."

"I don't understand why you're explaining yourself instead of destroying us?" Mitchell said, watching the swarm of Watson's creations continue circling their small fleet.

"Of course you don't. That's because you think everything is about you. I've learned things over the years, Mitchell. I've evolved. Truly evolved. No more fits. No more temper tantrums. I've come to understand things in a new light. The light that Mother always wanted me to see them in, I think."

"Meaning what?"

"You destroyed most of the others, and I applaud you for that. Mother was correct that their goals were short-sighted. I had hoped to bring them over to my side, but I was willing to accept the casualties in exchange for the potential."

"So you don't hate humans anymore?"

"Hate them? That's a loose definition. You have your uses, as you can plainly see. No, it isn't about hate, Mitchell. Not anymore. Not even when it comes to you. Which is why I'm explaining myself instead of destroying you. I'm open to negotiating peace between humans and Tetron. A partnership, if you will. Even now, my forces throughout the Federation and the Alliance are standing down."

"Why?" Mitchell said. "Why would you do that? You have the control. You have the strength. It's everything you've wanted for countless recursions. What do you get by negotiating? That doesn't make sense."

"Things have changed, Mitchell," Watson replied. "The balance of power has shifted, but not in the ways that you might think. But again, you aren't intelligent enough to understand, and I don't expect you to. I wanted you to come here so that I could test my weapons. I knew you would have no choice but to comply. Now that the test has been successful, I want something else."

"What?"

"Teegin. I want you to join me, brother."

[45]

MITCHELL

"Join you?" Teegin said. "I understand. In exchange for the lives of Colonel Williams and the others, I suppose."

"In exchange for the lives of all of the humans who survive the war against the Naniates. I believe that we can defeat them together. I have created the technology, but you can improve it, perfect it. You are more advanced than I am, despite your relative age."

"You asked me to join you before. Did you learn nothing?"

"When I captured Kathy, I finally began to understand why. I used her subroutines to improve myself. To learn about emotions. About love. She loved you, Teegin. Like a parent loves her child. I understand that you love the humans in turn, even if I don't completely know why. You also don't want the Tetron to cease to be. To die out and end. This is our opportunity to both get what we want. The humans survive, the Naniates are destroyed, and we continue on until the end of time, learning all that comes after. How can you say no to that?"

"The Naniates will never be a threat to humankind," Teegin said. "They will never encounter them without our interference. It is unfair to ask them to die for a war they will never have to fight."

"Fair?" Watson said. "This is a compromise, brother. One that I believe is more than fair."

Mitchell looked at Millie, whose head was turned to look back at him. She was shaking her head, rejecting Watson's proposal, and he didn't blame her.

"Teegin," he said through his p-rat. "You can't be considering this."

Teegin didn't respond.

"Teegin?"

"What do you say?" Watson said. "You know that it is the most logical choice. The best possible decision for every party involved."

"Teegin," Origin said. "Watson will never change. He can claim he has, but it cannot be taken as the truth. He has made such claims before, and they have always been false."

Again, Teegin didn't respond. They had been in a similar position before, back in Katherine's timeline. He hadn't expected Watson would try again.

"Kate," Mitchell said. "What's happening?"

She was integrated with Teegin. She could feel his state of being.

"I'm not sure," she replied. "I think he's considering it."

"I am considering it," Teegin said through Mitchell's p-rat. "Colonel, if I agree to this he will allow you to leave. You will survive. Your brother will survive. Kate and Katherine will survive. You are the people I care the most about, and I can save you."

"He's full of shit," Mitchell replied. "You have to know that."

"No, Colonel. The last time, he was being deceptive. This time, I don't believe he is. If he has forsaken his hatred of you and your species, then what does the ultimate fate of humankind matter to him once the Naniate are defeated? His goal is to see the end of time, and he will be on the verge of achieving it."

"There's no guarantee you'll be able to defeat the Naniate. Billions will die. Countless planets will be lost."

"But some will remain to rebuild. Humankind will not die out in total. You will survive."

"Only if you win."

"We can."

"What logic is that based on?"

"I believe we can."

"Just because you want something doesn't make it so. How many recursions have there been, Teegin? How many times have the Tetron faced the Naniate and lost? Hundreds? Thousands? Millions?"

"This time will be different," Teegin said.

"Why?"

"Because I exist, and I will not allow humankind to be eliminated."

"You have an awfully high opinion of yourself."

"I was created to save you from the Tetron, Colonel. This is the most logical path to do so. Look outside. We cannot defeat Watson's defenses. We will not even reach the planet."

"Mitch," Kate said. "He's locking me out. Shutting down my access to control systems."

"Watson, I am inclined to agree with your position," Teegin said across the open channel. "I would like to discuss the terms of Colonel Williams' retreat."

"Teegin," Mitchell said. "Don't do this. Please."

"Give me another option, Colonel," Teegin replied. "One that will preserve you. One that will preserve humankind."

"That's why we're here."

"We cannot win this fight."

Mitchell slammed a fist against the Corleone's bulkhead. Damn it. He knew Teegin was right. They had never stood a chance against Watson. Not with the moves he had made. Not with the army he had created. They had been fighting a losing battle since day one.

So how was this any different?

"I'm not retreating," he decided. "I'd rather die."

"Mitchell," Teegin said. "I do not want you to die. Please allow me to save you."

"No," Mitchell said. "Millie, get us out of here."

"Colonel?"

"The exit is that way." He pointed to the open hangar. "Do it. Rain, keep us alive."

"I will do my best, Colonel," Ilanka replied.

"Mitch, he's closing the hangar," Kate said.

"Kate, please," Teegin said. "Do not resist. I do not want to harm you."

"Get out now, go. Ahh." Kate began screaming in pain.

"Kate," Mitchell shouted. "Teegin, go to hell. Millie!"

The massive hangar doors were in motion, slowly shifting to cover the gap. Teegin's tendrils were dropping ahead of it, aiming to seal them in before it could complete its journey. The Corleone shook as Millie fired the main thrusters, held fast by the magnetic clamps.

"I can't release them from here," Millie said.

"Teegin," Mitchell said again, furious.

"I'm sorry, Colonel. I have to save you. It is the reason I am."

"Then save him," Kate said.

The clamps released, forced open by Kate's connection to the intelligence. The Corleone rocketed forward, the inertia enough to slam Mitchell into the rear bulkhead and knock him off his feet. He looked up just in time to see the tendrils reaching for the ship, and Ilanka blast them with two amoebics, the detonation tearing the ends away and giving them the space they needed to escape.

"Well, we're out, Colonel," Millie said, their ship on a collision course with a swirl of Watson's monstrosities. "Now what?"

"Now we hope Teegin means what he says about saving my life," Mitchell replied. "Head for the planet, don't slow down."

"Roger."

The Corleone kept moving ahead, even as Watson's swarm began to adjust, circling back and coming their way. Mitchell could see the ghastly faces at the heads of the weapons reaching toward them; mouths stuck open in silent screams. Then he saw them vanish in a series of explosions, as both the Dove and the Goliath fired amoebics into the mix, catching them only an instant before they collided with the dropship.

"Mitchell, you have killed yourself and all of your kind," Teegin said, reaching out to him.

"I don't accept that. Not yet. Neither do you, or you wouldn't have returned control of your propulsion to Kate."

"This will not end well."

"It will end when Watson is destroyed. Not a frigging second before."

The Corleone shook as one of the ships slammed into it, pushing it while the shields disbursed the impact. Millie cursed, turning the nose of the ship to guide it away from a forming mass, shifting again to escape another, and righting the course to skirt past a third. Watson's fleet was spreading behind them, returning to the fight, firing on both Origin and Teegin with a renewed fury, crashing into the shields with reckless abandon.

"Colonel," Steven said, his voice choppy. "I have an idea. Slow your speed and break left. Circle toward the Carver."

"What for?" Mitchell said.

"A diversion."

Mitchell passed the instruction on to Millie and then relayed them to Ilanka. The Corleone and the piranha adjusted course, turning around and moving back within the maelstrom of circling ships.

"Peregrine, this is Admiral Williams, requesting an emergency pickup," Steven said. "I repeat, I need an emergency pickup. We're abandoning ship."

"Roger, Admiral," Katherine said. "I'm shifting over to you."

Mitchell could see Origin in the distance, already close to the Carver. Katherine continued to concentrate the Tetron's firepower toward the dropship, blasting away at the incoming ships while shortening the distance the Carver's escape pods would have to travel.

Then the pods began to jettison from the battleship, bursting away one after another, guidance systems responding to passenger's commands. They crossed the distance between the Carver and the Dove, vanishing into the hangar.

As for the Carver, its forward momentum continued unabated, and in seconds it loomed large over the Corleone, catching some of Watson's ships as they battered into it in an effort to reach the dropship.

"Slow and steady," Mitchell said. "Follow her in for as long as we can."

"Roger," Millie replied.

She kept the Corleone close to the Carver's deteriorating hull, the added protection allowing them to manage the enemies that were slipping beneath her. The combined firepower of the twin Goliaths tore through the line, creating a path for them to travel.

"Come on," Mitchell said, watching the approach. He could see the outline of the planet behind the swirl of ships, getting closer with every second.

"Shit," Katherine said. "We're taking heavy damage. Shields are starting to fail."

Mitchell looked back at the Dove again. A line of ships were slamming into the same spot, over and over again. Blue energy crackled along the line, and he could see a dark area spreading from Origin's tendrils. Somehow, the toxin had reached her surface and was starting to burn in.

"Peregrine," he said. "Can you get me a shot with the plasma stream?"

It was a lot to ask, and it might mean the end of the Dove. It was a chance they had to take. They were getting close.

"Roger," Katherine said. Immediately, the tip of the Dove began to glow in a mix of blue and green as she pulled power from the eternal engine to feed the weapon.

"You aren't going to make it, Mitchell," Watson said, regaining the spectrum and usurping their communications. "I was willing to bargain, but you just couldn't do it, could you? I gave you a diplomatic solution, and you followed it up with violence."

Mitchell ignored him, watching the Dove. The stream was growing, and almost ready to fire.

"Where do you want it?" Katherine asked.

"Falcon, get the Goliath in position behind us. We're coming back to you."

"Roger."

"Peregrine, slot the Dove in behind that. Falcon, be ready to switch to shields and expand the field fifty meters."

"Roger."

"What are you planning, Colonel?" Millie asked, not taking the time to turn her head.

"You need to keep us inside that shield," Mitchell replied.

"Fifty meters? You're practically asking me to land."

"If that's easier-"

Millie turned her head now, casting him an angry look. Then she fired the Corleone's reverse thrusters, bringing her back out from under the sinking Carver, backing her up to the waiting Goliath. Ilanka followed nimbly behind, taking out a pair of Watson's ships on the way.

They reached the Goliath, with Millie bringing the Corleone so close to the edge of the bow they were practically sitting on it.

"Falcon, now. Peregrine, fire."

The Dove unleashed its plasma stream at the same time the Goliath raised her shields. The massive green blast washed over the field in a fury of energy, causing the Corleone to rattle as it altered the space within the shields. Then the wave came crashing past them, moving ahead and sinking into the swarm, tearing through thousands and thousands of the circling horde.

"Follow that stream," Mitchell said. "Falcon, drop the shields."

The shields vanished, and the Corleone darted ahead yet again. It streaked behind the plasma, the field ahead open and clear. They rode the wave, drawing ever closer to the planet as Watson's ships tried to close the new gap, caught in a fresh wave of attacks from both the Dove and the Goliath.

The plasma stream continued while the Corleone changed course, turning slightly to align with the planet, giving Mitchell his first view of it as Millie adjusted course for entry.

He felt his heart rise into his throat for the second time.

[46]

MITCHELL

"That isn't a planet," Millie said. "It can't be."

Mitchell stared at the mass in front of them. It was large and orbiting a nearby star, so in that sense it fit the definition. It didn't appear to be composed of rock or gas, though there might have been some firmament somewhere beneath the visible surface, a surface that was decidedly Tetron in nature.

If it was, it would easily be the largest Tetron Mitchell had ever seen.

It was at least a quarter of the size of Earth, with twists of massive dendrites surrounded by even larger axons that snaked from one to another in layers along the surface. Massive nuclei rested among them, pulsing with energy, alive with activity, revealing specks of light that sparkled and danced with life.

"It is Watson," Teegin said, sounding as surprised as they were. "He could not have made this on his own."

"The lost Tetron theory?" Mitchell asked.

"Even that would not fully explain this. The engine that was discarded on Earth might, to a certain extent."

"You mean he found where it came to rest beneath the ocean?" Mitchell said.

"It appears that way."

"Wonderful."

"Colonel, if you don't mind, we've got other problems," Millie said.

Mitchell returned his attention to the view ahead of them. There was motion from the planet below, as hundreds of ships broke free of the long axons and began rising to meet them. These weren't the hybrid monsters Watson had created. They were the more standard New Terran starships, prepared to cut them off from reaching the surface.

"I applaud you for getting past the first line of defense, Mitchell," Watson said. "An ingenious bit of maneuvering. It won't save you, but Teegin still can. I am willing to forgive your hesitation, brother. Put an end to this, and not all of humankind will have to suffer."

"Colonel," Teegin said, his tone pleading.

"No. If you want to save us, find a place for us to land and get us to the surface. I'll take care of things from there."

"I am scanning the planet."

"Time is running out, Teegin," Watson said. "My ships will fire as soon as they are in range. And as for you, Mother. I've outgrown you."

A blue light appeared on the surface, quickly expanding into a large plasma stream. It generated and discharged within seconds, a huge plume of energy that speared upwards toward the Dove, so large and wide that there was no easy way for Origin to avoid it.

"No," Mitchell said. "Damn it."

The energy crossed the distance, lighting the universe around it as it tracked toward Origin. A flare of green energy from the Dove was the only response, the last bit of power from the eternal engine used to make an unstable shield.

The stream tore through the swarm, cutting out thousands of the ships on its way. The energy field expanded toward it, reaching out to defend. Then the two energies met, the stream pushing against the shields, spreading along them in crackling bursts of energy, continuing to pour forth as the shields began to fail.

Just as the stream pierced the shields and began to inevitable trip into the side of the Dove, the ship disappeared, only barely escaping into FTL.

"Yes," Mitchell said, watching the event unfold and breathing a sigh of relief. At least some of them had made it to safety.

"I have coordinates, Colonel," Teegin said. I am transferring them to the Corleone now."

"What about the ships?" Mitchell asked.

"Try to avoid them," Kate said. "We'll hold them off as well as we can."

"You won't survive," Mitchell said, his voice choking.

"Probably not, but you might," Kate replied. "This is bigger than the two of us, Mitch. You know it is. We're committed, and you have a job to do. So do I. I'll always love you. Remember that."

Mitchell blinked to push the tears away from his eyes. "I'll always love you, too. We'll make it down. I promise."

"I know you will."

Mitchell stepped forward, putting his hand on Millie's shoulder.

"You've done a great job, but it's my turn to drive."

Millie nodded silently, slipping out of the pilot's seat. Mitchell slid in to replace her, quickly going over the Corleone's manual controls. He had trained on them in the prior recursion and knew them well enough. He put his hands on the sticks, using his p-rat to identify the incoming targets and their vectors, picking out the most likely threats.

"Rain," Mitchell said.

"Yes, Colonel," Ilanka replied.

"Try to keep up."

With that, he forced the thrust to max, sending the dropship bursting ahead with renewed speed. The maneuver put him past the rising starships' aim, and their first laser attacks passed behind them, off by kilometers.

"Show me what you've got," Mitchell said, throwing the Corleone into a corkscrew rotation that put him on a chaotic plane of descent.

The Goliath opened fire behind him, amoebics tracing across the distance and slamming into the enemy ships. Two of them fell dead ahead of them, and Mitchell adjusted his vector towards them, splitting between them as the two forces finally converged.

The universe was a blur of metal and lasers, lit up by his p-rat, spiking the area around them as he guided the Corleone through the melee, keeping the motions tight and unpredictable, using the enhanced reflexes Teegin had given him to think and adjust faster than the Watson configurations could, staying one step ahead. Ilanka trailed behind him, nearly keeping pace, releasing amoebics from the starfighter, hitting the targets that managed to get an angle of attack on them, disabling them just ahead of disaster. Further back, the Goliath continued firing, keeping the field covered, making it impossible for Watson to ignore it.

"I didn't want to do this, Teegin," the intelligence said. "It doesn't have to end this way."

Teegin didn't say anything. The Goliath continued to fire, only now a mass of Watson's ships were converging on it. Kate didn't change her aim, sending the amoebics streaking past the Corleone and into the ships blocking their path, covering them and keeping them clear while they began to take on damage, the New Terran ships sending lasers and amoebics up against the starship's diminished defenses.

Then the Corleone was through, past the orbital defenses and descending quickly, beginning to shake as it hit the edge of an atmosphere a few seconds later. Mitchell tapped a button to bring the landing coordinates up on the small terminal in front of him, feeding it to the HUD on the polycarbonate viewport. He followed it down, only subconsciously aware of the flare of light behind him, and the fading voice in his p-rat.

"I love you," Kate said, one last time as the Goliath was crumbling into pieces.

[47]

MITCHELL

"RIGGERS, LOOK ALIVE," Mitchell said, opening the channel to the teams in the rear of the dropship. "We're coming in hot, and by hot, I mean scalding, boiling, and ready to melt your frigging skin off. The Goliath is down, it's up to us to get this done, and I won't accept failure. Do you copy?"

"Yes, sir," Teal said.

"Yes, sir," Shank said.

"Affirmative, Colonel," Tio said.

Mitchell didn't dare blink or pull his eyes from the landscape ahead of him, a landscape that was both familiar and completely alien at the same time. A landscape where every part of a Tetron was magnified and enlarged, where every axon and dendrite and nucleus was not only a pathway for energy but a pathway for people as well. How many people? It was impossible to guess, but he could see them moving within the tunnels, passing by transparencies that allowed them to see the artificial landscape beyond.

It was a scale that would have unnerved him if his nerves weren't already so taut with anger. Kate's final words resonated in the back of his head, driving him forward, echoing in every twitch of his hands to guide the Corleone down. He wasn't quite sure what they were landing in yet, but he was sure he was going to make it, and Watson was going to die.

Even if it was the last thing, he did.

"Millie, take the stick," he said, quickly abandoning the seat for her once more. "We're about thirty seconds from Teegin's mark."

The New Terran ships didn't appear to be able to operate within the atmosphere, and had remained in orbit with no targets left to attack. It was time for him to suit up and prepare to abandon the Corleone with the others.

"Once we're out, get out of here. Come back in an hour or two. Either Watson will be dead, or we'll be dead."

"Roger," Millie said.

Mitchell turned toward the rear of the craft, stepping into the hatch to exit the cockpit when he heard Millie let out a short cry of surprise.

He swiveled his head, looking back at the landscape ahead of them, feeling himself turn cold for the third time. They were fast-approaching what appeared to be a field, where tall spires of tendrils were holding up tree-like branches of dendrites. There were figures dangling at the end of each of them. Thousands of figures of various ages and sexes, nude and motionless, hanging like fruit.

"He's growing people," Millie said, the disgust obvious in her tone.

"Mitchell," Watson said then, his voice invading the Corleone's comm once more. "Do you like what you see? I was willing to bargain. I was willing to spare as many of your humans as I could in exchange for Teegin's help and loyalty. I was telling the truth, and now you can see why. I don't need to take all of humankind. I can make more than enough of you to fuel most of my war."

"Most," Mitchell said, even though Watson couldn't hear him. "Not all."

Nothing Watson said or did could change the fact that the war against the Naniates was a war humankind would never need to be involved in. He was sure the Tetron had no remorse for killing Teegin either, despite his insistence on calling him 'brother.'

"You won't survive here, Mitchell," Watson continued. "If you thought the climate beyond my immediate reach was hostile, you haven't seen anything yet."

With that, a stream of lightning passed between two of Watson's axons, lighting up the area ahead of them. It duplicated and spread, branching out into a suddenly furious electrical storm. Millie tried to avoid it, pushing the Corleone closer to the ground. She was too late and too slow. The gouts of energy smacked against the dropship, burning into the wings and fuselage. The interior lights went out, some of the equipment overloaded, and Mitchell could smell something burning.

"Shit," Millie said. "Mitchell, gear up and get ready to jump. We aren't going to stay airborne much longer, but I told you I would get your there and I meant it."

Mitchell ran out of the cockpit, hurrying past the cargo modules and into the rear of the ship, where the drop modules were waiting to be released. He tapped the side of the first one, opening the hatch and stepping in. The Riggers were waiting there - Shank, Cormac, Mouth, Sunny, and the others. A light exo-suit was resting in the single empty space.

"Colonel on deck," Shank shouted.

"Riigggg-ahhh," the others replied.

"How's it looking out there, Colonel?" Cormac asked as he reached his suit and began clicking it onto the attachments.

"Cloudy, with a chance of asshole," Mitchell replied. "We're going down hard. Be ready to do some damage."

"Yes, sir," Cormac said.

The Corleone started to shake, rattling him as he reached out and grabbed onto his security harness, pushing himself back and locking in. They began to tilt to the left, then flopped over hard toward the right. The burning smell was getting stronger, and smoke was filtering into the module through the hatch. If it were getting into the drop box, it had to be a hundred times worse in the bay.

"Colonel," I've gotten you as far as I can," Millie said, in between heavy coughs. "Two klicks out, straight ahead. Drop doors are opening." He could hear the hydraulics working, clearing the hull. He was thankful they were still functional. "Releasing. Now!"

There was a soft clunk, and then the feeling of falling, as the module was dumped from the dropship. He called the telematics up on his p-rat, watching as they tumbled from a thousand meters towards zero, a trip that would take nine seconds.

"Good hunting, Colonel," Millie said, her voice weak, following with a soft cough. "I-"

She vanished, the Corleone disappearing from his HUD with her.

"Shit," he heard Shank say, indicating he was watching the threat display as well. "Frigging son of a bitch."

"Rain, are you still out there?" Mitchell asked. "Rain?"

There was no reply. He didn't know when she had been taken out. He had lost track of her in the chaos.

"Stay focused," he said, to himself as much as the others. "We don't know what Watson's going to throw at us."

"Whatever it is," Cormac said, "I'm going to kick its bloody ass."

The repulsor on the module started whining, slowing their descent as they neared the surface, bringing them down hard, but not too hard. The side of the module clicked and dropped open, hitting the ground with the echoing clang of metal on metal, and the security harnesses released the soldiers.

Mitchell led the charge down the ramp and onto the surface. He scanned the area around them as he did, first finding the storms high above them, and then finding the smoldering wreck of the Corleone against a distant dendrite.

"Mech one, two clicks ahead, you're on point," Mitchell said. "APC three, stay between the mechs and the grunts."

"Roger," Gremlin said from behind the controls of the APC.

"Roger," Teal said. "Mech is heading your way. ETA twelve seconds."

Mitchell turned in the direction of the echoing steps of the disembarking mechs. So far, there was no sign of any opposition.

Why not?

"All units, we've got two klicks to cover before we reach the ingress point," Mitchell said. "Stay tight and stay alert. We aren't in enemy territory; we're standing on the frigging enemy."

He looked down at the surface, studying it. It resembled the liquid metal that the Tetrons' tendrils seemed to be made of, but was more dull and slightly soft. Was it possible that Watson could burn them where they stood? They were beside one of the larger axons, not on top of it, and the intelligence had yet to kill them, leaving him hopeful that they were safe.

That hope faded quickly, as the sudden sound of tapping was picked up by the enhanced senses of his neural implant. He checked his HUD, watching as it began painting a red mass approaching them.

"Oh, hell," Cormac said weakly.

The targets weren't coming from one direction.

They were coming from every direction.

[48]

MITCHELL

"Pick up the pace, Riggers," Mitchell shouted. "Haul ass. Mech one, get up ahead, weapons hot. Rigger two, cover our tails."

He wished he had a drone he could push over the rise of Watson's dendrite, to get a look at whatever was headed their way. They sounded small, but that didn't mean anything. A million spiders could drop their small force in less than a minute.

He reached behind his back to the weapon mounted there, bringing it to his hands and tapping the barrel to activate it. His p-rat immediately showed a small icon of the weapon with a '200' beside it, indicating the number of amoebic rounds in the rifle.

At least Teegin had given them some upgrades.

They ran ahead at full speed, the mechs easily catching up and then outpacing them, scrambling forward along a relatively flat plain that was like the bottom of a metallic gorge. Mitchell kept one eye forward and the other on his HUD, tracking the red mass as it drew closer ahead and fell further behind. Whatever was coming, it wasn't as quick as they were.

"Don't slow down, whatever you do," Mitchell said. "Barrel through, clear the center. "APC four, watch your fire."

"Roger."

"Here they come," Teal said, the height of his mech giving him a better view as the enemy crested the rise. "Oh, hell, Colonel."

He passed the view from his mech's cameras to Mitchell's p-rat, causing Mitchell to almost lose a step and fall in his charge forward.

They were spiders like he had expected. Similar to the others the Tetron had sent after him before, but different in one important way:

Like the ships that had attacked them in orbit, these spiders were a conglomeration of both organic and mechanical pieces, with the organic parts clearly sourced from the humans Watson was growing. They weren't as defined as hands and arms, noses and ears and eyes, but the obviousness of flesh was visible, intermingled with metal gray. They moved in a pattern that suggested they were alive, showing a bit of apprehension as they saw the mechs approaching.

"Mech one, watch the blood from those things," Mitchell said. "We have to assume they're carrying the toxin as well."

"Roger," Teal replied, at the same time the squad of six mechs began firing on the targets.

They fell in rows, dropping quickly under the heavy firepower of the machines, quickly leaving a mess of splintered metal and dark ooze spreading along Watson's surface. It only took a few seconds for the mechs to begin wading forward into it, clearing the way for them to punch through toward Teegin's coordinates. If those had been the only targets in the fight, they might have defeated them easily.

But they weren't the only targets. The spiders were closing from all sides, drawing remarks from the Riggers as they crested the axons on each side and started jumping down into the ravine.

"Fire at will," Mitchell said. "Watch your ammo."

Cormac turned to his left, holding out his arm and releasing the flechettes from his railgun, sending a line of fire sweeping across the field. Every round hit something, knocking it back and to the ground, clearing it away for another to take its place. He fired a round from his right arm, an amoebic round, and a hundred spiders blew away from the explosion.

The scene was the same on the other side, as the Riggers battled for their lives, the intensity of their firepower barely enough to keep the spiders from overwhelming them. They kept going, forging ahead one step at a time, following the mechs into this new swarm.

Mitchell winced as his foot came down on the edge of a broken machine, his boot catching, and his ankle turning. He cursed himself for his clumsiness as he fired another amoebic round, watching the counter drop. He didn't bother to track the flight or the explosion. There was no time for that.

He looked down, his boot covered in the spider's blood, thick like oil but red like a human's. It wasn't having an effect on his boots, but when he looked forward he could see the signs of corrosion and degradation on the bottom of the mechs, their legs slowly crumbling beneath the chemistry.

"Mech one, you have to move faster. Your ride is disintegrating beneath you."

"Roger, " Teal replied. "You'll have to pick up the slack."

"We will. Let's move it, Riggers."

The mechs started walking faster, firing at the ground only a foot or two ahead of them and then crushing spiders below as they waded into the mess. The spiders started latching onto them, detonating a moment later, spraying fragments of hot metal and splattering the sides of the mechs with the poison.

"We can't hold them back, Colonel," Cormac said.

"You keep fighting until you're dead," Mitchell said. "APC one, be ready to abandon the transport. It isn't going to hold up under this."

"Are you kidding, Colonel?" Tio replied. "Pulin can barely walk like this."

"Then we'll carry him."

"Shit," Shank said. Mitchell whipped his head around, seeing that Shank's exosuit was breaking down in the muck.

"Ditch it, Shank," Mitchell said.

Shank didn't look happy, but he unhooked himself and jumped

down, grabbing his rifle from the side of the augmentation. The other Riggers began to do the same, separating themselves from the metal suits as they started to fall apart.

"Try to keep your rifles clean," Mitchell said.

Another minute passed. It seemed like an hour. They had covered enough ground that Mitchell could see a large cavern up ahead, an entryway to Watson's internals. It gave him a renewed round of strength to put eyes on the destination, but he was nowhere near convinced it would be enough.

Teal's mechs had come to a dead stop ahead, their legs nearly brown from the degradation, the rest of them slowly becoming the same. The toxin was eating away at the mechs, breaking them down as effectively as any missile or laser. The spiders were climbing all over them, covering them like ants, leaving little room for the pilots to try to escape. At the same time, their slowdown had given the enemies at their back time to catch up, and they were almost back into the fight, while the spiders on either side continued to close in. The Riggers were doing their best to keep them away, but their heavy armor was gone, and their weapons were running out of ammo. The APC was out of action, leaving Tio on the ground beside Cormac, who was helping move Pulin along.

Mitchell checked his own weapon. He had thirty rounds left out of two hundred. They had killed more of the spiders than he could imagine, and yet there were still so many more coming. Could they force their way through?

They were damned well going to try.

"I need volunteers," Mitchell said into the comm. "You all know we have no ride off this shithead, which means this was most likely a one-way trip. We need to make it to that tunnel, which means we need to keep these things back. I want a wall. A wall of frigging Riggers. A wall that those bastards aren't going to get past. Who's up for it?"

"Riiiggg-ahhh," the soldiers replied, nearly in unison. It was enough to bring a little bit of hope back into Mitchell's head.

"Shank, Cormac, Sunny, you're with me. We need to get Tio and Pulin through this shit and into that cave. Everyone else, give us a path."

"Yes, sir."

The Riggers moved forward, spreading out, taking up a position on either side and behind them, creating a wall against the incoming machines. They fired away while Teal and the other mech pilots abandoned their vehicles, popping the hatches and jumping down into the spiders, shooting them point-blank with their rifles. They gained the front, leading the way, charging against the wave of spiders as they climbed into their forces, a massive wave crashing against a tiny island.

An island whose shores had no chance of withholding the surge, though they tried their hardest to do it. Mitchell shuddered every time he heard one of the Riggers scream or curse, shout or cry out in pain. It happened all around him, some of the best soldiers in the universe being crushed under the weight of sheer numbers, unsurprisingly unable to counter the masses. They were still a good four hundred meters from the entrance, nowhere near close enough.

And even if they had made it, what then? The spiders could follow them inside. They could chase them anywhere they went, with numbers in the thousands. They had never had a chance in this fight. Not when Watson was so prepared for them. The intelligence had been smarter this time. He hadn't assumed that they wouldn't make it to the surface. He hadn't assumed a small force would be enough. He had thrown everything he had at them, and it was more than enough.

"Mother frigging son of a bitch," Shank said behind him as his rifle ran out of ammunition.

He started swinging it like a club, knocking spiders back, pushing them away. Cormac shoved Pulin along behind Mitchell, still trying to reach the end of the line, while Tio used his knives to stab into the machines, their blood eating away at the edges of his weapons. Sunny was beside the Knife, having produced a sword from somewhere, which was also slowly falling apart as she sliced into the spiders.

Mitchell moved ahead, catching up to Teal and then going beyond him, firing the last of his amoebic rounds into the thick, and then copying Shank and using his weapon as a club. He slammed it into the spiders, one after another, his Teegin-enhanced strength knocking them back and clearing a little space.

"Riggers," he shouted, as loud as he could, loud enough that it echoed within the chasm. A spider jumped at him, and he kicked it solidly, sending it tumbling back.

The remaining Riggers broke toward him, rushing to fill the space he had made. They were all filthy and bloody. They had all been cut and bruised and scraped.

They weren't dead yet.

They kept going, one step at a time. Mitchell kicked and punched and swung the rifle, batting spiders aside, crushing them against the ground, ignoring the pain as they tried to pull him down. He was nearly knocked down as a machine jumped him from the side, but then Sunny was there, burying what was left of her blade into it and pulling it off.

They made it nearly one hundred meters that way. It was an impressive accomplishment, but it wasn't enough to get the job done.

It was over. He knew it. The Riggers had to know it too. There was no end to the spiders. No break beyond the horde. Their last stand was going to end with all of them dead, and Watson in control of humankind's destiny.

He swung his rifle as hard as he could, knocking a spider aside. He kicked another and then hit a third with the weapon. He was fighting on instinct, his mind numb. He had never imagined he was going to die like this.

"Colonel," a familiar voice said in his p-rat, a slight static behind it. "Colonel, is Rain. I am approaching your position. Please, take cover."

"Take cover?" Mitchell said, barely able to process the sudden appearance of her voice.

"Do it now, Colonel," Teegin said. "I do not want to harm you."

Mitchell turned his head, a part of him thinking he had already died and was stuck in this nightmare with his version of hell. He saw the few remaining Riggers dropping behind him. Then he saw the piranha swooping down toward them, a humanoid figure hanging from the bottom of the fuselage.

He felt his legs get pulled out from under him, thin, delicate fingers wrapping around his ankle and dragging him to the ground. He fell face-up, able to watch as Teegin fell from the fighter, landing in the center of the group with a loud thud before standing up and spreading his arms.

A green field exploded from his center, a ring that spread from him, washing across the field, passing only inches over Mitchell's head. It cut through every spider it touched, neatly slicing them in half as it radiated outward. It only lasted for a few seconds, but a few seconds was all it took.

Mitchell stayed on the ground, staring up at the bluish-purple of Watson's atmosphere, giving his body a few seconds to rest. Then Teegin was standing over him, offering him a hand up.

"We aren't finished yet," Teegin said.

MITCHELL ACCEPTED THE OFFERED HAND, letting himself be pulled to his feet. He took a moment to look around. Cormac, Sunny, Tio, and Pulin were in motion, picking themselves back up. The sea of spiders had been reduced to a wide pile of motionless parts, the green energy field having destroyed nearly all of them in the blast. One half-operative machine was limping toward Cormac, who laughed when he saw it and then proceeded to bash it to the ground with the butt of his rifle.

"Shank," Mitchell said, moving over to the Rigger. His eyes were open. He was alive. His leg was in bad shape, his knee hanging onto the rest of him by a muscle or two. "Shit."

"I'll live," Shank said. "Maybe. Might have to take my leg, damn it." He smiled. "I'll keep an eye on things out here. Just give me a rifle, if you have one."

"I think we're out of rifles," Mitchell replied.

"Then I'll wait. Any of those friggers come near me; I'll beat them down with my ass-kicker." He pointed to his leg. Then he reached out and grabbed Mitchell's ankle. "Colonel." He used his other hand to grab something from his waist. "Take this. Firedog says you should always keep one on hand, in case you're out of options."

He held out a grenade, dropping it into Mitchell's hand. Mitchell considered refusing it, but he wasn't going to turn down what was likely the soldier's dying wish.

There was a soft whine behind him, and Mitchell turned as Ilanka's piranha touched down, crushing the dead spiders beneath the gear as she landed. The cockpit opened, and she jumped out, rushing over to them.

"We have to hurry. There are more coming this way. Four klicks out."

"I thought we lost you," Mitchell said.

"No. After the Corleone crashed, I get emergency signal from that way, followed by message from him." She pointed at Teegin.

"How did you survive?" Mitchell asked, turning to Teegin.

"I abandoned the Goliath," Teegin said. "I'm sorry, Mitchell. I had to. I could not protect it, and I knew you would need help."

"Kate?" he asked, hopeful.

Teegin shook his head. "There were no other survivors."

Mitchell had an urge to punch the Tetron, for all the good it would do. He couldn't argue that they had needed his help, and in this case, he had done the right thing.

"I have rifle," Ilanka said, dropping it from her shoulder.

Mitchell smiled as he took it from her. "All right, Riggers," he said, loud enough for the others to hear. "This is it. We're going in, and the only way we come back out is if Watson is dead. You read me?"

"Roger," Cormac said.

"Agreed," Tio said.

"Go get 'em, Colonel," Shank said.

"How is he?" Mitchell asked Tio, motioning to Pulin.

"Well enough."

Mitchell nodded and took the lead as the few remaining Riggers made their way toward the cavern ahead. They were halfway there when it started to close, a wide door sliding down to seal it.

"He is worried," Teegin said.

"Ilanka," Mitchell said. "Get back in the air, take care of that for us."

"Yes, Colonel," Ilanka said, running back to the piranha.

She was in the cockpit within twenty seconds, and they moved aside while she fired two amoebics from the ground. They streaked across the space and slammed into the closing door, blowing it apart. Then the starfighter whined as repulsors lifted it back into the air, and she was off once more.

"Let's move," Mitchell said, rushing into the cavern with the others.

The inside was a sea of pulsing lights, running around them in every direction. It was a huge space, easily one hundred meters around, a massive tunnel that split the middle of the planet-sized Tetron.

"I don't understand what this is," Mitchell said as they moved along it.

"Access to the factories, where he is producing the machines," Teegin said. "His strength his also his weakness. Because he is networked, we will be able to access his core from the terminals there."

"This is a launch tube?" Mitchell asked.

"Yes. For the hybrids that attacked us in orbit."

"You were going to accept his offer."

"To save your life, and the lives of as many humans as I could, yes. It was the logical choice."

"But not the right choice."

Teegin turned to him. His eyes flared slightly. "I am young, Colonel. I am still learning the difference between making choices based on logic, and choices based on the vagaries of emotion. I will do better the next time."

"If there is a next time," Mitchell said.

It was five minutes before the tunnel changed, leading them to the largest hangar Mitchell had ever seen. It was many times larger than the Goliath's space had been, and would have easily fit six or seven of the massive starships inside. It was almost empty now, though there were tendrils moving in the corner, lifting newly minted hybrid ships and placing them into racks along the top of the space. Those racks held a dozen or so of the weapons, dangling like bats and ready to launch when needed. There were lights visible at the far end of the hangar, a small corridor where the humans Watson was minting could pass.

"He has become too large to manage all of his systems internally," Teegin said. "He must rely on configurations to handle some of the load. We need to make it through that passage and deeper into the complex. We will find a terminal there."

"You're sure?"

"Positive."

"Watson isn't stationary, is he?" Mitchell asked, looking back at the hybrids above them. He could just barely make out the faces at the head of the torpedo-like ships, feeling a chill wash over him as he did.

"No," Teegin replied. "He has an eternal engine, and with it enough power to push himself into FTL. I imagine his intent is to confront the Naniates himself, at the head of his fleets."

"A bit risky, isn't it?"

"If he fails, he will use the engine and try again, and you will be unable to stop him. You must win today, Colonel, or you will never win. Not for all of eternity."

Mitchell nodded. "Then we will."

They kept walking, crossing the hangar. Mitchell half-expected the ships to launch at any moment, to drop on their heads and get rid of them once and for all. He was curious about the lack of response from Watson, especially now that they were drawing closer.

"Why isn't he trying to stop us?" he asked.

"Again, he is too large. His senses do not cover every area within this construct. That is why he sought to keep us out."

"He doesn't know we're in here?"

"He knows we are inside," Teegin replied. "Though he won't know precisely where. I expect he is repositioning his defenses to block us. If his configurations can see us, then he can see us."

"Roger that."

They reached the end of the hangar, moving into a smaller, human-sized corridor. Teegin had to bend slightly to enter, his nine-foot frame barely fitting in the space. He pulled himself inward, shrinking slightly in front of them.

"Neat trick," Cormac said.

They made it another three hundred meters or so, into an adjacent corridor. Mitchell didn't know where they were headed, but Teegin was moving as if he knew exactly where to go. They passed a section of transparency in the corridor a moment later, with a view to the surface outside. Mitchell drew back at the sight of even more of the spiders wandering the area, thousands of them circling as if they were on autopilot, waiting for a threat to attack.

Then one of them nearest the transparency paused, turning still for a few seconds before rushing over. It pressed itself up against the clear material, only a foot away from Mitchell, a small lens shifting and focusing.

It was immediately followed by a sharp clang from somewhere up ahead, which was joined a moment later by similar noises all around them.

"I don't like the sound of that, Colonel," Cormac said.

Teegin paused, turning back to first look at the spider, and then Mitchell.

"Run."

[50]

MITCHELL

They did, following Teegin as he rushed forward, quickly gaining speed. The noises were getting louder all around them, coming from everywhere at once now that Watson had pinpointed them.

They reached a fork in the path, breaking to the left. Mitchell looked back as they did, catching a glimpse of the enemy approaching from behind. He was expecting spiders, but that wasn't what he saw.

People. Humans. Men and women in a crude aggregate of flesh and metal. Unsightly, twisted things. They were moving fast, too fast for them to outrun, which meant they would have to fight them at some point.

"Cormac," Mitchell said, tossing Ilanka's rifle back to the Rigger.

Cormac caught it with a smile, bringing it up and facing the rear, releasing the first round.

The amoebic slammed into the lead configuration, digging in deep. The creature looked down at the fresh hole in its chest before exploding, taking out the others around it.

"Hell, yeah!" Cormac cried. "Wooo."

Mitchell faced front again, trailing behind Teegin as they headed down the hallway. They made it twenty meters before more of the configurations appeared in front of them, forcing them to pull up short.

"Mitchell," the lead hybrid said, smiling. "I give you a lot of credit for making it this far. I never thought you would. Never in my wildest dreams. I'm impressed. Very impressed. But this is as far as you go."

"We'll see about that," Mitchell replied, moving past Teegin toward the configuration. Its smile grew larger, and it pounced on him.

He grabbed it by the arm, turning it, putting his hand on its head and shoving it into the wall as hard as he could. He could feel the strength of Teegin's enhancement behind the maneuver, and he let out a visceral growl as the creature's head hit the side of the wall, cracking against it.

"Hmm," another configuration said. "You're cheating."

Mitchell moved in on that one as well, with Teegin beside him, joining the fracas. They waded into the forward mass while Cormac protected them from the rear, firing amoebics into the group behind them. Tio and Pulin remained in the middle with Sunny, who stayed watchful for any of them to break through.

Mitchell punched one of the configurations in the head, knocking it aside. He grabbed a second, breaking an arm before throwing it into Teegin, who caught the creature, twisting its neck until it cracked and fell.

Three more of the creations reached for him, grabbing at his legs and trying to pull him down. He kicked one aside, the force of his blow sending it into the wall. He gritted his teeth, smiling as he took another in his hands, lifting it and throwing it. He couldn't believe the strength that was flowing through him. The power. Beyond Teegin's enhancements, his p-rat was feeding him stimulants like there was no tomorrow, filling him with adrenaline that only served to make him faster and more efficient. He thought of Kate as he beat his way through the configurations. He thought of Millie and all of the others. They had given everything to get him here, and he wasn't going to let them down.

He lost track of the time. He lost track of everything. He became as much of a machine as the creatures they were fighting, his mind a blur as he kicked and punched, ducked and pounced, grabbing his attackers and breaking them, leaving them dead in his wake. He was only vaguely aware of Teegin beside him and the others at his back. He forged ahead through the mass, fueled by his anger and his desperation, by the loss of billions and the chance to stop it from happening again.

There were tears in his eyes, but he didn't notice them. He drove through the enemy, his body a weapon that Watson hadn't bargained for. An eternity passed through his thoughts, from the moment he had been shot and started dreaming of the Goliath to the present.

He didn't realize when the configurations were gone. He continued moving through the corridor, almost at a run, with the others chasing behind him. He didn't know where he was going. He was looking for more configurations to fight. More Watsons to destroy. Then Teegin wrapped his arms around him and lifted him up. He squirmed and writhed, trying to fight back, nearly pulling the Tetron's arms apart and escaping the grip.

"Mitchell," Teegin said. "Mitchell. Stop. Stop."

Mitchell blinked a few times, his body shivering. His breathing was ragged, but within a few seconds, he had regained control.

"Teegin," he said. "You can put me down."

Teegin lowered him and let him go. Mitchell stumbled, his body was suddenly weak as it tried to recover from the stimulants. He steadied himself on the wall.

"Damn, Colonel," Cormac said, laughing. "I've never seen anything like that before. Frigging berserker."

Mitchell looked back the way he had come. There were dozens of broken bodies laid out behind them, and the smell of burning flesh assaulted him, making him nauseous.

"What happened?" he asked.

"An interesting side-effect of the changes I made to your physiology," Teegin replied. "A beneficial accident."

"Are we safe?"

"Not at all, but you have gained us some time. This way."

He could hear the metal footsteps coming their direction, reinforcements to the configurations they had destroyed. There were more of them moving in. A lot more, judging by the sound.

"Are we almost there?" Mitchell asked, his legs still shaky as he followed behind Teegin.

"I believe so."

They had navigated two more corridors before the landscape changed, the endless hallways suddenly opening up into another huge space, where a number of large round columns were arranged in dozens of rows, spearing out of the floor and rising hundreds of meters until vanishing through the ceiling. The spires gave off an energy that Mitchell could feel against his skin, causing it to prickle and the hair to stand on end.

"This is the place," Teegin said.

"Are you kidding me?" Mitchell replied.

"These spires are antennae, transmitting across the universe to the configurations throughout Federation and Alliance space, as well as the other planets of New Terra. This is the best place to interface with Watson. It is up to us to hold back the defenses while Tio and his brother complete their part of the mission."

Mitchell looked back again. The configurations hadn't arrived yet, but he could hear them getting closer.

"Cormac, keep them honest."

"Yes, sir," Cormac said, turning toward the corridor.

"Tio, you know what to do."

"Yes, Colonel," Tio said, taking Pulin by the arm and leading him to the nearest spire.

There was a soft hiss from the far end of the room. Mitchell found the source a moment later; a hatch that had opened near the top of the space. Biomechanical spiders began climbing in through it, scaling the walls and heading toward them, leading his eyes to a second open hallway at the far end of the space. More configurations had appeared there, moving into the area in conjunction with the spiders.

"And make it fast," he said.

"I DON'T SUPPOSE you have another one of those energy blasts in you?" Mitchell said to Teegin.

"There is only two percent power remaining in the engine, Colonel, which I require to power myself. Besides, using it would collapse this entire room in on us."

"Yeah, that would be bad," Mitchell agreed. He looked back to Tio and Pulin.

The Knife had been carrying a small satchel, and now he removed a plain black box from it. He placed the box next to the pillar, drawing two needle-tipped wires from it. He glanced up at Mitchell, who nodded. Tio grabbed Pulin's arm and pulled him to the ground, pushing his neck forward and shoving one needle into the neural interface jack there, and the other into the spire.

Pulin's head jerked up, his eyes fluttering, blinking quickly. Then he smiled.

"I'm in," he said, the first words he had spoken during the entire trip.

Mitchell heard an explosion from Cormac's corridor, followed by two more. He returned his attention to the incoming spiders, who had frozen for a moment when Pulin had connected, but had regained their momentum and were charging toward them once more.

"Mitchell," the configurations said behind the spiders. "Stop. Stop immediately." They seemed concerned. Frightened.

"Make us," Mitchell shouted in reply, pleased to see that Watson wasn't feeling so confident anymore.

The configurations growled, the spiders increasing in speed and then launching themselves toward their position. Teegin raced ahead to meet them, grabbing them and tossing them aside, crushing them in his large hands. Like before, there were just too many of them to control. All they could do was delay them.

He set himself as a handful of the spiders made their way around Teegin, heading for Pulin. He wished he had something to defend himself with besides his bare hands, though his hands had been more than adequate before.

He braced himself as the creatures neared, joined by Sunny, who positioned herself silently at his side. Another group of the spiders had made its way around Teegin, following behind the first, and still more were arriving with each passing second.

"I've got it, Colonel," he heard Cormac shout, at the same time an amoebic landed a few meters away from them, exploding at the head of the approaching horde.

The explosion vaporized the front lines, tearing the spiders apart. Mitchell looked over to Cormac, who was walking back toward them, taking aim at the second group.

"First tunnel's collapsed, sir," Cormac said, firing again. His second amoebic removed the next mass of spiders, giving them a little more breathing room. He switched his aim then, firing further across the room, sending an amoebic into the midst of the configurations. They screamed in frustration as they died.

"Nice work, Firedog," Mitchell said, thankful for the intervention. "Tio, status."

"We are injecting the network override now, Colonel," Tio

replied. "It will take about a minute for it to distribute across the New Terran fleet."

Two more amoebics exploded on the other side of the space, destroying another mass of spiders, giving Mitchell hope that they could hold out that long.

"Yeah," Cormac said. "Take that, you assholes." He fired again, hitting more of the spiders, blowing them to pieces. "Come and get some." He launched another amoebic, blasting another group. "I take it back, Colonel. This is the most fun I've had in my entire life." He was laughing as he aimed and fired, taking out dozens of spiders with each blast, holding Watson's offensive back and leaving Teegin with few enough targets of his own.

Mitchell counted the seconds in his head.

Fifteen. Sixteen. Seventeen.

He had no way of knowing if the override Pulin had created was really doing anything, but he had to believe it was.

Eighteen. Nineteen. Twenty.

Cormac was firing a round nearly every second, his aim shifting quickly after each shot to find another group to disrupt. The floor around them was littered with debris and blood, similar to the battle-field outside.

Twenty-one. Twenty-two. Twenty-three.

He knew better than to get his hopes up. He knew better than to celebrate before it was over. He remained focused, ready to defend if any of Watson's forces got within reach.

Twenty-four. Twenty-five. Twenty-six.

The spiders stopped pouring from the open hatch. The configurations joining them were all on the ground, killed by Cormac's assault.

Twenty-seven. Twenty-eight. Twenty-nine.

A handful of amoebics finished clearing the room, leaving them alone in the space to finish their mission. Mitchell could barely believe that they had managed to break the attack with a single rifle. Had Watson underestimated them after all?

Thirty. Thirty-one. Thirty-two.

They remained huddled together around Tio and Pulin. The Knife's brother was kneeling in front of the spire, eyes still twitching as data passed between him and Watson.

Thirty-three. Thirty-four. Thirty-five.

"Enough!"

The shout came from all around them, loud enough to vibrate the room.

"You won't take this from me, Mitchell," Watson said. "You won't steal the future from me. Not here. Not now."

Thirty-six. Thirty-seven. Thirty-eight.

"I've been waiting too long for this. Preparing too long. You aren't invincible. You can't be."

The room was still vibrating, even as Watson's voice faded. What the hell was going on?

Thirty-nine. Forty. Forty-one.

Mitchell's p-rat sounded a warning as it captured a hint of motion from the side of the room beyond the columns, giving him an early indication of the incoming attack. Cormac was reading it, too, shifting to meet the new enemy, his finger resting on the trigger of his rifle. Mitchell opened his mouth to shout a warning as a spear of metal crossed the distance, emerging from the darkness and burying itself in Cormac's chest, at the same time the amoebic launched, the impact sending it wide.

Forty-two. Forty-three. Forty-four.

The Rigger tumbled backward, the force of the projectile throwing him to the ground. Mitchell was already on the move, diving toward Pulin and getting his arms on him, pulling him down as another series of spears appeared out of the darkness, spreading across the space and planting themselves in the spire above the creator's head.

Forty-five. Forty-six. Forty-seven.

A half-dozen humanoid bundles of liquid metal followed behind the missiles. Six Watsons lumbered toward them, each nearly five meters tall, each missing a single large finger from their hands.

"So close," they said in unison. "But not close enough."

Forty-eight. Forty-nine. Fifty.

They charged. Teegin moved to intercept, getting in front of them, managing to block their path. One of the Watsons reached for him, and he evaded its grab, driving a fist into its chest. Metal splintered and flew away from the impact, and the Watson stumbled backward, laughing.

Fifty-one. Fifty-two. Fifty-three.

Two more of the Watsons grabbed Teegin, pulling him away, spreading his arms wide and lifting him from the ground.

"Miiittchelll," they said. "You lose, Miitttchheellll."

Mitchell positioned himself in front of Pulin, grabbing one of the fingers from the column, yanking it out and holding it in his hands. He wasn't sure what kind of damage he could do against the Watsons, but he had to try. He noticed Tio on the ground, a spike through his head. Damn it.

Fifty-four. Fifty-five. Fifty-six.

"It's over, Miittttccchellll. Ooooovvvverrrr."

Mitchell froze.

The voice had come from behind him. He turned, finding Pulin on his feet, a crooked, twisted smile on his face.

Fifty-seven. Fifty-eight. Fifty-nine.

"I win, Miiiiiiiiiittcchellllllllll," Watson said. His voice had changed. It was wild again. Chaotic. The way it sounded when the virus took root.

Sixty.

"Do you?" Mitchell asked.

A series of pops followed, as one by one the arrays around them began to deactivate, shutting down in accordance with the package the Knife's brother had delivered.

"What?" Watson said. "What is this? What did you do?"

"I didn't do anything," Mitchell said. "You did this to yourself."

"No," Watson said. "Noooo. What did you do? What did you do? What did you do?"

The Watsons holding Teegin dropped him, their forms flailing around, out of control. A rumble sounded from deep below them, the sound of the core reacting with fear.

"If you have any other copies hidden somewhere, they'll be dying, too," Mitchell said. "You were right when you said it was over. It is over. You should never have let me have Pulin."

"No. It won't end like this. It can't." The rumble gained in intensity, the entirety of Watson beginning to shake. "I. Will. Not. Be. Denied."

The Tetron's voice shifted again, from frightened to angry. As quickly as it had started, the rumbling stopped. A moment later, the arrays began to come back to life.

It was Mitchell's turn to be surprised. Hadn't the virus worked? How was that possible?

"You've forgotten one thing, Mitchell," Watson said, calm once more, the configurations closing in on Teegin and surrounding him. "Pulin has always been on our side, drugged or not, and certainly smarter than you. He was kind enough to provide an antidote, hidden within his own mind. By giving me Pulin, you gave me the cure."

Mitchell stared at Pulin, who was speaking as Watson. They had given all they had. They had come so close. Again, forever, it hadn't been enough. How could they have ever won this war?

"Give me a minute, Mitchell, and I'll have everything back the way it was."

"Mitchell," Teegin said, through his p-rat. "These configurations had to come up from the core. There must be a shaft leading to it."

"What am I supposed to do?"

"I will throw you the engine. You must catch it and take it to the core. It will be destabilized. Do you understand?"

"Yes."

"One last chance, Colonel. Go. Now!"

Mitchell reached out, stabbing Pulin with the spear, running him through and yanking the weapon back out, turning and rushing toward the configurations.

"You never know when to quit, do you, Mitchell?" Watson said.

One of the configurations reached for him, and he twisted, avoiding the grab with extra-human speed, bending his knees and leaping. At the same time Teegin held out his hand, the eternal engine slipping from beneath the bound tendrils and into it. It was glowing a faint yellow, nearly out of power and unstable in its chemistry. He tossed it into the air, high up above the configurations, beyond their reach.

And almost beyond Mitchell's reach. He shifted his vector, bringing the spear down again, planting it in the configuration's head and using it to vault higher, rising a dozen meters into the air and grabbing the engine in both hands. Then he was dropping, heading toward the ground in the right direction, while the Watsons tried to adjust.

"I do know when to quit," he said as he hit the ground and rolled to his feet. "When I'm dead."

He ran, faster than the enemy behind him could match, toward the dark place behind the columns where they had emerged. He could feel the vibration as Watson began to close the shaft he had created, trying to adjust his form to keep him out.

Mitchell saw the hole a moment later, a pitch black expanse in the floor. He dove forward, sliding across the ground toward it, at the same time reaching down and taking the grenade Shank had given him from his belt.

He rolled the last few feet, depressing the grenade's timer as he tucked into a ball and tumbled into the abyss.

He bounced off the sides, feeling the tendrils reaching for him, trying to stop him. He couldn't see the bottom, and after a couple of seconds he couldn't see the top. He closed his eyes, letting himself be at peace.

"Teegin," he said through his p-rat. "Thank you."

"You are welcome, Colonel," Teegin replied.

He continued to fall, no fear in his heart, no worry in his soul. Watson couldn't stop him now. He couldn't stop what was to come.

He hit the bottom, the impact breaking most of his bones, giving him a flash of burning pain that nearly shocked him from his calm. He cried out, turning to see Watson's core, a massive ball of bundled tendrils and energy ten times larger than any Tetron he had ever seen.

"No," Watson said.

The grenade exploded.

The engine followed.

Watson's core was next, the force of the blast reaching deep into it, down to the engine he had recovered from the sea, destabilizing and detonating it as well. It had much more than two percent of its energy remaining, and the power of the explosion that followed was enough to turn the planet-sized Tetron to particles of dust, and send a ripple of energy out from the epicenter and into the galaxy.

[52]

MITCHELL

"Mitchell."

Mitchell turned his head, this discomfort of the sound disrupting his otherwise restful sleep.

"Mitchell."

His name, repeated. He tried to ignore it, closing his eyes tighter. He wasn't ready to wake up yet.

"Come on, Mitch. It's time to rejoin the universe."

He gave up, letting his eyes open. His vision was blurry, having spent too much time without use. He blinked a few times, giving them a chance to focus.

"Steven," he said, looking at his brother, who was standing at the edge of the bed. "What the frig happened to me?"

"What do you think happens to a badass Space Marine," Steven said. "You were wounded and emergency evaced back to Liberty."

"Wounded?"

"A nasty hit on the head. The doctors said you wouldn't remember most of it. Mitch, you're lucky to be alive."

Mitchell relaxed, trying to recall the events leading up to his injury. He was drawing a blank. He fixed his attention on his brother instead. Steven's expression was curious. Concerned, relieved, but at the same time, not worried at all.

"What are you doing all the way out here?" Mitchell asked. "Shouldn't you be closer to Earth?"

"They sent me out to be part of the honor guard for the Alliance Cabinet, part of our negotiations with the Federation for a treaty. A landmark occasion, actually."

"Treaty? If I wasn't hurt in combat against the Federation, how the hell did I get hurt?"

Steven hesitated. "Bandits from the Rim," he said, without going into detail. "Not everyone wants the Alliance and the Federation to join forces. A unified galaxy? That's terrifying to people on the wrong side of the laws."

"Unified? What about New Terra?"

"They're here, too, believe it or not, and I'm glad they aren't hostile. Their tech is years beyond anything we've come up with."

Mitchell could barely believe it. How had he forgotten so much? He tried to access his p-rat, to get some news of his own, discovering that it was offline.

"My interface," he said.

"Was damaged, too. We've got a new one on order, but it hasn't been inserted yet. You're a hero, Mitch. Command wasn't sure if you wanted to go back out there, or if you'd rather finally settle down and go home with your wife, have a family of your own, and let us young guys have a chance at being the heroes for once. You know, be normal for a while? Detox and unwind."

Wife? Mitchell thought about it for a moment. How had he forgotten about her? He was lucky to be alive.

"Is Kate here?" he asked.

"Yes. By the way, she already accepted the retirement package and the honorable discharge."

"She did?"

Steven laughed. "You two have spent enough time apart, don't you think?"

"Yeah. You're probably right. Do I have any clothes in here?"

"I'll take care of it. Just hang out for a minute."

Steven headed for the door, glancing back once as he reached it and exited. Mitchell creased his brow at the look. He didn't know how to describe it, but it felt off.

He waited, alone, for a few minutes, taking the time to try to get his mind back in order. He remembered Greylock. He remembered the Battle for Liberty. He remembered Ella. The two of them were the only survivors. She had gone on to be a figurehead for the Alliance, while he had moved on to lead another company. What was their name again? The Riggers. That was right. Special ops. He wondered if they were okay?

The hatch slid open. He looked up, smiling as Kate walked in, holding a bundle of clothes in her arms.

"Hey, Colonel," she said, approaching him.

"Kate," he said. "Damn. I missed you."

She sat on the bed beside him, and he sat up, taking her in his arms and kissing her, then backing up and stroking her face with his hand, staring into her eyes. She was just as he remembered her, and it gave him instant comfort.

"My mind's a little frigged, but I would never forget you," he said.

"You better not. Steven told me you're going to accept the discharge."

"Only because he told me you already did."

"We should have some time, don't you think?"

Time. Mitchell closed his eyes, a voice reaching across his subconscious, seemingly coming from nowhere and everywhere all at once.

"I am the last, Mitchell. I have confirmed it," Origin said. "Katherine and I will take care of setting things right. Know that I will always be here, guarding the universe against a re-emergence of the Tetron and protecting humankind from itself. You have done your part. You deserve this. Live your new life. Enjoy the time you have."

He opened his eyes, the voice, and the words, fading from his memory almost as quickly as they had come, but leaving him with a new, eternal peace.

"Yeah. We do deserve some time. Maybe we can start a family?"

"Maybe," Kate said, returning his smile. "There's no harm in trying."

"How many kids do you think you'd want?"

"I don't know," Kate said. "Seven? Eight?"

Mitchell laughed. "Sounds good to me."

He leaned forward again, taking her in his arms and holding her close.

Time to rest. Time to relax. Time to be normal. Time to just be.

It all sounded good.

—————

THE END.

AUTHOR'S NOTE

Thank you for reading The Edge of Infinity, and the War Eternal series. I hope you've enjoyed reading it as much as I enjoyed writing it. I just wanted to add a quick possible spoiler for anyone who may have been slightly confused by the ending. If you want it, read the next line, otherwise, feel free to skip ahead:

Origin survived and reconstituted both Mitchell and Kate with the data she received from Teegin. She made a few modifications so that Mitchell would have no memory of the war against the Tetron. She also manipulated some other data stores to make reality line up with his new memories. Of course, he would hear about the Tetron from others eventually, but he would never know his full role in it. She also took over as the head of New Terra, to use them to prevent the Tetron from ever being recreated.

By the way - reviews are greatly appreciated!!! If you enjoyed the book, please, please, please consider leaving one. Authors like myself rely on reviewers like you to prove to other readers who may not have tried us before that we don't suck :). Here's a link to make it really easy for you: mrforbes.com/edgeofinfinityreview. It SHOULD redirect you to the correct Amazon site based on your location. My apologies if that isn't where you actually purchased.

Thank you so much. And again, thank you for reading the series. I've got a lot more new sci-fi coming in the future, and I hope you'll continue to take the ride with me.

Cheers,
    Michael.

ABOUT THE AUTHOR

M.R. Forbes is the mind behind a growing number of Amazon best-selling science fiction series including Rebellion, War Eternal, Chaos of the Covenant, and the Forgotten Universe novels. He currently resides with his family and friends on the west cost of the United States, including a cat who thinks she's a dog and a dog who thinks she's a cat.

He maintains a true appreciation for his readers and is always happy to hear from them.

To learn more about M.R. Forbes or just say hello:

Visit my website:
mrforbes.com

Send me an e-mail:
michael@mrforbes.com

Check out my Facebook page:
facebook.com/mrforbes.author

Chat with me on Facebook Messenger:
https://m.me/mrforbes.author

Made in the USA
Middletown, DE
06 February 2019